"You said you'd stay,"
she told him.

"Until my job was done. This is what I do, Rachel. I figure out a recovery plan, then move on."

Her heart raced. "But you can't just abandon us."

"I've done all here that I can do."

"This puts me right back where I started. I don't know anyone capable of taking over the business," Rachel said. "I don't know who to turn to, who to trust. There must be some way I can get you to stay. I'll increase your fee."

Mitch pushed out of the chair. "That's not how I work."

"I'll double it again. Triple it."

"No."

She squeezed her hands into fists. "There must be some way I can get you to stay. Something I can do. Something I can say."

"Say you'll marry me."

* * *

The Hired Husband
Harlequin Historical #776—November 2005

Praise for Judith Stacy

The Nanny
"One of the most entertaining and sweetly satisfying
tales I've had the pleasure to encounter."
—*The Romance Reader*

The Blushing Bride
"Lovable characters that grab your heartstrings…
a fun read all the way."
—*Rendezvous*

The Dreammaker
"A delightful story of the triumph of love."
—*Rendezvous*

The Hired Husband

JUDITH STACY

HARLEQUIN®

TORONTO • NEW YORK • LONDON
AMSTERDAM • PARIS • SYDNEY • HAMBURG
STOCKHOLM • ATHENS • TOKYO • MILAN • MADRID
PRAGUE • WARSAW • BUDAPEST • AUCKLAND

ISBN 0-373-29376-3

THE HIRED HUSBAND

Copyright © 2005 by Dorothy Howell

www.eHarlequin.com

Printed in U.S.A.

Please address questions and book requests to:
Harlequin Reader Service
U.S.: 3010 Walden Ave., P.O. Box 1325, Buffalo, NY 14269
Canadian: P.O. Box 609, Fort Erie, Ont. L2A 5X3

To:
David—For always being my friend, no matter what
Judy and Stacy—For having the courage to
walk your own paths

Prologue

"I now pronounce you man and wife." The minister closed his Bible. "You may kiss the bride."

Rachel Branford glared up at her new husband. "If you even think about kissing me, Mitch Kincade, I swear I'll bite your lip off."

She stomped away.

Mitch stood at the altar watching his bride storm past the rows of empty pews, her quick footsteps echoing through the silent church. Back stiff, dark hair drawn in a severe knot beneath her hat, she wore her least favorite dress—she'd made a point of telling him so, the one time she'd spoken to him this morning.

The woman could throw a blanket of frost over everything around her, no doubt about it.

And still, he wanted her.

Even if she couldn't stand him.

Not that he blamed her, Mitch conceded, as he watched her bustle bobbing down the aisle. Not after the disaster her father had caused and her brother had compounded, the mess that she'd been left to fix…with her body.

But she'd given her word and she'd stuck by it. She'd gone through with the wedding. Why wouldn't she? Rachel had as much at stake in this marriage as he did.

Now, through that series of unfortunate circumstances, Mitch stood on the verge of having the one thing he'd fought for, sweated blood over and dreamed of for years. So close he could taste it.

"Vengeance is mine, sayeth the Lord," Mitch mumbled.

"Excuse me?" the minister asked.

Mitch glanced back at him. "Nothing. Never mind," he said.

The minister shifted uncomfortably. "Well, uh, congratulations." He cleared his throat. "And…good luck."

You'll need it, his tone implied.

Mitch didn't disagree.

Drawing in a breath, he popped on his bowler and headed down the aisle after his bride. He'd have what he wanted from Rachel Branford.

One way or the other.

Chapter One

Three weeks earlier

"Another problem?" Rachel whispered. "No, Uncle Stuart, that can't be."

Stuart Parker shook his graying head kindly and leaned closer. "Please, Rachel, we must talk. Privately." He bobbed his wiry eyebrows toward the other side of the room.

Across the large bedchamber Rachel's father, Edward Branford, lay in bed, the nurses who attended him huddled nearby.

Her father. The man who'd told her bedtime stories, hugged away her adolescent broken heart and supported her at her mother's funeral just months ago, now lay propped against his pillows, eyes closed, pale, drawn… dying? Rachel's heart broke anew each time she looked at him.

"Rachel, please?" Uncle Stuart said.

She led the way out of the bedchamber and down one side of the twin staircases that wrapped the marble foyer. The house, located in the most fashionable district of the city, normally bustled with people and the sounds of life, yet had been like a tomb for weeks. The servants crept about silently, visitors stayed just long enough to inquire about Edward Branford's health, then quickly departed. Her younger sister and brother rarely ventured out of their bedchambers.

In her father's study, Rachel closed the door behind Stuart Parker. He was her father's oldest, closest and most trusted friend. "Uncle" was an honorary title.

The scent of her father's cigars, the smell of the leather furniture nearly overwhelmed Rachel, and for a moment she wished she'd taken Uncle Stuart to one of the sitting rooms. But she sensed this "problem" he wanted to talk about was important, and here in her father's study seemed the best place for such a discussion.

Uncle Stuart drew in a breath. "I'm afraid I have bad news."

"More bad news?" Rachel asked. "Is that possible?"

She didn't see how it could be. Nor how her family—what was left of it—could bear up under any more troubles.

Not quite a year ago Edward had gone into semiretirement and turned over the day-to-day operation of his massive business holdings to Rachel's older brother, George. Then came the train accident that had taken Ra-

chel's mother—and so much more. But thank goodness
George was at the helm of the family empire.

Or so Rachel had thought at the time.

A new fear pierced her heart. "Is this about Georgie?
Did the investigators learn anything about him?"

"No," Uncle Stuart replied, "I'm afraid not."

Rachel's shoulders slumped. Now when she needed
her brother the most, he was nowhere to be found. A few
weeks ago George had disappeared. Simply vanished.
The police and private detectives continued to investi-
gate, yet had uncovered no information. At times, Rachel feared the worst.

She turned to Uncle Stuart. "What's your bad news?"

"I received a visit from Mr. Rayburn today."

"From the bank?" Rachel asked. "What did that pom-
pous old windbag want?"

"He came by as a courtesy to tell me…" Stuart
paused. "To tell me that your father's bank accounts are
all nearly…empty."

"Empty?" Rachel reeled back. "No. It must be some
sort of mistake."

"There's no mistake, Rachel. I went to the bank with
Rayburn and reviewed the accounts myself."

"But—but that's impossible. How can they be
empty?" Rachel waved her arms. "Look at this house.
One of the biggest in the city. Father has business holdings throughout the entire state. Hundreds of employees. He has a whole town named after him up north. We
can't possibly be—"

"It's true," Uncle Stuart said, more forcefully this
time. "Your father's financial empire is teetering on col-

lapse. Your family is nearly penniless. You could lose everything."

Rachel's breath came in short puffs as she gazed up at Stuart. "But—but where did it go?"

Stuart shook his head. "I don't know."

Rachel touched her fingers to her temple. "Oh, my gracious, what will people think?"

On top of everything they'd endured these past months the family could become destitute? There'd be talk, vicious talk. The unbearable notion of her family being fodder for the city's rumor mill caused Rachel to cringe inwardly.

"Come sit down," Uncle Stuart said, reaching for her.

"No. No, I'm fine—or I will be when this situation is handled. We must get to the bottom of this, Uncle Stuart. Right away. Before anyone finds out," she said.

"I agree completely," he replied, stroking his chin.

"We must go down to Father's office and find someone who can look into the situation—" Rachel stopped herself. "No. No, we mustn't do that. If we alert the employees, word will get out. Everyone will know what's happened."

"True, true," Uncle Stuart said, nodding thoughtfully. "Once it's known that your father's business is in trouble, it could bring on even worse financial consequences."

"Oh, yes. Of course," Rachel said, realizing her uncle was right, even if that aspect of the crisis hadn't been her first concern.

A quiet moment passed with only the ticking of the mantel clock to keep them company.

"You'll need someone who can analyze the books,"

Stuart said. "Someone who can figure out what happened and come up with a solution, a plan to return the business to solvency."

"We must find someone from outside the city," Rachel insisted.

"Of course. After all, we don't know who's involved with the disappearance of the funds. Who do we trust? In whom do we confide? Where do loyalties lie?"

Anger welled in Rachel. A thief, a trader in the heart of her father's business? Stealing from them? Ruthlessly, callously leaving her family in this grave situation?

George floated into her mind. If only her brother were here he'd know what to do, how to handle the problem, how to solve it.

"Do you think—" Rachel clamped her lips together, holding back her own words. She'd very nearly suggested that Uncle Stuart look into the problem himself. But with her uncle nearly as old as her father and no longer as sharp as he'd once been, the job would undoubtedly prove too taxing for him.

"Do you think we can find someone who isn't already involved in Father's business?" she asked instead. "Someone knowledgeable who can be trusted?"

Uncle Stuart raised a brow. "Looking for a knight in shining armor?"

"I'll settle for a bookkeeper who can keep his mouth shut."

"I already have someone in mind," Uncle Stuart told her. "An outsider. A man who knows nothing of the situation, except what he'll discover in the account books and ledgers. He'll be totally impartial with nothing to gain financially—beyond his salary."

"Who is he?"

"Mitch Kincade. I met him during my last trip up to the Bay Area. He's helped out in similar situations."

"What are his qualifications?" Rachel asked.

"A financial genius, he's been called."

"Can he be trusted?"

"Implicitly," Uncle Stuart said. "I learned of him from the highest sources."

"This sort of thing happens often?" Rachel asked, troubled to think of other families suffering the same sort of problems.

"Yes, unfortunately." Uncle Stuart shrugged. "But sometimes it's only suspected, not confirmed. Other times a company might want an outsider to check into things as a way to keep the partners honest. And there are occasions when a fresh perspective from an outside source might reveal ways of doing things better."

"If this Mr. Kincade is so intelligent, why doesn't he run his own company?" Rachel asked. "Why is he working on salary for other firms?"

"There's some prestige in being a hired gun," Uncle Stuart pointed out.

"What about his background?"

"Nothing that caused a problem for his other employers. His credentials and references are beyond reproach. He's worked for several men I know and maintains a sterling reputation." Uncle Stuart looked down at her. "I've covered your immediate debts, Rachel, but I can't do so forever. Something permanent must be done to contain this situation. And with George gone and your father ill, I'm afraid the problem falls squarely on your shoulders. What do you want to do?"

Impatience zinged through Rachel. The answer was obvious, of course, and she wanted to get this Mr. Kincade here *yesterday.*

Yet her mother's face floated across her mind. The two of them had spent their time planning social functions, attending teas, redecorating the house room by room. Weighty issues? Matters of finance? Women involved in business? It simply wasn't *done.* What would people say? It wasn't her place. How many times had Rachel heard her mother say those things?

She'd have do it quietly, Rachel decided. Give the problem over to this stranger, let him come up with a plan. Then let him implement it and avoid the scandal.

She lowered her lashes, hoping to look demure when what she really wanted to do was race to San Francisco herself and drag that Mr. Kincade down here tonight.

"Do you think he can come right away?" she asked.

"I'll see to it," Stuart said.

"People will wonder why we've brought in this hired gun, as you call him, and given him free rein into Father's business affairs," Rachel said.

Uncle Stuart thought for a moment. "He'll stay here at the house. You can explain that he's a friend of the family, come to visit and offer assistance."

Rachel shook her head. "Entertaining a guest so soon after Mother's death and during Father's illness? It's highly inappropriate."

"Then we'll say he's a very dear, old family friend,"

Uncle Stuart told her. "Besides, it will be excellent cover for Edward's illness. Everyone will think the company records are being brought to the house for your father to review."

Rachel might have mumbled a little curse if her uncle hadn't been in the room. The very last thing she wanted was to attempt to entertain a guest, especially a withered-up, boring accountant. She'd seen the prune-faced bookkeepers at her father's offices, hunched over their ledgers, squinting at columns of figures. Having such a man underfoot would surely be a trial. Yet she'd have to do it.

"All right, then. It's settled," she said. "How long will this take?"

"Two weeks, three at the most," Uncle Stuart said.

Rachel sighed with relief. Thank goodness. In only a few weeks time, her life would be back to normal.

Chapter Two

"This one must be a dog. A real dog."

"Wouldn't be the first," Mitch Kincade said and glanced across the hansom cab at his friend sprawled on the leather seat. They'd arrived at the train station barely an hour ago and headed immediately for the Branford home.

"She's what—twenty years old? Isn't that what the old guy, Parker, said? And she's not married?" Leo Sinclair leaned his head back and laughed. "She's a dog, all right."

Mitch turned his attention out the window and watched the streets of Los Angeles roll past. In truth, he'd scarcely noticed the details of the Branford family that Stuart Parker had related to him two days ago in San Francisco. All Mitch cared was that Parker had showed up in person—the sign of a desperate situation—and hadn't blinked an eye when Mitch quoted his fee.

"Bet me. Come on, bet me," Leo said, still not letting the topic drop.

"I won't bet you."

"Because the ol' girl's a dog and you know I'm right," Leo concluded. "And because you've still got change from the very first dollar you earned and wouldn't risk it to save your best friend's life."

"You're my best friend," Mitch pointed out, "so it should be obvious why I wouldn't squander my money on such an endeavor."

Mitch saw a little grin pull at Leo's lips; he seemed pleased at being reminded that the two of them were, in fact, best friends. Fate had thrown them together nearly twenty-five years ago when Mitch was only seven and Leo but five; circumstance kept them together.

"You and your visions, your plan," Leo said and waved his arm. "Why can't you relax? Enjoy life? All you do is work. Why can't—"

"—I be more like you?" Mitch shook his head, but admitted to himself that, at the moment, the notion had appeal. The afternoon was warm and though he'd tossed his suit jacket and bowler on the seat next to him, he wasn't nearly as comfortable as Leo appeared to be in his trousers, open-collar shirt and work boots.

"And there's something wrong with that?" Leo asked, sitting a little higher on the seat. "I go where I want. Do what I want, when I feel like it. Take this trip. I was free to come down here with you on a whim. Nothing to hold me back. I've already had enough structured time in my life, and so have you."

Mitch looked away, wanting no further reminders of the years he and Leo had spent growing up.

"Don't tell me you really aren't considering it," Leo

said. "Marrying this Branford girl, I mean. The ugly one. You'd do it."

"The hell I would," Mitch grumbled.

"Not even to get what you've really been after all these years?" Leo asked.

Wealth and power. Mitch had made no secret of wanting both for as long as he could remember. The wealth he could manage on his own, and he was well on his way to amassing enough money to launch his own business empire.

But there was only one way to achieve real power: acceptance among the wealthy elite. For someone like Mitch, the sole option available was to marry into it.

He'd been offered the hand of many of the daughters of his wealthy clients, clients whose financial futures he'd saved. But he'd turned them all down. Mitch intended to build his empire himself and be beholden to no one.

That way, no one could take it away.

"Just don't be surprised when her father tries to push her off on you." Leo grinned, then slouched low in the seat, folded his arms across his chest and closed his eyes.

Mitch was glad for the peace and quiet, yet it offered no respite from his thoughts.

The Branford family. More stupid rich people. He knew their kind. Just because people had money it didn't make them smart.

But Mitch was smart. That's why people of that social circle came to him, begging for his help, paying him well—very well—for his expertise, his ideas, his solutions.

The Branfords would be no exception. Mitch knew it. He'd take his fee and be on his way in no time, his wallet fatter, his clients forever in his debt.

He didn't make it easy for them, though. Mitch never accepted a job when first presented. He insisted on meeting the principals, hearing firsthand what the situation was. Then he accepted the work.

Mitch picked them. He never allowed them to pick him.

The hansom swung around a corner, rousing Leo. He sat up and gazed through the window, then turned to Mitch, his eyes wide. "Jesus…"

Mitch turned. Outside, the West Adams District passed before him. A neighborhood of staid elegance and a solid, stately air. Wide, palm-lined boulevards. Grand mansions.

The hansom pulled into a driveway of an imposing residence, towering three stories high. Ivory in color, trimmed in deep blue, decorated with carved scrollwork and gingerbread, it sported numerous balconies, a turret room and a black slate roof.

"Looks like you've hit the motherlode this time," Leo said.

A very old, very familiar knot twisted in Mitch's belly. He fought it off.

"Whatever they're paying you, ask for more," Leo advised.

"Maybe I'll do just that," he murmured.

The hansom drew to a stop just steps away from a large covered entryway surrounded by potted palms and blooming flowers. Mitch shrugged into his jacket.

"What are you going to do while I'm working?" he asked.

"Knock around a little. See the sights. Meet some people."

Mitch nodded. It was more of a commitment than he expected to get from his wandering friend. Leo was apt to disappear for weeks at a time, and return looking worse for wear.

"Watch yourself," Mitch said.

"Don't I always?"

"No." Mitch pulled his wallet from the inside pocket of his jacket and peeled off several bills. He held them out to Leo. After a moment's hesitation, Leo took the money and shoved it deep into his trouser pocket.

"These people can tell you where to find me if you need anything," Mitch said, nodding toward the house as he returned his wallet to his jacket.

"Try not to yack when you first lay eyes on the Branford's ugly-duckling daughter," Leo said with a smile.

"Good advice," Mitch said, letting Leo have his fun.

He put on his bowler and climbed out of the hansom. The waiting driver accepted Mitch's fare and tip, then climbed up top again and headed out of the driveway, leaving Mitch alone.

He turned and gazed up at the house. Huge. Expensive. So spectacular that Mitch's stomach knotted again.

Once more he shoved down the old feelings. He wanted no part of them. Would tolerate none of the memories.

And the Branford's ugly-duckling daughter? He wouldn't give her a second look. All he wanted to see was the flash of green when he received his fee.

An old gray-haired butler opened the door when he rang, relieved Mitch of his bowler and gave him entrance.

"You're expected, Mr. Kincade. This way, sir."

Mitch followed the butler across the foyer, past the twin staircases that swept up to the second floor, and into a sitting room.

"Refreshments for you, sir," the butler said, gesturing to a small, round table near the settee. "The others will join you shortly."

Mitch glanced around the room as the butler's footsteps faded. A lady's sitting room, he guessed. Pale pink, flowers, ruffles. On the little table sat a maroon-and-ivory-colored tea service, trimmed with gold. Thin plates, cups and saucers. Trays of miniature cakes. The room smelled of food, tea and cleaning polish.

How many servants had worked to prepare the tea, the cakes? How many had labored to clean this room? Mitch wondered. How many hours of work? How much sweat? How many aches and pains?

He walked to the tea table. He wasn't usually received in the homes of his clients. They met in bars, restaurants or offices to discuss business. Seldom in their homes. That's the way Mitch wanted it. Clients, desperate for his help, always did it his way.

He picked up one of the teacups. Thin. Light. Delicate. Where had the set come from? How long had it been in the Branford family? Someone with exquisite taste had selected it. Someone who knew about such things, had access to them. Someone used to having money.

Returning the cup to the saucer, Mitch gazed around the room. Everywhere he looked he saw fine, expensive things. The sort of fine, expensive things he had been allowed to look at a long time ago, but not touch. Not own. Not have for himself.

The house, for all its grandeur, seemed to close in on him. Memories surfaced. Hiding under tables and around corners. Peeking out. Watching, afraid of being caught.

Mitch gave himself a mental shake. His fee just went up.

Rachel hiked up her dress and dashed down the staircase, her mind whirling. She'd heard the door chimes and was relieved to escape her younger sister's bedchamber and her latest crying fit, yet distressed to think that the visitor might be the accountant Uncle Stuart had hired, and that he'd arrived early.

Early. And she wasn't ready to receive. Rachel touched the back of her dark hair as she hurried across the foyer. She hadn't checked the sitting room to ensure the servants had set it properly. She hadn't yet selected the floral bouquet from the garden to scent the room. She hadn't had time to think of appropriate topics so that she could make conversation with the dull, boring bookkeeper who awaited her.

Rachel cringed inwardly. What would her mother think of her?

She paused near the entrance of the sitting room, smoothed down the front of her green skirt and drew in a breath to calm herself. It certainly wouldn't do to rush into a room short of breath and lacking in composure.

Rachel had been alarmed when Uncle Stuart had reported that this Mr. Kincade—her knight in shining armor, her uncle had called him—insisted upon meeting with her and the family before making his decision on accepting the job. So much was riding on this meeting. She had to make sure everything went well.

Rachel called upon each and every hostessing skill her mother had ingrained in her since early childhood, lifted her chin and walked calmly into the sitting room.

Then stopped. A tall, broad-shouldered man wearing a dark suit stood with his back to her near the tea service. Her gaze swept the room, then landed on the man once more.

Where was the accountant? This wasn't him.

Alarm filled her once more. Had Mr. Kincade been insulted that she was late? Had he left? Had her best chance of saving her family's financial future simply walked out because of a lapse in her hostessing skills?

The man turned his head, saw her, then came around slowly to face her. Rachel's heart thudded into her throat, setting her pulse to pounding. A jumble of emotions swept her, all too confusing to name.

Except for one. This wasn't her accountant. It couldn't be.

This man was huge. Tall. Muscular. Square everywhere—jaw, shoulders, knuckles. And he was handsome. Thick brown hair and blue eyes just short of being beautiful.

This couldn't be her Mr. Kincade. Never in her life had she seen an accountant who looked like this.

He studied her for a moment, seemingly as lost as she, then came forward. "Miss Branford? I'm Mitch Kincade."

"No, you're not."

He paused and his brows drew together. "I'm positive that I am."

"You're Mitch Kincade?" Rachel's gaze swept him from head to toe, then landed on his face once more. "You're my knight in shining armor?"

Rachel's cheeks flushed. Good gracious, had she actually said that aloud?

Mitch's lips twitched. "You probably don't recognize me because I left my white steed out front."

Then he smiled and the most glorious warmth welled inside Rachel, making her smile in return.

"Yes, I'm sure that's it," she said, her voice little more than a breathy whisper.

They stared at each other for an awkward moment, then Mitch asked, "Are you Miss Branford? Rachel Branford?"

"Oh, yes." Rachel felt her cheeks warm. "And I'm so pleased to meet you. Thank you for coming."

He kept looking at her—studying her, actually—until Rachel realized she suddenly couldn't think of a single thing to say.

"Would you care for some refreshment?" She blurted out the words, thankful that something intelligent had finally floated through her mind, and walked to the tea service. "I have—"

Rachel stopped, frozen in horror. This was the wrong tea service. Here it was mid-April and the servants had put out the winter service.

She pressed her lips together, holding in a gasp and silently berating herself. She should have checked it herself, should have made sure the table was properly set. This simply wasn't done. No wonder Mr. Kincade had been staring at the tea service when she walked in.

Rachel turned to him, sure her cheeks had grown even more pink. What could she say? How could she possibly explain this social insult?

"Is Mr. Parker here?" Mitch asked.

A few seconds passed before Rachel realized what he'd asked. "Not yet. But I'm sure Uncle Stuart will be here shortly. Would you care to sit down?"

Hell, yes, he wanted to sit down. Mitch moved to a chair and managed to stay on his feet until Rachel lowered herself onto the settee at his right.

This was Rachel Branford? The ugly duckling of the family?

But she was lovely. Tall, slender. Nicely filling out the front of her shirtwaist. Big brown eyes. Coral lips that made him want to—

"How was your trip?" Rachel asked.

Mitch shifted uncomfortably in the cramped chair. He wasn't much for making small talk, especially now, looking at Rachel.

She sat erect, back straight, hands folded primly in her lap, feet placed firmly on the floor. A lady. A genuine lady perfectly at ease in this elegant, dignified setting.

"Fine," he said. She gazed at him, as if expecting more conversation. Mitch cleared his throat and tried again. "The train—"

"Run!"

Mitch surged to his feet as a young girl swept into the room, tears streaming down her face.

"Run!" she shouted at Mitch, then pointed a finger at Rachel. "Get away from her!"

"Chelsey, please." Rachel rose and said to Mitch, "My sister."

"Run now! While you still can!"

"She's fifteen," Rachel told him in a low voice, as if that explained everything.

Mitch looked back and forth between the two of them, bewildered. Chelsey, in the throes of an all-out hissy fit, and Rachel, somehow managing to remain calm and composed.

Chelsey approached Mitch, not bothering to wipe the tears from her puffy eyes. "She'll take over your life! She thinks she runs everything around here! Everything!"

"Chelsey, please, this is hardly the time," Rachel pleaded. "We'll discuss your situation—"

"It's not a *situation!* It's my education!" Chelsey drew in an anguished gulp of air. "You're ruining my life!"

"Chelsey—"

She flung out both arms, as if beseeching the heavens. "And no one cares!"

Mitch was nearly overcome with the need to do something. Intervene, get to the bottom of the problem, comfort one of them—both of them. Do something.

But his attention darted to the doorway as a young man ambled inside. Dark haired, brown eyed. He vaguely resembled both Rachel and Chelsey. Their brother, surely.

Mitch guessed the boy fell between the two of them in the family line, probably around sixteen years old.

He ignored Mitch and his sisters, as if he hadn't noticed any of them in the room, and went to a low cabinet beside the fireplace. Opening the door, he withdrew a bottle of whiskey, then turned.

Mitch's chest tightened. The left sleeve of his shirt was knotted just below his shoulder. The boy had lost his arm.

"Noah?" Rachel called, making Mitch realize that both she and Chelsey had fallen silent. "Noah, please come meet our guest, Mr. Kincade."

With practiced ease, the boy pulled the cork from the bottle with his teeth, then caught it in his fingers as he turned up the bottle. He kept walking.

"Noah?"

Rachel spoke again, and Mitch heard the quiet desperation in her voice. A knot wound so tight in his stomach that Mitch didn't think he could bear it.

Noah managed a salute in Mitch's direction with the bottle, then disappeared out the door.

A heavy silence hung in the room. No one moved. No one spoke.

Then Chelsey turned to Rachel. "I hate you," she declared, then put her nose in the air and stomped out of the room.

Mitch watched her go, his gut aching. He turned to Rachel. Her cheeks had lost their pretty little blush. They were white now. Her hands were clenched in front of her. She looked small and frail, suddenly, yet she stood straight, as if she'd put up a wall to protect herself from...everything?

Mitch took a step toward her. Then stopped.

No. No, he couldn't do this.

"I hope you'll excuse my family," Rachel said softly, unable to meet his eyes. She straightened her shoulders. "Uncle Stuart should be here shortly. He can explain the details of—"

"No." Mitch shook his head. "No, our deal is off. Forget it."

He strode out of the room.

Chapter Three

"Wait! Mr. Kincade! Please, wait!"

Mitch didn't acknowledge the plea he heard behind him as he headed toward the foyer. He was getting out of this place—now.

"Please?"

The desperation in Rachel's voice touched his conscience. Mitch stopped and turned. Rachel, dress hiked up to ankles, rushed toward him. He fidgeted. He had to get out of here. Leave, and not look back.

But something about Rachel held him in place. A tug he couldn't fight, at the moment.

"It's the tea service, isn't it," she said, squeezing the words out as if they pained her.

He frowned down at her. "The tea—"

"I knew it," she declared. She pressed her lips together and, for an instant, Mitch thought she might cry, though he didn't have the slightest idea why.

"This is my fault. All my fault," Rachel insisted. "I should have made sure the tea service was—"

"What are you talking about?" Mitch asked, walking closer.

"It's a winter service. Completely inappropriate for spring. I saw you eyeing it when I walked into the room," Rachel said.

Mitch just looked at her. She thought he knew the tea set—of all things—was wrong? That he was gentleman enough to realize the error?

For an instant Mitch didn't know what was worse: to tell her that he didn't know one tea service from another, or to reveal the real reason he wouldn't accept the job.

He decided to take the easy way out.

"Stuart Parker mentioned that things have been difficult for you and your family," Mitch said.

Rachel gazed up at him, her eyes wide with hope. "You're not leaving because the tea service is all wrong?"

A proper tea service. Why the hell would a person give a damn one way or the other about a tea service? But reputations were made—or destroyed—because of just such details. Mitch had forgotten that.

Rachel leaned a little closer and rose on her toes. The fragrance of her hair wafted up to him. A most delightful scent. She touched his arm.

"Please, Mr. Kincade, if you would just hear me out?"

She whispered the words. Her sweet breath brushed Mitch's ear warming him, yet somehow sending a chill down his spine.

"Won't you please come back?" she breathed into his ear. "Let me explain things. I don't want Chelsey or Noah—or the servants—to overhear us."

Indecision seesawed through Mitch, a condition that

he almost never experienced. A head full of old memories warred with the vision of this woman standing before him. He knew what he should do. Knew what was best for him. No question about it.

But the warmth of her body so close to his called to him. Made him want to ease forward just a bit. Brush against her soft—

"Please?" she whispered.

Mitch drew back, drawing on a familiar store of willpower. All right, he decided. He would listen. Just listen to what she said, then leave.

He gave her a brisk nod then was annoyed with himself because the little smile she gave him pleased him so. He followed her swaying bustle down the hallway and into the sitting room once more.

"We'll have some tea," she told him, as if that would make things better.

Wrong service or not, Rachel Branford looked perfect with the delicate cup and saucer in her hand. Easy, practiced motions. Flawless movements. Grace and charm. She'd done this all her life, obviously.

Mitch accepted the tea, though he didn't really want it. He preferred a steaming mug of coffee with cream and lots of sugar.

"Would you care for a cake?" Rachel asked, gesturing to the tray on the table.

The little cakes on the platter held no appeal for Mitch. He was hungry, but he craved beef with potatoes smothered with gravy. He doubted such a meal had ever been served in this house.

"Thank you for staying, Mr. Kincade, for hearing me out." Rachel sank onto the settee and sipped her tea.

Mitch's cup rattled in the saucer as he sat down and placed it on the table beside him.

"I suppose Uncle Stuart told you that our family situation is…well, desperate," Rachel said.

Had Parker told him that? Mitch didn't remember, nor did he care. Every family, every company he worked for had a sob story of some sort. An illness, a death, a disgruntled ex-employee, a crooked partner. Mitch never listened to the details. All he cared about was doing his job and collecting his fee.

"It began last year," Rachel said, "when Father turned the business over to my brother Georgie. A few months later my mother…well, she—"

"Died?" Mitch asked.

Rachel glanced away for a moment, then looked at Mitch again. "The train derailed. She and Father were taking Noah to look at colleges."

"That's how your brother lost his arm?" Mitch asked.

"Yes, and I think that was the start of Father's health problems, too. Seeing them there in the wreckage…" Rachel shook her head as if shaking away the vision, and set her teacup aside. "Father's been in decline since. A minor stroke, the doctors said. But it's more than that. They can't seem to pinpoint exactly what's wrong."

Mitch just waited.

"With Father ill, Georgie took complete control of the business several months ago." She shook her head. "If only Georgie were here I'm sure he could handle everything."

Mitch frowned. "He's away now?"

"He didn't even tell us he was leaving. We don't know where he is or when he'll come back."

Mitch paused. "Your brother, who ran the business, disappeared suddenly, then shortly thereafter the family money vanished also?"

"Yes, isn't it terrible? At times, I fear something dreadful has happened to him."

Mitch shifted in the chair. "You don't think it's more than a coincidence?"

Rachel looked up at him with wide, innocent eyes. "Whatever do you mean?"

Of course, there could be several reasons why George and the money's disappearance coincided, other than the obvious. Mitch decided not to pursue it with Rachel.

"Georgie is my half brother, actually. My mother's son from a previous marriage," Rachel explained. "But Father never treated him any differently than the rest of us. He gave Georgie his name, educated him."

"Turned the business over to him?"

"Oh, yes. Of course," she said. "And I just know that as soon as Georgie returns, everything will be fine. The police are looking, and a detective agency of some sort has been engaged. We've learned nothing about his whereabouts, though. I just hope—"

"I'm sure he's fine," Mitch said, wanting to relieve her distress. Making her feel better suddenly seemed important to him.

"Noah is having a particularly difficult time of it," Rachel went on. "And Chelsey…well, Chelsey is a situation that must be handled, also. So you can see, Mr. Kincade, that our circumstances are, indeed, desperate."

Mitch nodded. "They are."

She leaned forward a little. "So you'll reconsider? You'll stay and help us?"

"No."

A few seconds passed before his words seemed to dawn on her.

"But you just said you understood—"

"I do understand," Mitch said. "But it doesn't make any difference."

"You know my father's holdings are vast and complicated. You come highly recommended," Rachel said. "There must be something I can say that will convince you to stay."

"There's not."

She sat up straighter. "Then why come all this way? Why get my hopes up just to refuse the work?"

"I don't have to give you a reason," Mitch told her. "I choose my clients, not the other way around."

"You must help us." Rachel gave him a hopeful little smile. "After all, that's what knights in shining armour do."

"I'm not here to rescue you," Mitch said, though he knew that's what she wanted. He knew her type. He'd seen it dozens of times. Pampered and spoiled by a life of leisure. Circumspect, reserved, a slave to social status. And now she was completely out of her element after being thrust into these dire circumstances, and expected someone else to fix the problem.

"Then your reason must be…" Rachel nodded. "Oh, I understand."

Mitch frowned. "Understand what?"

"That after arriving here, you can see that you aren't up to the task." Rachel smiled pleasantly. "It's perfectly all right. I wouldn't want you to take it on if you can't handle it."

Mitch uttered a laugh. "Let me assure you, Miss Branford, that I've untangled finances far more complicated than those of your father. I checked before I came here so I know what I'm talking about. I can have this job finished in less than two weeks."

"Then you are the perfect man for the job," Rachel insisted. "You are the only one who can help us."

Mitch pushed out of the chair. "Listen, Miss Branford, I'm not your preacher, your helpful brother, or your knight in shining armor. I do this for money. That's all."

"Fine. If that's what you care about, then that's what you'll have. I'll double your salary."

"No."

"Triple it."

Mitch shook his head. "I don't want to work for you."

"Quadruple it."

He glared at her.

Rachel got to her feet and drew herself up. "We're talking about my family, Mr. Kincade. Name your price."

"I don't want the job."

She flung out her arms. "You don't want four times your usual fee? For less than two weeks work? Really, Mr. Kincade, what sort of businessman are you?"

"Do you even know what my salary is?" he demanded. "Do you have any idea?"

"Whatever it is," Rachel told him, "it's nothing compared to the survival of my family."

He'd be a fool to turn it down. The sum was impressive. In his mind, Mitch reviewed the ledger he kept that tracked his money and thus his dream, and imagined the balance shooting upward. That much closer to the things he'd worked for his entire life.

And all he had to do was stay here.

"Well?" Rachel asked.

A few moments dragged by while Mitch wrestled with his conscience, old memories and the ache in his stomach it all caused. Finally, the money won out.

"All right. I'll do it," he said. "For four times my usual fee."

"Good. Then it's settled." Rachel drew in a breath. "I've already prepared a very nice room for you overlooking the rear gardens. You'll—"

"You expect me to stay here?"

"Well, yes, of course."

"No." Mitch paced a few feet away.

"You must stay with us," Rachel told him. "And you must work here, too."

"No," Mitch said. "That's out of the question."

Rachel huffed. "Fine. Then I'll pay you five times your salary."

He swung back to face her. "You don't even know if you can afford that."

"Then you'd better see to it that I can," she told him.

A long moment dragged past with the two of them glaring at each other. Finally, Mitch broke the silence.

"Just so we're clear," he said. "I don't care about you or your family. I'm here to do a job. That's all."

She drew herself up and raised an eyebrow. "I don't

know what sort of services you've provided for your previous employers, Mr. Kincade, but all I need you to do is the job for which you've been hired."

"I expect to be left alone to do just that."

"You can work in my father's study. No one will disturb you."

"Fine."

"Fine."

They glared at each other for another moment, then the reality of his decision and the situation it left him in struck Mitch like a kick in the knee. He'd finish this job. Get it done and leave.

And in only a few weeks, he'd have his old life back again.

Chapter Four

Everything would be all right now. Wouldn't it?

The thought ran through Rachel's mind once again as she sat on the settee, watching the late-afternoon shadows crawl toward her across the sitting-room floor. Yes, everything would be fine. Mr. Kincade had come highly recommended. At this very moment he was in Father's study discussing the situation with Uncle Stuart. He'd fix their problem.

If he kept his word and stayed.

Another wave of anxiety rumbled through Rachel, setting her heart to beating faster. Mitch had said from the outset that he didn't want the job. He'd refused it outright, initially. She'd had to bribe him with more money to get him to agree to stay.

But what if he changed his mind? What if he simply up and left?

Was that fear the reason she felt so anxious?

Rachel glanced down at the tablet in her hand and the

blank page that taunted her, and realized Mitch's potential abrupt departure was one of the many troubling things on her mind right now.

The pages of her tablet should be nearly filled by now. The guest list. The menu. Flowers. All those things still needed to be put into motion.

Usually, preparing for this sort of event delighted her.

Usually, she and her mother did it together.

With a heavy sigh, Rachel pushed the tablet away. She'd work on the luncheon preparations later.

Mitch came into her thoughts once more at the sound of his voice rumbling in the background. Not loud enough that she understood his words as he spoke with Uncle Stuart in the study down the hall, but a constant companion as she'd sat here.

The image of him filled her mind. Tall. Yes, he was certainly tall, strikingly tall. Broad shoulders. Big hands. They'd looked ridiculous earlier holding the teacup. Was he seated behind the desk in Father's study? Had he taken off his jacket? Loosened his necktie? Opened his shirt collar…

Rachel gasped and hopped off the settee as if her own thoughts had given her a pinch. Good gracious, what had come over her, imagining Mr. Kincade—an accountant, of all things—without his shirt on?

Commotion at the sitting-room door caught Rachel's attention. She turned, grateful for the distraction and expecting to see Chelsey in tears again, but found Claudia Everhart rushing into the room instead. Rachel hadn't even heard the door chimes.

Gracious, had she been that deep in thought over Mitch Kincade's chest?

"Rachel! It's happening!" Claudia announced, her eyes wide, her cheeks as pink as the frothy gown she wore. "Tonight!"

Rachel gasped. She and the pretty, blond Claudia had been friends for years. That look on her face could mean only one thing.

"Graham?"

"Yes!"

"Tonight?"

"Tonight!" Claudia rushed to Rachel and clasped her hands. "Mother told me that Graham has asked to speak with Father. Tonight! He intends to ask Father's permission to marry me. I rushed right over here. You're the first to know!"

Rachel shared a quick hug with Claudia. "Graham Bixby asking for your hand. He's the perfect husband."

"Oh, yes he is, isn't he?" Claudia sighed. "The Bixbys are one of the finest families, and Graham is so handsome and so refined, and so dignified. He's terribly successful. He's—he's perfect."

"He'll look gorgeous in his tuxedo," Rachel said, smiling along with her friend. "Your groom waiting at the altar for you."

"Oh, and our wedding will be perfect. Absolutely perfect—" Claudia gasped and her eyes widened. "Oh, goodness, Rachel. How thoughtless of me. Rushing over here, prattling on about my news when you—"

"Don't give it a thought," Rachel insisted, forcing aside the unpleasant memory.

"But if things had been different, you and—"

"Please," Rachel told her, shaking her head. "It's over and done with."

"Benjamin Blair," Claudia said, disdain in her voice. "He should be shot for—"

"Has your mother started planning?" Rachel asked, anxious to talk about something different.

Claudia smiled. "Mother started planning a year ago when Graham asked permission to court me."

Rachel's heart swelled with delight over her friend's good news. Claudia Everhart and Graham Bixby would truly make the perfect couple. They would have the perfect wedding, the perfect reception.

"I must get back home," Claudia declared, rushing out of the sitting room. "I have to decide what to wear this evening when Graham comes over."

"Something pink," Rachel suggested, hurrying alongside her. "It's your favorite color and it will—"

Mitch Kincade and Uncle Stuart stepped out of the study, stopping Rachel and Claudia in their tracks. Rachel's gaze jumped between the two men. Mitch looked taller, sturdier, stronger next to her aging uncle.

And his shirt collar was buttoned up tight.

Rachel felt her cheeks color as the very unladylike thought zipped through her mind.

"Good afternoon, ladies," Uncle Stuart said with a smile.

Pleasantries were exchanged and, finally, Rachel had to introduce Mitch. She'd made thousands of introductions. Why did this man unnerve her so? Because he held the future of her family in the palm of his hand?

Or was it something else?

"Claudia, I'd like you to meet Mr. Mitch Kincade," Rachel said. "Mr. Kincade is one of our family's oldest and dearest friends, and he's visiting with us for a while."

Mitch seemed to bristle slightly at Rachel's introduction, but gave no indication of anything amiss as he and Claudia exchanged greetings.

"Will you stay for supper, Uncle Stuart?" Rachel asked.

"No, dear, I must get home." He turned to Mitch. "I'll be speaking with you soon. Good afternoon, ladies."

Mitch nodded to Rachel and Claudia as Stuart disappeared down the hallway, then returned to the study.

Claudia leaned close to Rachel, her gaze on the study door. "Oh, my…where have you been hiding him? He's gorgeous."

"Claudia! Have you forgotten about tonight?" Rachel asked.

"Graham is handsome, but Mr. Kincade…"

"He's only here out of respect for Father," Rachel insisted, hoping she sounded sincere. "When he heard about Father's illness, he rushed down here to help out, if needed."

"Lucky you," Claudia murmured.

"Go home," Rachel told her, taking her elbow and urging her toward the foyer. "You've got the perfect man coming to ask for your hand."

"You'd better prepare yourself for what will happen when word of Mr. Kincade gets out. Every young woman in the city will try and steal that man right out of your own house." Claudia said, with a crooked grin. Then she gave Rachel a quick hug. "I'll give you the details tomorrow."

"You'd better," Rachel called as her friend hurried out the front door.

In the silence, Rachel's smile faded. Claudia's life was set, it seemed. Tonight she'd become engaged to Graham Bixby, a truly perfect man, presenting Claudia with a truly perfect future to look forward to. While Rachel's life…

She fought off the sadness that crept into her thoughts and drew in a breath. She'd make it perfect again, just as it used to be. And the place to start was with Mitch Kincade.

Another troubling thought from earlier landed squarely in Rachel's mind once more. What if he left? Before he finished his work here?

That brought on another recollection of Benjamin Blair. Determinedly, Rachel shoved it into the deepest recesses of her mind and focused once more on her family.

If Mitch threatened to leave, she'd forbid it, Rachel decided. Though he hardly seemed like a man who did anything that didn't suit him, she would force him to stay. Somehow.

In the meantime, she had to get on with things. Mitch had insisted he be left alone to work, but that was impossible. He was a guest, after all. To ignore him simply wasn't done.

When Rachel entered the study she found Mitch seated at the desk but his gaze was trained on the doorway, as if he'd expected her to walk in. He got to his feet immediately and Rachel thought once more how out of place he looked here among the ledgers and account books stacked up around him.

Surely the man was better suited for outdoor work, something physical, something in the sunshine, something that required no shirt.

Rachel winced and tried to force the heat from her cheeks. Good gracious, what was wrong with her?

Mitch seemed to be lost in his own thoughts and didn't appear to notice her momentary distress. Rachel pushed on.

"Would you care for anything?" she asked. She glanced at the tray she'd sent to the study during Uncle Stuart's visit and saw that, while the coffee had been drunk, the fruit and cakes hadn't been touched.

"No. Nothing," Mitch said.

"If you want anything—anything at all—all you need do is ask."

To Rachel's horror, the words came out in a breathy little whisper. She'd spoken them countless times to other guests but now they sounded like a wistful—and illicit—invitation. Mitch drew in a quick breath and his chest expanded. His gaze dipped to her breasts, then jumped back to her face, causing her to tingle all over.

Their eyes held on each other for a long awkward moment, then Mitch plopped into his chair and scooted under the desk. He snatched up a pencil and dropped his gaze to the open ledger in front of him.

As much as she wanted to, Rachel couldn't just run from the room. She pressed her feelings down and sent her mind in search of something intelligent to say.

Good gracious, what had happened to her hostessing skills?

"Did, uh—" Rachel cleared her throat and tried again. "Did you and Uncle Stuart get things handled?"

Mitch looked up at her, seemingly grateful that she'd asked this harmless question.

"He gave me what I need to get started," he said, then gestured to the ledgers and account books stacked around him and the others still in crates waiting to be opened. "But there's a lot yet to do."

"Yes, I'm sure there is," Rachel said. "Is Uncle Stuart coming back to help?"

"I don't need any help," Mitch told her. "I'll analyze the books and make my recommendations. I have no authority in your father's business. It's up to Parker whether or not to implement my plan."

"Uncle Stuart and my father, of course," Rachel said.

Mitch hesitated a moment. "According to Parker, he and your father drew up agreements years ago placing each other in charge of their finances, in case either became incapacitated, as your father is now."

"I didn't know."

Mitch shrugged as if that didn't surprise him. "Your uncle has already agreed to my first recommendation, selling off some warehouses to generate cash."

"Warehouses? Don't we need those?"

His eyebrow quirked. "I don't usually explain myself."

"Do you usually receive five times your normal salary?"

Mitch glared at her for a quick moment, then said, "You won't need your warehouses if the business goes under and there's nothing to store."

"Oh, well, of course," Rachel said, feeling a little

foolish. She offered an apologetic half smile. "I've never been privy to the workings of the family business."

"No reason for you to be," Mitch said. "I'm sure you had other…important matters to attend do."

The upcoming luncheon causing her so much anguish flashed in Rachel's mind. It hardly seemed important compared to "generating cash" for the family.

"I can show you to your room now," Rachel said, in a hurry to get this portion of her hostessing duties over and done with.

Mitch dismissed the idea with a wave of his hand. "I'm sure I can find it on my own," he said.

"You are our guest," Rachel reminded him.

He turned back to his ledger. "I'm a hired worker, here to do a job."

"We don't allow the hired help to wander through the house, either."

Mitch's gaze came up quickly and pinned her with a look Rachel didn't know how to interpret. A hint of anger, a flash of embarrassment along with something more. Something different. Something she'd never seen before, certainly not on a man's face.

But whatever it was passed quickly and Mitch pushed himself to his feet. "In that case, Miss Branford, I'd be pleased to have you accompany me to my bedchamber."

Chapter Five

Mitch walked alongside Rachel through the hallway and up one side of the twin staircases while she talked about the history of the house, the neighborhood and other things he wasn't really listening to.

Walking with a woman required some attention, and he had to remind himself to shorten his strides. Though he didn't really hear Rachel's words, the melody of her voice wound through him.

Women's voices were pleasing. Light. Delicate. Almost like music. Music accompanied by the rustle of clothing, the brush of gentle footsteps. Rachel was no different.

Mitch glanced down at her beside him on the stairs and his heart thudded harder in his chest. Rachel's lilting voice seemed to call to him, draw him closer, suggest things not meant to be suggested between the two of them.

And her clothing. The rustling of petticoats under her

skirt. How many were they? What sort of fabric caused the sound? How long would it take to slip them off?

Mitch pressed his lips together, trying to fight off the familiar response to such a thought. It didn't work. This unexpected desire presented itself with a special urgency. He dropped back a step, thinking the distance would help, but then his gaze homed in on her bobbing bustle and swaying hips. Mitch groaned aloud.

Rachel stepped and turned back to him. "Is something wrong?"

That innocent face, those big brown eyes turned up to him, the fragrance of her hair wafting over him. Mitch nearly groaned again.

"Nothing's wrong," he managed to say.

She looked at him for another few seconds then headed up the stairs. At the top she turned right down the hallway, bobbing and swaying with each step. Mitch's condition worsened.

Halfway down the hall, Rachel opened a door and stepped inside. She stood there for a moment, as if inspecting the room, then moved in and allowed Mitch to follow.

"This room is one of my favorites," she said. "It overlooks the rear gardens. They're especially nice this time of year. I thought you'd enjoy the view."

"The view is spectacular," Mitch mumbled, his gaze still on her backside.

"Your baggage was delivered from the train station," Rachel said, gesturing across the room to what Mitch supposed was the dressing area. "But your valet wasn't there."

Valet? She expected him to have a valet? Mitch's desire cooled. He had no valet. Never had. But Rachel thought it natural that he would.

"I'm sure Joseph won't mind attending you," Rachel went on. "With Georgie away, Father ill and Noah… well, I'm sure he'll have time. If that's all right with you, of course."

"That's fine," Mitch mumbled, not sure just what he was supposed to do with a valet.

Rachel waited for a moment, then finally said, "Does the room suit you?"

He obliged her with a quick look around. The furniture was massive and ornately carved. Mahogany, Mitch thought, with black marble tops on the stands and dresser. There were spiral carvings on the bedposts, oversize claw feet on all the pieces, and a lion's head carved in relief amid a fan crest on the armoire and headboard. A large floral arrangement, that surely Rachel had selected herself from the garden, sat atop the dresser, its blues picking up the colors of the room.

Mitch had never slept in a bedchamber this grand. He'd seen such a room, but only to peek inside when no one was looking.

"Mr. Kincade?"

Rachel's voice freed him from the memories.

"The room is fine," he said.

She looked relieved. "Supper will be served at six. We'll eat in the—"

"That's not necessary," Mitch told her.

Rachel huffed. "Why are you making it so difficult to extend you even the simplest courtesy?"

"I made it clear to you when I accepted this job that I'm only here to work. Nothing more."

"Yes, you're here for the money. I do remember that," Rachel said. Then she smiled. "The cost of your meals won't be deducted from your fee, if that's what you're worried about."

Mitch just looked at her, fighting off the urge to smile back.

"Besides, we haven't had a guest for supper in a while," Rachel said. "A new face at the table will be welcome."

"Fine, then," Mitch agreed.

Rachel headed for the door. She stopped and looked back. "If there's anything you need, anything at all, all you need do is—"

"Ask?" Mitch finished the sentence for her, remembering her remark in the study that had set his blood to boiling and brought a blush to her cheeks.

Rachel smiled sweetly. "Yes, just ask…Joseph."

She disappeared out of the room, closing the door behind her.

Desire roiled through him again. God, how he wanted her.

Mitch found his way to the dining room at six sharp. He was certain that somewhere in the house was a breakfast room and a formal dining room for larger gatherings.

But this room held a small table that seated six. The room was cozy, decorated in shades of green. The table was set with china, crystal, linens and a floral arrangement. It sparkled in the light of the overhead chandelier.

All that silverware. Mitch studied it. Which fork, which spoon for which dish? And the stemware. So many different pieces.

Rachel and her younger sister took his attention. They were arguing. Or at least Chelsey was arguing; Rachel seemed to be doing her best to stay calm and fend off the barrage of hostile words and accusations.

They stopped abruptly at the sight of Mitch. Rachel looked embarrassed, Chelsey angry.

"Good evening," Rachel said.

She seemed relieved at seeing him, even though her smile was forced, and for some reason that pleased Mitch.

"Let's all have a seat, shall we?" she suggested.

Mitch seated both Rachel and Chelsey across the table from each other in the spots he was certain they'd occupied all their lives. The two end positions, designated for their mother and father, remained conspicuously empty. Mitch took the chair next to Chelsey.

Noah ambled in a few minutes later and murmured a brief greeting as he sat down. The boy looked pale and drawn. His clothes—shirt and jacket, but no necktie—hung loosely on him. His brown wavy hair curled around his collar. Mitch hadn't noticed these things earlier when he'd seen Noah. He couldn't help but notice now that the boy smelled of liquor.

Rachel made an attempt at small talk as the soup was served which brought a contemptuous response from Chelsey. Noah remained silent. When the main course was served—beef, maybe, and something green—Noah looked at his plate and his cheeks flashed bright red. He rose from the table and walked away.

"Noah?" Rachel called. "Noah, please, don't—"

"There. You've done it again!" Chelsey shouted.

"Chelsey, please don't raise your voice at the supper table," Rachel said, casting an embarrassed look at Mitch. "We have a guest and—"

"You always worry about the wrong things!" Chelsey declared. "Like that ridiculous luncheon! You care more about that stupid occasion than you do us!"

"Chelsey, that's not true—"

"That horrid Mrs. Chalmers means more to you than we do!"

"Of course not—"

"It's true!" Chelsey burst into tears and raced out of the room.

It was all Mitch could do to stay in his chair. He wanted to go after Chelsey and find out why she was crying, then give the cook a verbal lashing for embarrassing Noah with the meal preparation.

But the look on Rachel's face kept Mitch from leaving the room. Mortified, embarrassed, troubled. Yet she kept her chin up and blinked back tears of her own. He wanted to round the table, slip his arm around her, lay her head against his shoulder and make everything all right for her.

Yet he didn't dare.

Instead, Mitch caught Rachel's gaze across the table.

"Thanks for insisting I join you for supper. These family occasions are certainly special," he said and smiled.

For a few horrible seconds, Mitch thought Rachel might actually burst into tears at his gentle teasing. Then she smiled. Then she laughed. A quick giggle that took the edge off her emotions.

"I wanted your first evening with us to be memorable," Rachel told him.

"And you've succeeded beyond your wildest hope."

They shared another moment of smiling silence. Then Mitch asked, "Is there a reason Chelsey dislikes you so much?"

"I'm ruining her life," Rachel reported.

"I see," Mitch replied, though he still had no idea what was going on between the sisters.

Rachel's smile faded. "But I truly wish I knew what to do about Noah. He's sullen and moody, almost never speaks. He stays locked up in his room nearly all the time."

And he drinks too much, Mitch thought.

"The doctor insists this is normal, that Noah needs to come to terms with…what happened…in his own way." Rachel shook her head. "But I feel so helpless, and I don't know what to do. I don't even understand what's wrong."

Mitch didn't offer his opinion. Who was he to butt into this business? The business of a real family?

Rachel pushed her plate away. "I've lost my appetite. But finish your meal. There's dessert, of course."

Mitch looked down at his plate. Chicken, he thought now, or maybe not. Something green. No potatoes. No gravy.

He'd starve to death if he didn't get this job finished soon.

"I can't eat anything else, either," he said and rose from the table.

Mitch considered excusing himself, going to the study and getting in another hour or so of work on the Branford family business. But that idea held no appeal as he found himself walking alongside Rachel up the staircase. When they reached the second floor she turned to him.

"You'll stay, won't you?" she asked.

In the flickering light of the hall sconces, Mitch saw quiet desperation and hope in her expression. And something else also. Fear.

"Of course, I'll stay," he said, his words harsh. "I told you I would."

She didn't seem put off by his tone. "Yes, but I know you didn't want this job. If…if you were to leave—"

"I won't. I'll stay until the job is done."

She gazed at him, wanting him to say more, he was sure.

"What is it?" he asked, unable to stand the suspense. "What more assurance do you want?"

She hesitated another moment. Then, as she'd done earlier today in the foyer, she rose on her toes and whispered in his ear. Her breath, her sweet voice, sent a shiver through him, dissolving his irritation at having his intentions questioned.

"You can do this, can't you? You can really figure out what's wrong with Father's business and fix it?"

He looked down at her and nodded. "I'm very good at this."

Rachel gave him a hopeful smile.

"I'm very, very good at this," he told her.

She seemed to relax a little and her fear morphed into

something that resembled trust, hinted at faith. Mitch's chest swelled, bringing on a myriad of emotions, few he'd ever experienced.

"Thank you." She gave him a little smile, then turned and walked down the hallway to her bedchamber. At the door, she looked back, then disappeared inside.

Something within Mitch, some part of him, seemed to tear away and go along with her.

He ducked into his room and stared into the darkness.

He had to get this job done and leave this place.

Quickly.

Chapter Six

Waking to find another person in his bedchamber was disconcerting enough, but a man?

Mitch couldn't even remember the last time he'd awakened with a woman in his room.

Morning sunlight drifted in through the tall windows as Mitch went about dressing. When he'd awakened and found a man creeping around his room, his first thought had been that a burglar had broken in. He'd vaulted out of bed and nearly given the gray-haired fellow a heart attack before realizing it was Joseph, his valet.

His valet. Mitch shrugged into his white shirt. He'd never had servants before, beyond the maids who worked at the hotels he called home when he traveled. He hadn't known exactly what to do with Joseph.

He'd allowed the valet to draw his bath, arrange his shaving kit in the bathroom, lay out his clothing for the day, brush his suit and buff his shoes. But he'd drawn the line when the valet had tried to sift talc in his underdrawers and hold them while he stepped in. He'd sent Joseph on his way.

The bedchamber was silent now as Mitch closed the buttons on his shirtfront and eased cuff links into place. He looked down at his gray trousers. This suit had hung with the two others he owned in the massive redwood closet built to hold dozens more. His few shirts, undershirts, drawers, socks and other belongings took up only a fraction of the space in the dresser.

He'd considered buying himself another suit before making this trip, but had decided against it. He didn't want to pay the extra charge to have it rushed.

Mitch wondered now if that had been a mistake.

But his suits—few though they may be—were of the current fashion. He knew because he watched what others wore. Powerful, wealthy men always dressed well. Mitch paid attention to everything and everyone around him and figured things out as best he could.

He looped his necktie beneath his collar and stood at the beveled mirror to tie it, anxious to get downstairs, to get to work, to finish this job and leave. He tucked his shirttail into his trousers, fastened them and pulled his suspenders into place.

Mitch had to remind himself not to make the bed, to leave it for the servants. But he put his clothes away and tidied up the bathroom just the same.

No use getting too comfortable living in these circumstances; no servants awaited him at home, in the room he rented over the bakery.

Rachel floated into his mind. If she knew his real circumstances would she be appalled? Would she pity him?

Would she laugh?

Mitch swept his jacket from the rack where Joseph had hung it this morning and stood by the window as he shoved into it. Outside, just as Rachel had promised, the view was spectacular. At least an acre of grounds, Mitch estimated, surrounded the house. Brick walkways, fountains, shrubs, flower beds, towering palms. And with the morning sunshine just seeping over the horizon—

Rachel.

Mitch's heart lurched and he leaned closer to the window. Yes, it was Rachel. He hadn't expected to see her, of all people, up at dawn and outside on the grounds. Yet there she sat on a little stool before an easel, facing the sunrise, painting.

Another side of this woman he hadn't anticipated. She was a lady, of course, as she'd been raised to be, with all the social restrictions necessary to maintain that illusion. Rachel was soft and vulnerable, too.

But he'd seen a streak of grit and determination in her when she'd negotiated his increased salary, brought about by her love and concern for her family. Rachel was a tigress fighting for her loved ones. He hadn't expected that from her pampered lifestyle.

Nor had he expected himself to be so completely attracted to her.

His body had yearned for her from the moment he'd laid eyes on her. He'd never felt such a strong pull toward a woman—ever. The mere rustling of her skirts drove him crazy with desire. He wanted to hear her voice, smell her hair, learn everything there was to know about her.

But that wouldn't happen. It couldn't.

Mitch turned away from the window and stalked out of the room. He knew who he was, knew where he came from.

He also knew where he was going, and nothing would stop him from getting there. Not Rachel and her rustling petticoats. Not his own want for her.

He was here to do a job. That was all. He had a plan—a plan he'd made long ago—and he'd stick to it. He'd have what he wanted in this life. And nothing, not even Rachel Branford and her rustling petticoats, would stop him.

A strange sensation zipped up Rachel's spine seconds before she heard the brush of shoes against the grass. She knew—somehow, she knew—who approached.

"Good morning."

Mitch's rich voice floated over her. She turned to find him standing a few feet away, gazing at her intently. So intently that for an instant she forgot how completely unprepared she was to see anyone—especially him—at this early hour.

When she'd looked out her window and seen the spectacular sunrise, she'd thrown on a day dress, no corset or petticoats. She twisted her hair into a careless knot, grabbed her art supplies and hurried outside. She'd kicked off her slippers to feel the grass against her toes and set to work trying to capture the sunrise.

She wasn't fit to be seen by anyone. It simply wasn't done.

Yet he looked so handsome standing there. From her

seat on her little stool, he seemed even taller. The color of his suit and the necktie he wore complimented his hair, his eyes.

Eyes that, for a moment, seemed to see straight through her and know that her heart beat a little faster at the sight of him.

Determinedly, Rachel turned back to her easel. "I have only a few minutes to scrutinize the sunrise," she told him, dabbing at her sketchbook with her brush.

He stepped closer and positioned himself beside her. His nearness sent a rush through her, producing a wiggly trail of paint across the paper.

"Is that supposed to be the sun?" he asked, leaning down, squinting at her work.

"Yes." Rachel picked up more paint with her brush and swept it across the paper.

He leaned in a little farther until his face was even with hers. "Your sun looks like a circle."

"I'm not painting the actual sun. I'm capturing its colors." Rachel put down her brush and sighed. "Or trying to. What I need is a spectacular shade of pink, but I'm not finding it this morning."

"You're quitting?" Mitch asked.

"Yes, for now." Rachel rose from the stool.

"Can I see your other paintings?" Mitch asked.

"No," she said, holding the sketchbook closer. Occasionally, she showed her work to others, but never the things she'd put in this particular book.

"Why not?"

She backed up a little. "It's…personal."

"I was in a museum once," Mitch said, easing a little closer. "There were pictures of naked people all over the place. Is that what you've got in your book? Naked people?"

"Are you offering to model?" she asked.

Rachel gasped. Her eyes widened. Goodness, had she actually said that aloud? Heat rushed up her neck and fanned across her cheeks. She saw Mitch draw in a quick breath and his gaze dip—and not to the sketchbook she clutched below her bosom.

How embarrassing. How humiliating. Rachel wanted to melt into the ground and disappear. How could she have said that aloud—how could she have even thought it?

Then Mitch reached out and cupped her chin. He lifted it until her gaze met his.

"Now there's a spectacular shade of pink," he said softly, rubbing his thumb over her cheek.

Her embarrassment fled. He'd done that before, turned her emotions with a look, a word…now with a touch.

Mitch leaned down and kissed her. He splayed his fingers across her cheek and touched his lips to hers. Rachel gasped as he settled his mouth over hers and moved with exquisite slowness.

He lifted his head and gazed into her eyes.

"You're a bit pink now yourself," she whispered.

"Shall I model for you?"

She smiled gently, caught up completely in this private moment with him. "Is that covered in the exorbitant fee I'm paying you?"

He grinned. "No extra charge."

She looked at him for a few seconds, as if considering his offer, then shook her head. "I'm afraid that simply isn't done."

"My offer stands."

"How very generous of you."

He studied her and for an instant Rachel thought he might kiss her again. Instead, he backed up a step.

"I'd better get inside and earn my fee," he told her.

Rachel watched as he headed toward the house, her head spinning slightly. Good gracious, what had just happened?

And how would she ever be able to ask Mitch the question that meant so much to her—without thinking of their kiss?

How the hell was he supposed to stay away from the woman when even the sound of her voice drew his attention? Sent his imagination reeling? Ratcheted up his desire?

Mitch pushed himself out of the desk chair and paced across the study. He'd been here since breakfast trying to work, trying to concentrate, trying to keep thoughts of Rachel out of his mind, and he'd failed miserably.

He'd tried to keep his body under control, but had failed miserably at that, too.

He'd kissed her. This morning in the yard he'd leaned down, put his mouth on hers and kissed her. Then he'd offered to model nude for her painting.

Mitch shook his head. Good God, what was wrong with him? He had to get Rachel out of his mind.

That was proving more difficult as the day passed.

Earlier, her friend had arrived and the two of them

had been in the sitting room down the hall ever since. Whatever the two were discussing must have been important—to them, anyway. Mitch had heard nothing but giggling, gasping and a steady low murmur, all of which kept reminding him of how sweet Rachel's kiss had been, kept him from concentrating on his work.

He paced to the door and gazed down the hall. He couldn't see inside. What was Rachel wearing? he wondered. The same yellow thing she'd had on this morning when he'd looked out his bedchamber window and seen her painting at her easel? Had she changed clothing?

He hoped so. If he walked in on her now and saw her dressed as she'd been this morning—obviously without the armor of under things women wore—he didn't know how he'd control himself.

Still, he wondered what sort of clothing she might have changed into. If he walked past the doorway, glanced inside he could—

Mitch drew himself up and pushed the thought from his mind. What the hell was wrong with him? Determinedly, he stalked back to his desk.

A few minutes later, the voices of the women grew louder. A cloud of the most delicate scent floated into the study. Mitch looked up as Rachel and Claudia walked past his doorway, heading toward the foyer.

Blue. She had on blue. A fresh wave of desire surged through Mitch. He leaned sideways, watching her drift down the hallway until he nearly fell out of his chair. He caught himself in time but sent a stack of ledgers tumbling onto the floor.

"Damn it…" Mitch grumbled under his breath as he dropped to his knees, gathering the ledgers.

Good God, what was he doing? Acting like a schoolboy instead of a grown man. Letting Rachel occupy so much of his thoughts that he—

"Mr. Kincade?"

Mitch's head jerked up and he saw Rachel walk into the study. He dropped the ledgers again.

"Let me help you," she said, coming toward him.

"No," he barked, grabbing for the ledgers.

To his horror, she sank to her knees beside him. Her scent cascaded over him. She was so near that if he leaned forward, just a little, he could touch her. Kiss her. Lay his mouth against hers and once more feel the warmth of—

"Are you ill, Mr. Kincade?" she asked, gazing at him with concern.

Mitch drew back, clutching the ledgers against him, unsure whether or not she'd spoken.

"You look a little flushed." Rachel smiled. "A little pink."

He was pink and flushed, all right. And if he didn't get some distance from her quickly, he'd lay her back on the floor—

"Mr. Kincade?"

He struggled to his feet and needed to slide into his chair, but he couldn't leave her on the floor—for his own good as well as hers.

He offered his hand and she took it. Her small, soft palm pressed against his, sending his desire up another few notches. Another hot wave crashed through him.

How could this keep happening? When he only touched her hand?

Thankfully, Rachel got to her feet quickly. Mitch dropped into his chair and snatched up a pencil.

"I'm—I'm busy," he grumbled, opening a ledger and flipping through the pages.

She lingered at his side for a moment, looking down at him. Then she bent low. From the corner of his eye, Mitch saw her bosom, filling out the front of his shirt-waist, coming closer. Then her breath brushed his ear.

"Your ledger is upside down," she whispered.

Mitch's cheeks flamed. They actually burned. He couldn't remember a time—not once in his entire life—when that had happened.

He ground his lips together, pushing through his embarrassment and looked up at her. "I told you I'm very good at this."

"I can see that you are, Mr. Kincade," she said, giving him a knowing, secretive smile.

Mitch smiled back. He couldn't help it. Rachel had seen his embarrassment and allowed it to pass without calling attention.

He wished he'd kissed her on the floor when he'd had the chance.

"I wanted to see if there's anything you need," Rachel said, easing around to the front of the desk again. "I can have Cook make your lunch now, if you'd like."

Rachel, or the cook, or somebody had decided on his morning meal for him and brought it to him in the breakfast room. Oatmeal and fruit. He'd been hungry again fifteen minutes later.

"Nothing now," Mitch said, thinking maybe he could sneak into the kitchen later and scrounge up a real meal.

"Oh, well then. All right."

Rachel gave him a quick smile but didn't leave. Silence yawned between them. She ran her finger along the edge of his desk.

How pretty she was. The thought ran through Mitch's head as the afternoon sunlight beamed in through the window, highlighting her hair, turning a few strands golden. Her brown eyes sparkled. Her pink lips glistened.

If she didn't leave soon, he was going to round this desk and kiss her. On the mouth. Right here in her father's study.

"I, uh, I was wondering how things are going?" she said, gesturing around the room to nothing in particular.

"Fine," Mitch said, though he hadn't made as much progress as he'd expected to. But that was Rachel's fault, thanks to his body's reaction to his every thought of her.

Rachel gave him another smile and he tapped his fingernail on the desk. Still, she made no sign of leaving.

"Did you want to ask a question?" Mitch asked, coming to his senses and realizing that something troubled her.

"Well…" She cleared her throat and looked at him. "Yes, just something small, really. Before Georgie left he mentioned a factory he was thinking of purchasing. I wondered if you knew whether or not he'd done that."

"A factory?"

"The City Ceramic Works. A Mr. Prescott owned it."

Mitch's gaze bounced around the room to the crates of documents he still had to review. "I haven't seen anything about it. Not yet, anyway."

"Oh." She sounded disappointed.

"But I'll look for it," he said quickly. "I'll find out what's going on with it and—"

Mitch stopped as Chelsey swept into the room. She drew herself up and narrowed her gaze at Rachel.

"I'm going out," Chelsey declared, pushing her chin higher. "Trudy telephoned. She's home for two days. She invited me over. And I'm going!"

"Please give Trudy's family my regards," Rachel said.

Chelsey shot her one final scathing look, whipped around and stomped out of the study.

The girl had worn on Mitch's nerves the first time he'd laid eyes on her. He didn't know how Rachel managed.

"Is there a reason she's so unhappy?" Mitch asked. "Any reason at all?"

"Chelsey wants to finish out the term at the Franklin Academy for Young Ladies. It's in San Bernardino. She's attended for two years," Rachel said. "She misses her friends and her studies. I understand that."

"Then why isn't she attending now?"

"She hasn't attended since Mother died."

"Why not?"

"Because the family is in mourning. It simply isn't done." She spoke the words as if the reasoning should be obvious.

"Does that have anything to do with the luncheon she spoke of at supper last night?" Mitch asked.

The reserve Rachel seemed to wrap tightly around her a moment ago, slipped completely. Her shoulders sagged and she pressed her fingers to her forehead.

"That luncheon…"

Mitch jumped out of his chair at the distressed look that had overcome Rachel. He didn't know how a luncheon could do that to a person, but he had to find out.

"What about it?" he asked, the words coming out more harshly than he'd intended as he rounded the desk to stand next to her.

With some effort, Rachel drew herself up. "It's the La-La luncheon," she said gravely.

Mitch stopped. "What's a la-la luncheon?"

"The Ladies Association of Los Angeles," she said. "The La-La's, for short. It's the premiere women's organization in the city, and the upcoming luncheon is the single most important event on our annual calendar. The luncheon is always—always—hosted here, in our home."

So far, this didn't seem like too big a problem to Mitch. "And...?"

"Mrs. Aurora Chalmers—she runs everything in the city—expects me to host the event, as always."

"And...?"

"And it's really Mother's event. She always plans it, arranges things and does a beautiful job. But this year—"

"Your mother's dead."

Rachel nodded, sadness causing her shoulders to droop farther.

"And it's too upsetting for you to do it this year," he concluded.

She nodded again.

Mitch shrugged. "Then don't host the luncheon."

Rachel came to life then. "I can't back out. Good gracious, what will people think? What will they say?"

"What difference does it make what people think or say?"

She looked at him as if he'd taken leave of his senses.

"It makes all the difference in the world," Rachel declared. "What sort of reflection would that be on Mother, if I didn't host the luncheon? What would people think of her? Of the family?"

"Let me get this straight," Mitch said. "Chelsey can't return to school, but you can host a luncheon?"

"These are two entirely different circumstances," Rachel insisted. "There are parties, dances and outings at the school. This luncheon is for a service organization."

Mitch didn't really see the distinction, but he let it go and said, "You don't have to host the luncheon. Not if you don't want to."

Rachel's shoulders sagged again. "I'm afraid you simply don't understand."

She left the study. Mitch's heart ached watching her go. She was right. He didn't understand.

Chapter Seven

Rachel couldn't muster enough of an appetite for supper, Chelsey hadn't returned from her friend's house and this was one of Noah's days to lurk on the staircase, so Rachel told Cook what to prepare for Mitch and went into the rear garden.

Evening shadows slid across the green grass as Rachel settled onto a bench surrounded by blooming shrubs. She looked at the tablet she'd brought outside with her. All afternoon she'd tried to work on the luncheon arrangements. She had yet to accomplish anything.

Of course there were lots of other things on her mind. Her father, for one. Dr. Matthews had come by the house today, as he did several times each week. She'd pressed him for details but the doctor had said nothing new, nothing hopeful. It irritated Rachel that he was always so evasive.

Though she hated to admit it to herself, she'd enjoyed the quiet of the afternoon, made possible by Chelsey's absence. Her younger sister had no problem making her feelings known on each and every issue that crossed her path.

Unlike Noah. Though she'd seen him several times today, skulking through the upstairs hallway, peering over the railing and dawdling on the staircase when he thought no one was looking, he hadn't spoken to Rachel. She'd learned months ago to ignore him on days like this.

Dr. Matthews had looked in on Noah, but the doctor had refused to answer any of Rachel's questions about her brother. Everything was proceeding "as expected," he'd assured her, though Rachel didn't feel assured at all.

Her heart fluttered a bit as Mitch Kincade's image floated into her mind. His presence here was unsettling, but Rachel didn't know just how or why.

She did know that the big, strong, capable man had become completely flustered in the study this afternoon, pretending to read his ledger upside down. And it had brought on the strangest reaction in Rachel. She'd wanted to comfort him, make things better, see him without his shirt on—

Rachel gasped and shook her head at her own disconcerting thought. Yet that wasn't as bad as this morning when he'd kissed her. Right there in the garden. For any neighbor who might be up at that hour to see. Or any of the servants who may have glanced out the window.

Rachel's insides seemed to hum at the memory of Mitch leaning closer, his scent wafting over her, then his lips closing over hers. Was that recollection the reason she'd accomplished so little today? Could a kiss do that?

For an instant she considered discussing it discreetly

with Claudia. She was officially engaged now. She might be willing to talk about men. She'd come to the house today showing off the gorgeous diamond and ruby ring Graham Bixby had presented her with, and given Rachel all the wonderful details of the upcoming nuptials.

Rachel sighed heavily as dusk settled over the garden. She was happy for Claudia. Happy and, perhaps, just the smallest bit—

The French doors that led inside opened, drawing Rachel's attention. Mitch stepped out. Her heart gave an unexpected little jerk.

He stood on the porch for a moment, hands thrust deep in his trouser pockets, gazing out over the garden. He looked solid and strong standing in the dim light. After a moment, he spotted her. Rachel saw the quick intake of his breath, the straightening of his shoulders. He hesitated, glanced back inside as if deciding something, then walked over.

"I hope you'll forgive me for not joining you for supper," Rachel said. "I had Cook prepare one of my favorite dishes for you."

"Nothing like a plate of vegetables after a hard day's work," Mitch said. "And fruit to top it off."

She slid over a little on the bench. "Would you like to join me?"

He looked down at her for a long moment. Even from a distance she sensed the heat rolling off him.

He glanced at the tablet on her lap—at least, she thought it was the tablet he was looking at.

"I'm working on the luncheon preparations," she

said. He glanced again at the tablet, at the blank page staring up at both of them. "I'm not getting very far," she admitted.

"You don't have to put yourself through this, Rachel," he said softly. "If your friends don't understand that, then hell with them."

Rachel gasped. The idea. The very idea. Could Mitch really mean that? She couldn't imagine.

Of course, Mitch didn't know the situation in its entirety. He didn't know that Rachel's father had married beneath himself when he married her mother. A woman from outside their elite social circle, a widow once married, with a young son.

Rachel had watched her mother struggle to be "good enough" in the eyes of Father's friends. Always careful to do exactly the right thing. Always worried about what other people thought. With the best of intentions, she'd impressed upon Rachel to worry about the same things. The actions of one family member were a reflection on them all.

Her father never seemed to notice the subtle slights, the whispers that her mother endured; she'd been too proud to bring them to his attention. Rachel often wondered if his love had been worth it.

She placed her tablet aside and got to her feet. "I feel like a walk through the garden this evening."

Mitch hesitated a moment, then fell in step beside her as they headed off across the lawn.

"I saw your friend here today," he said. "Claudia."

"She's officially engaged now to the most perfect man," Rachel said.

"You don't sound very happy for her."

She paused, surprised that Mitch picked up on the subtle tone in her voice. "I'm happy for her. Really."

"But?"

"Well, maybe I'm just a little envious. Claudia's life is perfect now."

"I suppose that depends on your idea of 'perfect,'" Mitch said, as they passed a bubbling fountain.

"Everyone has an idea of their perfect life. A dream of what they want their life to be." Rachel glanced up at him. "Don't you?"

"No."

"Surely you have a dream."

"No."

"Everyone has a dream—"

"I have a plan. There's a difference."

"What's your plan?"

He didn't answer for a long time and Rachel wondered if he'd respond at all. Maybe she had no business inquiring.

"My plan," Mitch finally said, ducking to avoid a low-hanging palm branch, "is to build my own business."

"Really?" Rachel asked, a little surprised. "Uncle Stuart seemed to think your status as 'hired gun' to the wealthy was your goal."

"A means to an end," Mitch said. "I need sufficient resources and, of course, the right investment opportunity."

"And that's your idea of a perfect life?" Rachel asked. "Managing your own business?"

Mitch glanced down at her and she saw a fierceness in his gaze that startled her.

"That, and the things that come with it," Mitch told her.

"You mean a nice house and fine horses and all the usual trappings of success?"

"I'm talking about power," Mitch said. "And the only way to get power is with money."

"That's important to you? Being powerful and wealthy?"

"Damn right it is."

She studied him for another moment. "And that's your idea of a perfect life?"

"Hell, yes."

They walked in silence through the darkened yard. Mitch felt an impatience to get back into the house, continue his work on the Branford family finances, finish this job and collect his fee. Get on with his own life, make his long-awaited plan a reality.

Rachel had asked him about his dream. He had one, of course, but it was so secret Mitch rarely allowed himself to think of it, let alone speak of it.

He preferred to focus on his plan. Work for the wealthy, the elite of society. Make connections that would serve him later. Amass the money he'd long ago decided he needed. Search out the right opportunity to launch his own financial empire.

It was a lesson hard learned many years ago. With money came power, and with power no one could take things from you. No one could steal you away in the dead of night, ship you off, tear your life apart, leave you helpless.

Yes, power was what Mitch wanted. He'd have it, and nothing would stand in his way.

The breeze shifted and the delightful scent that was Rachel's alone tickled his nose. Mitch had never before strolled the lush grounds of a grand mansion at dusk, in the company of a beautiful woman who smelled this nice. The urgency to get inside and back to work faded.

"What about your dream?" Mitch asked. "Is it to get married, like your friend Claudia?"

"Ah, yes. Marriage. A woman's path to fulfillment. Family being the reason for her existence."

Mitch was certain he heard the ring of sarcasm lurking in her words.

"I guess marriage isn't your dream," he concluded.

Rachel caught his gaze quickly then looked away but not before he saw the sadness in her face. Mitch was sure he knew her answer even before she spoke.

"My dream is just that. A fantasy. Impossible to attain." She stopped suddenly and looked up at him, the closing lights from the house highlighting the determined lines of her face. "I want to turn back time. I want to go back a year to when my mother was alive, to when Father was well, when Georgie ran the family business and Noah had both arms and Chelsey was happy at school. That's my dream. An impossible one, as you can easily see."

Mitch nodded slowly, the want in her voice winding through him, tearing at an old wound he knew would never heal.

"I guess we all have a moment like that," he said softly. "A moment that changed our lives, a moment when everything went to hell."

They stood facing each other in the garden for a long,

silent moment until Mitch couldn't bear the past pressing down upon him, made worse by the hurt he saw in Rachel's expression.

"So since you can't have your dream," Mitch said, forcing a lighter tone into his voice, "what else do you want? What sort of plan do you have for yourself?"

Rachel jumped and drew back a little, startled, as if he'd just asked if he could peek under her skirt. "Nothing. Nothing, of course."

She'd responded so quickly, so forcefully Mitch suspected it was a lie. When she kept talking, he knew it was a lie.

"Why, for a woman to have a plan—a business plan?" Rachel shook her head vigorously. "It's simply not done. What would people think? I mean, really, it couldn't possibly happen. It just couldn't."

Mitch's desire for her returned unexpectedly. Whatever she was going to such great lengths to deny must be something grand. He had to know what it was.

But before he could ask, the excitement left Rachel's face and she turned away.

"I really should get inside now."

She didn't wait for him, just started walking, leaving Mitch to follow. She kept her chin up, her eyes forward, her gait swift as they entered the house. She didn't speak a word, which only made Mitch more curious, more anxious to know what was on her mind. When she stopped suddenly in the front hallway, he nearly ran into the back of her.

"Oh, dear…" Rachel turned toward him, shielding her eyes as if she'd seen something she shouldn't.

Mitch followed her line of sight toward the entryway.

"No…no you shouldn't…." she murmured, trying to block his path.

He sidestepped her and saw the butler across the foyer as he disappeared silently down the hallway. Then he spotted Noah on the stairs, and his breath caught.

The boy sat crouched on a step, desperately clawing at an envelope held between his knees. With only one hand, he struggled to open it, his lips pressed together, his brow drawn in frustration.

It was one of the most pathetic sights Mitch had ever seen.

Noah's gaze came up, impaling Mitch. Embarrassment flashed across the boy's face, then anger. His gaze bounced from one of Mitch's arms to the other, and his expression turned to one of such hatred that it stunned Mitch.

Noah crushed the envelope in his hand and raced up the staircase taking the steps two at a time, his empty sleeve billowing behind him.

A rage exploded in Mitch. He turned to Rachel.

"Why doesn't somebody help him?" he demanded. "How can you leave him to struggle with things that he can't possibly accomplish? How can you—"

Rachel touched his arm, and as she'd done before, rose on her toes and leaned close to his ear.

"It's from Madeline," Rachel whispered.

Mitch eased back, still angry but now confused.

"The letter. It's from Madeline," Rachel said quietly. She glanced up the staircase and watched for a moment before continuing. "Madeline Jacobsen. She's a lovely girl. Her family moved in down the block a little over a year ago. Noah and Madeline were inseparable from the moment they laid eyes on each other. Love at first sight. But not that silly schoolboy and girl love. It was as if their souls entwined at their first meeting, joining their hearts and minds. The two of them are absolutely perfect for one another."

"And all she can do is send him a letter?" Mitch asked, bitterness in his voice.

"It's all Noah will allow. He refuses to see Madeline— or anyone, for that matter—ever since the…accident."

Mitch's frown deepened. "Do you mean that none of Noah's friends have been to see him since he lost his arm?"

"They came, at first. But he wouldn't see any of them."

"And he hasn't been anywhere? He hasn't been out of this house since last year?"

Rachel sighed wearily. "He won't go anywhere. Not even into the gardens. We all tried to talk him into it but he refuses. Dr. Matthews said we shouldn't force him. He'll have to do things in his own time."

"So he just sits here, day in and day out? Doing nothing? Cut off from everyone and everything?" Mitch asked.

"Except for his letters from Madeline." A smile touched the corners of Rachel's mouth. "His other friends finally gave up, but not her. She writes to him twice a week. Every week. And, as you can see, Noah lives for those letters."

"Christ…" Mitch turned away, his anger bubbling and his heart aching with the need to do something.

"I wish I understood."

Rachel's wistful words took Mitch's attention. She gazed up at him, looking utterly lost.

"I wish I understood," she said again. "Noah and Madeline are perfect for each other. They've loved each other since the moment they met. He refuses to see her, but she won't give up on him. Why doesn't he see how much she cares for him? How much she loves him?"

The anger, the rage left Mitch, in its place an emptiness so painful that he turned away from Rachel and pounded up the staircase. In his bedchamber he tore off his suit and pulled on his faded denim trousers and scuffed work boots, then headed for the attic.

Joseph had cleared a spot in the spacious room, as Mitch had requested. Under the flicker of the bare electric lights hung the punching bag Mitch kept in the room he called home and took with him when he traveled. He threw open the windows and pounded the bag until sweat poured off his brow and soaked his white undershirt. He kept at it, punching and jabbing, dancing back and forth until his arms hurt. But he couldn't stop. Not yet. Not until the ache in his body drove away the pain in his heart and mind, and the want of the secret dream he longed for.

He pushed himself harder, but tonight not even the physical punishment chased away the image in his head.

Noah and Madeline.

Oh, to be loved like that....

Chapter Eight

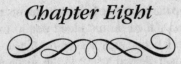

Stupid rich people.

Mitch sat on the leather seat of the hansom cab gazing out the window but seeing little of the Los Angeles scenery that passed by. The creak and sway of the carriage had kept him company since he'd bade goodbye to Stuart Parker a short while ago and headed for the Branford home.

Stupid rich people. Long ago Mitch had developed that opinion of most of the clients he worked for, yet he'd found a welcome contradiction these past few days as Parker had introduced him to the businessmen of the city.

After spending several days in the Branford home going over a portion of the company books, journals and records, Mitch had needed to get out, see the company holdings and assets in person. Standard procedure, in his line of work. Not everything could be properly assessed from studying contracts, journal entries or accounting ledgers. Mitch had to look for himself, judge for himself in order to make a sound recommendation.

Stuart Parker, anxious to please, as all his clients were, had personally taken Mitch for a tour of most of the buildings, lands, factories, warehouses that Edward Branford owned. An impressive portfolio that had taken several days.

Parker had also done what most of Mitch's clients did. He'd introduced him to other businessmen in the city, showed him off at business lunches, taken him to the city's most prestigious gentlemen's club for brandy and cigars.

Mitch was pleased to realize that some of the men were already aware of him by reputation. Those who weren't, upon hearing of his solid background, were anxious to meet him, talk with him, ask his opinion on business and investments.

Even old money wanted to associate with the smart newcomer, regardless of his background.

Mitch had discovered years ago that his past, the details of his personal life were of no consequence to his clients or the businessmen he met. They wanted Mitch's knowledge, they wanted to hear his opinion, his feeling about the economy or his gut reaction to an investment opportunity.

With Stuart Parker's glowing recommendation and business connections, Mitch knew he was on solid footing with the men he'd met in the city. He'd spotted several men whom he was certain would ask for his help. Potential clients. Potential business contacts. For that, Mitch was grateful.

He was grateful, too, that things had gotten easier for him over the years. Mitch sank a little lower on the hansom seat and allowed memories of his very first business venture to play through his mind. Still, over twenty years later he remembered it with pride.

His career as a newsboy had begun with great promise and the anticipation of rich rewards. He'd lasted about fifteen minutes on the street corner until an older boy bloodied his nose and tried to take his newspapers.

But at the ripe old age of twelve, Mitch had already tangled with more than his share of bullies and engaged in regular fistfights. Big for his age, Mitch was the frequent target of other boys trying to prove themselves.

He'd defended his street corner for four days in a row, soundly beating the older boy and his friends until they finally left him alone. Then the bastard who had the gall to insist he be addressed as "uncle" learned of Mitch's newfound income and insisted on a cut.

Mitch could fight him but knew he'd never win. So he'd attacked the problem from a different angle. Unbeknownst to his "uncle," Mitch recruited friends and put them to work selling papers. Mitch provided the muscle. He had no compunction about beating the tar out of anyone who stood in his way of earning money. Soon Mitch found other older boys who watched over the younger ones doing the selling. He collected the money, paid his employees, gave his bastard uncle the modest cut he expected and pocketed a tidy profit.

Mitch smiled at the memory. Then, on impulse, he reached inside his jacket pocket and drew out a small, slim book. The cardboard cover was worn thin with age, the pages dog-eared and crinkled in places.

Mitch held it in the palm of his hand, then traced his

finger over the twine he'd used to thread through the holes he'd punched so many years ago when he'd made the little book himself.

He opened it. Inside, a careful listing of every dime he'd ever earned. Long ago he could have afforded something nicer in which to track his income but Mitch liked this little ledger. A reminder of how far he'd come.

Also it was a reminder of who he was and what he was. Mitch shifted uncomfortably on the seat as Rachel flashed in his mind. For the past few days he'd left the house early, eaten at the little restaurant he'd found and walked the streets of the West Adams neighborhood until it was time to meet Stuart Parker. He'd returned late each evening. He hadn't seen Rachel at all.

What had she been doing while he'd been with Stuart Parker? Mitch wondered. Had she given in to the pressure of her friends and decided to host the luncheon? Was Chelsey still ranting and screaming at her? And Noah. Had Madeline sent him another letter?

Mitch slid the little ledger back into his pocket and admonished himself for having such thoughts. The Branford family wasn't his concern, beyond their finances. He'd have to make himself remember that.

Hayden, the Branford's butler, shot Mitch a look of profound relief as he opened the door and gave him entrance. Mitch knew why immediately upon stepping from the vestibule into the foyer.

Noah slouched in the doorway to the sitting room, drinking whiskey from a bottle.

Chelsey stood on the staircase, sobbing. "Why are you so determined to ruin my life?"

"Rachel!" Dr. Matthews called, following her across the foyer.

"No," she declared, hurrying away.

"Rachel, you must listen!" the doctor said, pursuing her.

"Why is everyone trying to ruin my life?" Chelsey beseeched.

"Rachel—" Dr. Matthews called.

She spun to face him, but caught sight of Mitch and stopped abruptly.

Dr. Matthews saw him, too. "Thank God you're here, man. Maybe you can talk some sense into this young woman."

Rachel flushed. "I'm perfectly capable of making up my own mind—"

"She's impossible!" Chelsey swept down the staircase, pushed her way in front of Rachel and the doctor, and turned her tearful face up to Mitch. "If you're going to help anyone, help me! Please!"

"This is a serious issue," Dr. Matthews said. "It must be addressed—"

"I've already addressed the matter," Rachel insisted.

"You haven't. Not to my satisfaction." The doctor turned to Mitch. "I need your support on this."

Rachel's gaze bored into him, daring him to speak.

"Please, talk to her!" Chelsey wailed.

Over all their heads, Mitch saw Noah, the look on his face one of unmasked contempt. Then Mitch's gaze swept the three other people in the foyer, all staring up at him, waiting for a response. A warm glow shot through him.

He turned to Dr. Matthews first, rested his hand on the doctor's shoulder and guided him toward the door. "I'll discuss the matter with Miss Branford right away."

"But—"

"Thank you for coming." Mitch eased him through the front door as Hayden passed the doctor his bowler and satchel. Mitch thought he saw a twitch of a conspiratorial smile on the old butler's face.

"You've got to do something about her!" Chelsey rushed toward him, jabbing her finger toward Rachel. "Why won't anyone listen to me! Why—"

"Chelsey." Mitch spoke her name just sternly enough and just loud enough that it silenced her. "I'll listen to your problem, but not your screaming. Go upstairs and calm yourself. Come back when you can tell me exactly what you want, along with three reasons why you should have it."

Chelsey stared blankly at him, as if the idea of presenting a calm, thoughtful argument hadn't occurred to her. Mitch suspected that was true.

"All right, I will," Chelsey said. She threw Rachel another indignant look, sniffed and headed up the stairs.

A calm fell over the house at the sound of Chelsey's fading footsteps. Hayden slipped away. Noah disappeared, leaving Mitch alone in the foyer with Rachel.

She looked irritated. She looked frazzled. She looked…beautiful.

At once, Mitch regretted the days he'd been away. He regretted the time he'd spent with Parker and the other men talking about business and the economy, labor and shipping costs. He should have been here.

"Where have you been?" Rachel demanded.

Mitch's heart lurched. The challenge in her words was oddly appealing, causing his pulse to rise. "I was—"

"I had no idea where you'd gone, no idea what you were doing." Her chin pushed up a little and her spine stiffened. "I've been here for days now, wondering what's going on."

She was angry and trying to hold back in true lady-like fashion. Beneath that controlled facade of hers lurked the hot-blooded woman he'd glimpsed before.

Mitch's desire for her heated up instantly.

"I'm not used to accounting to anyone for my where-abouts," Mitch pointed out.

"Well, things are different now," Rachel informed him. "You're part of this household. You can't just go running off, not telling anyone what you're up to."

"Did you think I wasn't coming back?" he asked.

His question seemed to irritate her further. "No, of course not."

"Then why are you upset?" he asked and eased a little closer. "Because you missed me?"

She gasped. Her anger vanished and her cheeks flushed. "Well...I, uh..."

Then her gaze met and held his. Mitch's heart hammered inside his chest. He lost himself in the brown of her eyes. He could have stayed lost there forever—happily so—if she hadn't spoken.

"I don't know why Dr. Matthews involved you in this problem," Rachel told him, a hint of irritation returning to her voice. "I've already made up my mind."

"I know," Mitch said simply and headed down the hallway toward the study.

"You know?" she asked, following.

Mitch looked down at her. "You're a smart woman, Rachel, more than capable of making a decision."

She paused, his comment surprising her. She couldn't recall anyone saying those words to her before. Ever.

"Oh. Well, thank you," she murmured as she watched his big, broad back disappear into the study.

Records from other Branford holdings that had been delivered in Mitch's absence were stacked in crates around the room. Incoming mail that had accumulated lay in neat piles on the desk, waiting to be opened. He flipped through a few of the envelopes.

He looked so calm, so at ease. She'd missed him.

The notion flew through Rachel and she knew it was true. When he'd walked into the house a few minutes ago, relief had swamped her. Everyone in the room had turned to him. He'd dispatched the doctor and stopped Chelsey's crying fit with so little effort.

A new wave of emotions roiled through Rachel. What was it, the feeling that had claimed her? She didn't know. Her irritation with Dr. Matthews? Yes, that was it. It must be.

"Dr. Matthews wants Father to go to a convalescent hospital," she blurted out. "He wants to send Father away."

Mitch looked up. "And you don't agree?"

"No, of course not," Rachel insisted, the very idea causing her heart to ache. "Father belongs here at home, with his family. I couldn't bear the thought of him being in a strange place with no loved ones nearby."

Mitch just looked at her. If he agreed or disagreed with her feelings, she couldn't tell. From his expression, his thoughts seemed to be somewhere else entirely.

Then she realized what she'd said. Mitch surely spent most of his time in strange places with no loved ones nearby. But just how he felt about it, Rachel couldn't guess.

"Then the matter is settled," Mitch said.

"It is?" she asked. That was it? That was all he had to say? He was giving her his complete support for no other reason than that he trusted her judgment?

He looked up at her and tilted his head a little, as she'd seen him do so many times already when he studied the journals and ledger entries. A thoughtful look, as he tried to glean everything possible from his observation.

Having that look directed at her was a bit disconcerting. It made her heart beat a little faster, for some reason.

"You carefully considered the doctor's recommendation," Mitch stated. "You thought it through, decided what was best for your father. Didn't you?"

"Yes," Rachel told him, uncomfortable beneath his stare for another reason now.

Anxious suddenly to change the subject, she walked a little closer to the desk and gestured at the stacks of mail.

"I received the weekly report from Mr. Edgars," Rachel said.

She could see Mitch's mind working, as if mentally searching the family records to locate the name.

"Edgars Detective Agency, the firm engaged to search for your brother," Mitch said.

"Mr. Edgars came by the house today."

"For the fees the man is charging, I'd expect him to hand deliver his reports etched in silver," Mitch grumbled.

"We shouldn't need their services much longer," Rachel said. "Several possibilities have developed. Mr. Edgars is sure he'll find Georgie quickly."

"I guess that would solve many of your problems."

Rachel sighed heavily. "I just know if Georgie were here, he'd make everything all right."

Mitch looked at her without responding and Rachel decided he'd probably heard enough of the family problems.

But she was wrong. Mitch settled onto the corner of the desk, making himself a little shorter.

"What's wrong with your sister now?" he asked. "Anything new?"

"She's adamant about going back to school."

"Maybe you should let her."

"And she'd learn what from that?" Rachel asked. "That if she screamed loud enough, long enough, she'd get her way?"

Mitch looked at her for a moment, in that reasonable way of his. "Is something else going on between the two of you?"

"No," Rachel insisted. But she had to look away, unable to meet Mitch's stare.

He touched her chin, gently bringing her face around to him. "Sure?"

Rachel's heart ached with a need to lean into his palm, drape her arms around his neck, rest her head against his wide shoulders. She imagined his strength seeping inside her, bolstering her, making her stronger, too.

Yet she didn't do any of those things. She didn't dare lean on Mitch—or any other man, for that matter.

When she didn't answer, Mitch rose from the desk and left the room, then returned a few moments later with Chelsey. She'd dried her eyes but her cheeks were pink. Mitch eased onto the desk again, the two sisters in front of him facing each other.

"Chelsey," he said, "please state exactly what it is you want, and three reasons why you want it."

"It's all I've ever wanted! I've always—"

"Chelsey." Mitch's stern voice quieted her. "I don't need the show, just the facts."

She looked slightly embarrassed, but continued. "I want to go back to school. I want to—"

"Don't tell me." Mitch gestured to Rachel. "Tell your sister."

The two sisters faced each other looking awkward and unsure.

"I want to finish the term," Chelsey said, "so I don't get too far behind in my studies. And because I miss my friends. And because it's—it's so sad living here."

"Now, Rachel," Mitch said. "Give Chelsey three reasons why she can't go back to school."

"Because it's not proper for you to be gone. And…and…" Rachel gulped, emotions swelling inside her. "And because it's so sad living here and I'll miss you terribly."

Tears sprang to Chelsey's eyes. "You will?"

"Yes!" A sob tore from Rachel's throat as emotions held inside too long suddenly broke free.

"Wait—no." Mitch hopped off the desk.

Chelsey burst into tears, too.

"I didn't mean for you to get upset," he said.

The sisters threw themselves together.

"I didn't want you to cry," he exclaimed.

Rachel ignored him and hugged her sister, both of them sobbing. They cried together for a long while, then pulled apart, swiping at their tears.

"I didn't know you'd miss me if I left," Chelsey said. "I've been so awful to you."

"You're still my sister."

"I'm sorry."

"I'm sorry, too," Rachel said. She gulped. "You can go back to school."

"I won't disgrace the family," Chelsey told her. "I heard those things from Mother, just as you did."

"Go pack your things," Rachel told her. "You can leave in the morning."

"Thank you." Chelsey gave her sister a big hug, then threw her arms around Mitch. She dashed out of the study.

Rachel watched her go, then turned to Mitch. More than ever, she wanted to lean against him, soak up his strength. But he looked bewildered, unsure whether or not he'd done the right thing.

Rachel smiled. "This is for the best. I can see it now. Thank you."

Mitch shrugged. "You're welcome...I guess."

"I'd better let you get to work." Rachel headed for the door, then turned back. "I thought about what you said about the luncheon, about not hosting it. But I can't turn my back on the event."

"You don't sound very happy about it."

"I'm not," she admitted. But nothing could be done except to go forward. Otherwise, what would people say?

"Then maybe you should host the luncheon in a way that will make you happy?" Mitch suggested.

Rachel gasped softly, the notion zipping through her mind. "Change the luncheon? I couldn't possibly do that."

"Why not?"

"Because," she told him.

He raised an eyebrow. "Because…?"

"Because it's always been Mother's luncheon. Her linens, her china, her floral arrangements." Rachel drew in a breath. "Are you suggesting that I change everything?"

"Wouldn't that make your mother proud?"

Rachel considered it for a moment. Would her mother be proud of her? If she took control of the occasion, put her own individual stamp on it, wouldn't that show the ladies that her mother had raised a daughter who could carry on despite everything? Would that be the ultimate tribute to the memory of her mother?

And maybe, just maybe, Rachel wouldn't miss her mother quite so much. Maybe she could actually enjoy the event.

"My goodness." Rachel pressed her palm to her forehead as dozens of ideas swept through her mind. "I have so much to do. I've got to start over, completely."

She rushed from the study. She needed her tablet. She wanted to make notes. She had to contact Claudia and arrange a shopping trip. She needed new…everything.

Rachel stopped short in the hallway as an unwelcome thought brought her plans to a screeching halt. She turned and went back into the study. Mitch waited exactly where she'd left him a moment ago.

"Can I afford this?" she asked.

Mitch thought his heart would break. The excitement, the sheer joy he'd seen on her face only a moment ago had vanished and in its place he saw the worry that he'd witnessed too many times already. The urge to take care of her, make things better for her rose in him with an intensity he'd never experienced before.

"Of course," he said. "Get whatever you want."

A half smile pulled at the corner of her lips. "Really?"

No, not really. The Branford family could ill afford to spend their money on a luncheon, of all things, not with all the expenses involved with running a household this large.

But Mitch couldn't tell Rachel "no." He wouldn't. It was his job to handle the family finances and—short of dipping into his own funds—he'd find a way to pay for the things Rachel wanted.

"Get whatever you want. Whatever you need," Mitch said.

She hesitated. "You're sure?"

"I told you," he said and gestured to the ledgers around him. "I'm very good at this."

A big smile bloomed on her face. "Oh, this is going to be the best luncheon ever. It's going to be perfect."

Mitch smiled as Rachel dashed from the room. He turned and surveyed the ledgers, the accounting of the sources of the Branford funds. He'd have to find a way to make the money available to Rachel.

And he knew exactly where to start.

Chapter Nine

The door chimes broke Mitch's concentration as he sat behind the desk in the study. He glanced at the mantel clock across the room. After five. Too late for visitors. Too late for the postman.

Madeline's letter? Mitch hurried to the door and gazed down the hallway to the foyer. Rachel had told him that the young girl wrote to Noah twice a week. Mitch didn't know which days, but he wanted to be ready, just in case.

As he watched, Hayden crept from the vestibule with a large box wrapped in brown paper tucked under his arm. Among the butler's many duties, he delivered all letters and packages that arrived at the Branford house. He'd overseen the placement of the many crates of family records that littered the study.

Hayden nodded respectfully to Mitch as he passed, and disappeared into the sitting room. A few second later, he returned and went about his business elsewhere in the house.

Had Madeline sent Noah a package? Was the boy waiting in the sitting room?

Mitch went to the doorway and was relieved to see Rachel inside, alone. She stood with her back to him at the little writing desk, the box lying open, a froth of white tissue paper around her.

The early evening shadows cast her in pale light. Somehow, she seemed to shine. Mitch's heart tumbled. Such a beautiful woman.

He glanced back down the hallway, knowing what he should do, what he ought to do, what was best for him. But he just couldn't seem to bring himself to do it.

"Something for the luncheon?" he asked, walking in.

Rachel whirled around, her eyes wide as saucers. She spread her arms to block his view of the box.

Mitch had thought that something she'd bought for the luncheon had arrived. But the blush on her cheeks told him nothing of the sort was in the box.

"What is it?" he asked.

"Nothing!" Rachel spun around and batted at the tissue paper.

Mitch eased up behind her and tried to look over her shoulder. She glanced up at him, dodged right, then left, desperate, it seemed, to block his view. Now he had to know what was in the box.

"Did you buy a dress?" he asked, seeing the light blue fabric through the thin paper.

Rachel grabbed the lid and smashed it onto the box. She turned to face him. "It's—it's nothing."

Was she worried he'd be upset that she'd spent money? He wondered.

"What is it?" he asked again.

The pink on her cheeks deepened. "It's something… personal."

"Since when is a new dress 'personal'?" Mitch asked. "Is it for you to wear at the luncheon? Let me see."

She drew herself up and spread her arms wide. "I told you, it's personal."

"How personal can a dress—"

Mitch froze as he realized that the items in the box were Rachel's undergarments. Then his heart slammed against his chest and heat soared through his veins.

They were undergarments and they were colored.

Mitch's desire for her flamed. Colored underwear. Miss What-Will-People-Say, Miss That-Simply-Isn't-Done wore colored undergarments. She probably had them specially made in secret, shipped to the house in a plain wrapper so no one would know. Surely she had a conservative ivory flounce sewn on the edges of her petticoats so no one would suspect.

Mitch gulped. He wanted her. Right here, right now. He wanted to lay her back on that box of blue underwear and—

"If you'll excuse me?" Rachel snatched up the box and hurried from the room.

Mitch watched her go, watched the sway of her hips, the swing of her skirts as she disappeared out of the door. He clenched his fists. It took all the willpower he could muster to keep from going after her. He'd never wanted a woman the way he wanted Rachel.

When he'd first met her, his heart had ached for her. His body wanted hers from the start.

If his head ever agreed with the rest of him, God knows what he might do.

The house in the dead of night caused no trepidation for Rachel. Darkness, shadows, silence were as welcome to her as daytime's bright sunlight and the voices of her family, the servants and visitors. This place was her home and she was always comfortable there.

Except for tonight.

Rachel's bare feet skipped up the staircase, tracing a well-practiced route that avoided the occasional creaking riser. Noise was her enemy tonight. She wanted no one to realize her intentions at this late hour.

At the top of the staircase, she turned right, her nightgown and robe flying behind her as she hurried down the hall. She pushed her long hair over her shoulder and stopped in front of Mitch's door.

She needed him. Now.

Rachel raised her fist to knock but stopped herself. She glanced up and down the hallway. Someone might hear the noise. Her father was incapacitated and Chelsey's room lay a good distance away, but the servants seemed to hear, see and know everything that went on. And the very last thing Rachel intended to do was attract attention.

She turned the doorknob, slipped inside Mitch's bedchamber and closed the door behind her. Darkness enfolded her as she clung to the knob, not daring to turn around.

She was in a man's bedchamber. Mitch's room. Her heart beat a little faster at the realization. Moments ago, downstairs, all she could think of was to get to him. But now that she was here…

Rachel drew in a fortifying breath, turned and surveyed the room. Her gaze landed on the bed.

Empty.

Empty? She ventured closer, seeing in the dim light that the coverlet hadn't been disturbed. The adjoining bathroom was dark and empty, too. Where had Mitch gone?

Rachel pressed her lips together. She hadn't seen him downstairs just now. Had he left the house? Hurrying to the window, Rachel gazed outside onto the rear lawn. No unusual shadows moved about the grounds.

Disheartened, she left the room, considering what to do next. Who could she turn to now?

A faint light caught her attention from the end of the hallway along with an odd thumping sound. Rachel followed it to the attic entrance and went up the stairs.

Mitch. Her breath caught at the sight of him.

Across the cluttered attic he pounded his bare fists into a big, heavy bag suspended from the rafters. Boxing. It was all the rage, with participants attaining a sort of celebrity status. Rachel knew of the sport, though she didn't understand the allure of men beating each other bloody.

Seeing Mitch brought her a sudden appreciation for the effort and froze her on the top step.

Wide, square shoulders. Huge arms, bulging with every punch and jab. Damp hair hanging over his sweating forehead.

The business suits he always wore kept secret the strength of his body. Now, the sleeveless white undershirt, damp with sweat, stuck to his chest and rippled belly. His soft, worn denim trousers clung to places a lady should never look.

Rachel looked. Warmth spread through her, somehow locking her in place, binding her to the sight of Mitch.

He stopped suddenly and his gaze fell on her. An unexpected heat covered her cheeks and she nearly ran back down the steps. But she couldn't bring herself to leave.

"What—what are you doing?" Mitch asked, breathing heavily, his hands at his sides.

A moment ago he'd looked nearly spent from pounding the bag. Now he seemed spun up, ready to pounce— on something. But he wasn't angry. Rachel wasn't sure what it was.

"I saw the light on," she said, gesturing vaguely down the stairs. "I was in your bedchamber and I—"

"You were in my room?" he asked, his eyes dipping to take in the length of her.

"Yes, I needed you—"

"Oh, Christ…" Mitch grabbed a towel from atop an old dresser and plopped down onto a tiny three-legged stool. He plastered the towel over his face.

Rachel hurried to him. "I need you."

He dragged the towel down and gazed up at her, his breathing quick and heavy. A few more seconds passed without him speaking until Rachel supposed he wasn't going to.

"It's Noah," she said. "Downstairs. I couldn't wake him. I don't want the servants to find him. I think maybe he's…"

Mitch nodded. He dragged the towel over his face

and around his neck, then tossed it aside and rose to his feet.

Rachel fell back a little at his strength and great height rising in front of her. Heat rolled off him. A masculine scent engulfed her. It seemed to call to her, somehow. Urge her to do something very unladylike.

Mitch stared down at her, a hunger in his gaze that had nothing to do with proper decorum. Rachel felt her cheeks flush again.

Was he going to kiss her? The thought skittered through her mind. Did she want him to?

Before she could decide on an answer, Mitch turned sharply and left the attic. Rachel followed, the cooler air of the second-floor hallway a welcome relief.

"He's in the library," Rachel explained, hurrying alongside Mitch. "I couldn't sleep so I went to find a book. I found him on the floor."

In the library near the rear of the house, a solitary lamp burned on the desk. Noah lay facedown on the floor near the leather sofa.

Rachel knelt near her brother's head. "I couldn't rouse him. Is he all right?"

Mitch dropped to one knee and turned Noah over. An empty liquor bottle rolled from beneath him.

"He'll be fine," Mitch said. He grabbed the boy's arm and hoisted him over his shoulder.

Rachel led the way upstairs to Noah's room. Mitch dropped him on the bed and waited while she pulled the quilt over him. They went into the hallway and closed the door.

"He drank too much, didn't he?" Rachel asked.

Mitch nodded and she said, "I don't know what to do about him."

"Nothing you can do tonight," Mitch pointed out.

They walked down the hallway and stopped at the door to Rachel's bedchamber.

"I didn't know you boxed," she said. "You seem very good at it."

He stood in front of her. "I'm good at a lot of things."

That strange heat seemed to emanate from him once more. It overtook Rachel, urged her closer to him. She held back.

"Thank you for your help," she said. "I know you didn't expect this sort of thing when you agreed to work here."

Mitch angled his body closer and braced one arm on the wall behind her head. His closeness, his strength robbed Rachel of words. She thought of only one thing to say.

"I missed you while you were gone," she whispered.

Mitch eased back a little and Rachel thought he'd turn and leave. Instead, he bent down and kissed her.

He slid his lips over hers, sending a quiver through her. One of his arms curled around her. He splayed his palm across her cheek. A warmth bound them together.

He deepened their kiss, slipping his tongue inside. Rachel gasped, then sighed at the wonder, the delight of it. He blended their mouths together for a long, exquisite moment.

Mitch lifted his head, but held her in his embrace. Rachel made no effort to pull away. She remained in his arms, gazing up at him. They stayed that way for a long time, just the two of them, bound together by unseen forces.

After another moment, Mitch backed away. Rachel's heart lurched. She didn't want him to leave. She craved his nearness, his heat, his scent.

He seemed to know that, somehow. Mitch hesitated for a few seconds, then turned and headed down the hallway. Rachel ducked into her room and fell back against the door.

Good gracious, what was happening to her?

Chapter Ten

The journal entries blurred before Mitch's eyes and turned into colors. Yellow? Pink?

Or the pale blue he'd seen yesterday?

He snapped the ledger closed and shifted in his chair. All he'd been able to think of this morning was Rachel's underwear, and those thoughts kept his desire for her humming until he could hardly sit still.

Did she wear the colored undergarments everyday? He suspected so. Did she pick a color at random or per-haps something that matched her dress?

What was she wearing today? The pale blue set he'd seen her open in the sitting room?

He pressed his lips together, imagining—not for the first time—what Rachel might look like in the blue un-dergarments. Stretched out on the bed, her long, lovely legs peeking from the folds of silky blue, an identically colored chemise hanging off one shoulder.

Mitch shook his head, clearing his mind. It was just

these thoughts that had driven him to the attic last night to work out his frustration on the punching bag.

The attic. Mitch moaned. In the attic last night, Rachel, quite obviously, had on no underwear at all. It was as if Mitch's overwhelming desire for her had somehow summoned her. She'd simply appeared at the top of the stairs, her hair falling around her shoulders, her swells and curves outlined by her loose-fitting nightclothes. It was almost more than Mitch could bear.

Yet he'd better learn to bear it.

Mitch picked up the ledger and forced his mind back onto the columns of figures. He was here to do a job and thoughts of Rachel and her underwear would only distract him, prolong his work, and thus his misery.

Determinedly, he pulled a tablet from the desk drawer and turned to a fresh page. He had to finish his analysis and come to a decision. He still had a number of things—

They matched.

The notion flew into Mitch's mind with an intensity that drove him from the chair.

They matched. Rachel's undergarments matched her dresses. Surely her desire for perfection extended to her own wardrobe. That could only mean that the color of whatever dress she wore was complemented by undergarments of the same hue. With a green gown, she wore green underwear. Blue with blue. Purple with purple. Black with—

The mental image of Rachel in black undergarments sent Mitch bolting for the door.

* * *

She'd seen him so many times now, how could her heart still lurch at the sight of him?

Rachel moved closer to the sitting-room window as she watched Mitch striding across the rear lawn. He usually took a walk in the middle of the day, a stroll through the neighborhood to clear his mind, she guessed. No one could remain cooped up in an office behind a desk all day.

But right now he appeared in a terrible hurry, though she couldn't imagine why. And he seemed hot, too. The day was overcast and cool, but he'd pulled down his necktie and popped open his collar.

A little shiver passed over her at the memory of last night. Mitch in his undershirt. She'd never seen a man dressed that way before. She couldn't imagine any man—not even Claudia's precious Graham Bixby—looking so fine.

Along with memories of Mitch's broad shoulders came another thought about last night. Rachel had had no man to rely on in a long time, and Mitch filled that hole in the family so easily, so effortlessly. They all ran to him with problems. And he seemed to have the answers.

Last night when she'd stumbled upon Noah on the library floor, she'd been afraid he'd hurt himself. Without another thought, she'd run to find Mitch.

He was so strong, so capable she knew he could get Noah upstairs and into his room. She knew, too, that he'd keep the incident to himself. She certainly didn't want the servants to learn of it. Goodness knows, they talked among themselves and to the servants of the neighboring households.

What would people think?

A plume of heat swelled in Rachel. What would people think, indeed, if they'd seen the two of them kissing outside her bedchamber? He'd taken her breath away. Made her forget, just for a few moments, all her troubles.

Could Mitch make her feel that way all the time?

The door chimes once again interrupted Mitch's concentration. He'd trained himself to listen for them, these past few days.

He shoved out of his chair, grabbed the letter opener from his desk and left the study. If this was another delivery of colored underwear, he didn't know what he'd do.

That concern proved groundless when he saw Noah coming down the staircase and Hayden crossing the foyer, a single letter lying atop the small tray he carried. It was from Madeline, surely. Noah must have been watching from the upstairs window and seen the family servant deliver it.

"Just a minute," Mitch called. "Let me see the letter."

The butler paused. His troubled gaze darted to Noah, who'd stopped on the bottom step. Mitch walked past the boy, glimpsed the anger in his expression and his want to race ahead and claim his treasured letter.

But Noah didn't move. Mitch knew he wouldn't. Mitch was bigger and stronger. And he had two arms.

"I'm making a change," Mitch said, stopping in front of Hayden. "From now on when you bring me the mail I want you to open it for me."

The butler just looked at him.

"Like this." Mitch picked up the letter from the tray and saw that it was, indeed, addressed to Noah. He sliced through the envelope with the letter opener. "I want you to do that for everyone in the family. Understand?"

A knowing smile quivered on the butler's lips. "Yes, Mr. Kincade. I understand completely."

Mitch presented Hayden with the letter opener, then turned to Noah and held out the envelope.

The boy didn't rush forward and grab it, but Mitch knew he wouldn't. A myriad of emotions played across his young face: fear, suspicion and finally, begrudged gratitude. He swiped the envelope from Mitch's hand and darted up the staircase.

Mitch watched him disappear down the hallway, then turned to Hayden. "Thank you," he said.

"No, thank you, sir." The butler nodded and left.

Mitch returned to the study and the analysis he'd spent the last hour working on. He knew what his recommendation would be. It wasn't even a close call. But Rachel had asked about it specifically, so he'd put in the extra effort, double-checked figures and thought it through again.

At last, Mitch put down his pencil and sat back in his chair. His initial impression had been correct. The purchase of the factory Rachel had asked him to check on was simply out of the question.

The business would be a good investment, though. Mitch had visited the site and spoken with Mr. Prescott during the time Stuart Parker had shown him around the city. Rachel's brother's interest in the business made sense. A new direction in which to expand the Branford holdings was good.

But with the family's current cash situation, there wasn't enough capital for the purchase and the expenses to follow. Mitch would recommend that they pass on the deal.

He rose from the desk and straightened his necktie. He'd break the news to Rachel himself. He owed it to her. Besides, he hadn't seen her all day. He didn't know what color dress she'd chosen or what color—

"Damn…" Mitch shook his head. He had to stop thinking about underwear.

He found her in the sitting room where she spent most of her afternoons. She stood by the window gazing out. And wearing amethyst.

Light purple beneath? Or dark, to match the dress? Mitch forced down another wave of wanting.

She turned as he walked into the room and Mitch saw a little frown on her face. He hadn't noticed it a moment ago, as things that couldn't be seen occupied all of his thoughts.

"What's wrong?" he asked, images of undergarments receding to the back of his mind, replaced by the concern that had hummed through him since the first day he entered this house.

"Nothing, really." She managed a small smile. "Did you need something?"

As any proper hostess should, Rachel was always trying to feed him. The problem was, Mitch had more appetite than Rachel or the cook staff were prepared for. He kept from starving by stopping in at a little restaurant he'd found during one of his daily walks, and by fixing himself something to eat late at night after the cooks had all retired to their quarters for the evening.

"I'm ready to make a recommendation to Stuart Parker about the factory you asked about," Mitch explained. "The one your brother wanted to buy."

Rachel's face brightened. "Mr. Prescott's factory? I thought you'd forgotten."

"I remember everything," he said, the image of her in her nightclothes flashing through his mind.

She didn't seem to notice.

"Are we going to buy it?" she asked.

"No," Mitch said.

"No…?"

Rachel gazed up at him with the hope that surely she'd heard wrong. Mitch's stomach knotted with regret, as if he'd failed her somehow.

"It's not feasible right now," he said.

"But isn't there something you can do?" she asked, looking up at him with those big brown eyes of hers. "Sell or restructure something? Jiggle things around, somehow?"

Mitch considered going over the details of the purchase another time. He hadn't realized it meant so much to Rachel. Yet he knew his decision wouldn't change.

"I've already looked at it from every angle," he told her. "It's not a smart move right now. I won't put your family in that situation."

Her shoulders slumped. "Oh…"

"Maybe at a later date," Mitch offered, overwhelmed with the need to say something positive. "In a year or so when things are running more smoothly."

"A year…" Rachel's gaze dropped to her hands and she sighed heavily.

Mitch moved to her side. It took all his strength not to slip his arm around her shoulder and draw her against his chest. She was upset and he had to make things better.

"I'll take another look at it," he told her. "I'll go over everything again and see what I can do."

She looked up at him. "But you really don't think you can make it work, do you."

"No." It was the hardest word he'd ever spoken.

"Well, then I guess that's that." Rachel sighed again and drew herself up, then offered an apologetic smile. "Sorry to make such a fuss. I know you're doing your best."

"Is there some reason your brother wanted the factory that I'm not aware of?" Mitch asked.

Rachel shook her head quickly and stepped away from him. "I don't mean to take it out on you. I'm sorry. I'm disappointed about something else, that's all."

Now what was wrong? Mitch had never felt so helpless in his life.

She gave him another half smile, as if she read his expression.

"It's nothing," Rachel insisted. She nodded toward the writing desk. "Claudia just sent me a note. We'd planned a shopping trip this afternoon to pick out table linens and other things I need for the luncheon. Now she can't go."

"I'll go with you."

Her eyebrows shot up. "You want to go shopping?"

Damn right he wanted go to. He couldn't recommend buying her the factory she wanted, couldn't make her father well, or bring back her mother or locate her older brother, or get Noah another arm.

But he could see that she got her shopping trip.

"Sure," Mitch declared. "You can show me what you want for the luncheon, table linens or forks or whatever."

She laughed gently. "Do you know anything about picking out linens?"

"I've always wanted to learn."

Rachel eyed him for a moment, as if making up her mind, then said, "Well, if you're sure..."

"Let's go." He nodded toward the door.

"I have to get dressed first."

"Get dressed? You look fine."

"I'll be just a few minutes."

Rachel hurried past him and Mitch turned, following her out of the room. He spotted Noah in the doorway and stopped.

Mitch didn't know how long he'd stood there or how much he'd overheard. The boy didn't say anything, but after a moment, he walked away.

Mitch didn't give it another thought as he headed for the study to get his jacket. Because for the first time in his life, he was going shopping with a lady.

Chapter Eleven

"Which do you like the best?" Rachel asked.

Mitch waited at the foot of the staircase as Rachel descended carrying a hat in each hand. Nearly an hour had passed since she headed up to her room to get ready for their shopping trip. He couldn't imagine what she'd done in that amount of time. She had on a different dress now, a dark green one, but that was about it. What had taken so long?

"I can't decide," she declared, holding out the two hats. "Which one should I wear?"

Both were wide brimmed, decorated with flowers.

"They're the same," Mitch said.

"They're completely different." She held out each in turn. "This one has pansies and this one has irises."

"Oh." He studied them again. "They're both nice."

"But they each give a totally different effect. Let me show you." Rachel turned to the mirror above the chest in the foyer and placed one of the hats on her head. She turned to him. "What do you think?"

He thought she was beautiful. The hat dipped low over one eye, tilting at a provocative angle.

"Or, this one." At the mirror again, Rachel tried on the other hat. She turned back to him. This one sat a little higher on her forehead, displaying her entire face.

"I like them both," Mitch said.

"But which one looks best?"

He thought for another few seconds. "The first one."

Rachel heaved an exasperated sigh and flung her arms out. "Now I have to go change my dress."

"Change your—"

She whipped around and headed up the stairs again.

"Why are you changing your dress?" Mitch called. "It's fine."

She didn't answer.

"I've already waited an hour," Mitch called, waving toward the hall clock. "Why are you…?"

All he could do was stand there as the last swish of her skirt hem disappeared down the upstairs hallway. Mitch pressed his palm to his forehead. What had just happened?

From the corner of his eye, he caught sight of Noah. The boy uttered a disgusted grunt and walked away.

"What?" Mitch went after him.

Noah glanced back only long enough to give him a disapproving head shake.

"What?" Mitch demanded.

Noah turned back, suddenly looking wise and confident.

"You don't have sisters, do you," he declared, not asking a question but rather making a statement, as if the answer was a foregone conclusion.

"No," Mitch admitted.

"Wife? Aunt, mother, grandmother?"

"What are you getting at?"

"They do this all the time," Noah told him, gesturing toward the upstairs. "Never—and I mean never—tell them you like a particular hat or dress better than another."

"But she asked me."

"It's a trap," Noah told him. "Believe me, whatever you pick, it will be wrong."

"What am I supposed to do when she asks me?"

"Tell her they both are perfect. She looks beautiful in each. Tell her you can't decide."

"But what if I really like one more than the other?"

"Then you run the risk of having to wait until she changes again."

"Like now."

"Exactly," Noah told him. "You may as well find something to do. It will be another hour before she's ready to go. Oh, and one more thing. No matter what, don't agree to eat at the Peacock Tea Room today."

"Why not?"

"You don't want to eat there. Believe me."

Mitch nodded. "Right. No Peacock Tea Room. Got it."

Noah looked as if he doubted it, and headed on down the hallway.

Mitch returned to the study and went back to work. An hour later, he and Rachel were finally in the carriage, heading out of the driveway.

It had been worth the wait. Seated across from her, Mitch's only thought was how beautiful she looked.

She'd changed into yet another green dress that looked to Mitch to be no different from the last. But she was smiling now, arranging her skirt and talking about the trip ahead.

"Wilshire Boulevard has the best shops. We'll go there." Her smile broadened. "Then we'll have lunch at the Peacock Tea Room. How does that sound?"

Mitch didn't hesitate. "Sounds perfect."

The smile Rachel received in return made her stomach flutter. The sensation caused her to look away from him, out the window at the neighbors' houses rolling past.

It was strange sharing a shopping trip with a man. Rachel couldn't remember one single time when her father had escorted her mother on such an occasion. When they were all younger, Chelsey, Noah and Rachel had accompanied their mother. Noah finally rebelled, refusing to go. Chelsey preferred to stay home and read, usually, until finally it was simply Rachel and her mother.

The joy of those treasured memories brought with it the sadness of her mother's absence. Rachel forced aside the turbulent thought. She sat a little straighter on the leather seat, focusing instead on the day that lay ahead.

And her shopping companion.

Though she'd made Mitch's acquaintance only a short while ago, she knew some very important things about him.

He was a hard worker. Smart. Decisive. She knew he ate very little, especially for a man his size. She knew he liked his solitude. She knew he boxed.

Her gaze drifted across the carriage.

She knew what he looked like in his undershirt.

His gaze darted to meet hers, as if sensing her study of him. Rachel looked away. After a moment, her eyes found him again.

His kiss. She knew that about him, too. The taste of his mouth. The feel of his lips. And he gave off an incredible amount of heat. On cold, winter nights how nice it would be to snuggle close, indulge in that warmth.

Rachel's thought startled her. Good gracious, what had come over her? Thinking such things. How unladylike. It simply wasn't done.

Shifting on the seat, Rachel smoothed down her skirt, directing her thoughts elsewhere. It came to her then that, aside from these few facts, she knew very little about Mitch. His background was a mystery to her while he knew everything there was to know about the Branfords. Their finances, their troubles, their living arrangements. Everything.

Rachel decided it was high time the scales were evened, and with some clever questioning, she could accomplish that.

"Do you like Los Angeles?" she asked, keeping her voice light, conversational.

Mitch nodded thoughtfully. "It's a nice place."

"It's different from San Francisco, though, isn't it?" she asked. "That's your home? San Francisco?"

"Both cities are prosperous. Lots of commerce. Not as much rain here, though."

Great. She'd maneuvered him into talking about the weather.

"What about your family?" she asked, trying for something more direct. "Do they miss you while you're gone?"

He uttered a half laugh. "Families. There's always something to be dealt with. You know that."

How easily he'd avoided answering even one of her questions. He'd deflected them all, given her no real information. And with practiced ease, too. As if he'd confronted these very questions many times before and successfully sidestepped them all.

Why?

A stunning thought made Rachel's breath catch.

"Are you married?" she asked. It came out as an accusation, rather than a question.

That got his attention.

Yet he didn't blurt out an answer. A frown creased his forehead and his eyes narrowed.

"No one ever asked me that before," he said.

"I think I have a right to know," she told him.

"Because I kissed you?"

Her cheeks warmed. "You didn't answer my question."

"Would you have let me kiss you if I were married?" he proposed.

"Of course not," Rachel told him, then was annoyed with herself for responding. "You still haven't given me an answer."

"I have a very low opinion of married men who cheat on their wives," Mitch told her. He glanced out the window for a moment, then back at her. "No, I'm not married. Not engaged. Not courting anyone."

She felt relieved, for a reason she didn't want to think about.

"Marriage isn't part of your plan?" Rachel asked, remembering the night they walked through the garden together when he'd told her of his desire to attain wealth and power. "You think it would be difficult to follow your plan with a wife and children in tow?"

"Don't you?" he countered.

"I think that would depend on the wife."

Mitch seemed to consider this for a moment, then asked, "What about you? I've seen no suitors coming or going since I've been at your house."

Benjamin Blair roared into Rachel's mind, the man who'd called on her regularly only a few months ago. She pushed the bitter recollection aside, as she'd done so often before.

Now, since her mother's death, it wasn't proper to receive a gentleman caller and that suited Rachel fine. She seldom met a man she found interesting. A man she wanted to learn more about.

Or one she wanted to see without his shirt on.

Rachel waved away Mitch's comment, hoping also to banish the image from her mind.

"I am far too consumed with family matters at present," she told him.

Mitch hadn't really expected a different answer from her. Even if accepting a gentleman caller were socially acceptable at this point, he doubted Rachel would have done so. Her family commanded her attention, their reputation and well-being uppermost in her mind.

"Here we are," Rachel said as the carriage rolled to a stop. Mitch climbed out first and assisted her to the sidewalk.

Pedestrians bustled along the walkways, men in suits and women wearing the latest fashion, bunched together with folks of the working class. Horse-drawn carriages and delivery wagons crowded the street, vying with the trolleys for the limited space. Utility lines crisscrossed overhead. All manner of businesses were housed in tall buildings—banks, shops, restaurants, hotels.

Mitch took it all in with a slow, even sweep. He loved the city. The people, the sights, the sounds. The opportunities. The chance to be as big as the city itself.

Then Rachel's hand closed around his elbow, shrinking the world and closing out the sound.

"Let's start here." She pointed to a nearby store.

The smile on her face touched him. Today the potential of the City of Los Angeles could wait. Today he was shopping for table linens.

They went from store to store all along the street. The clerks knew Rachel by name. They brought out their best wares. Mitch stood at her side as she considered the items, listening, learning.

"In the linen, silver and crystal of the supper table one reads the story of the hostess's personality," Rachel explained.

"The story of the hostess's personality?" Mitch repeated.

"Certainly. Her taste is reflected in the correctness, or the incorrectness, of the table arrangement," she explained. "One must be careful not to overburden the table, of course, as it's easy to do."

Mitch nodded, taking it in. When she asked for his opinion, he remembered Noah's advice and remarked that he liked them all. That seemed to please Rachel just as well; he was sure she already knew what she wanted, anyway.

Other times he followed along behind her through the store aisles because he had no idea where she was going or what might strike her fancy and cause her to stop suddenly. Besides, the view was nice from the rear.

He carried packages. He went where she wanted to go. He listened. He leaned down when she wanted to whisper in his ear about someone she spotted in the crowd. He smelled her hair and watched her bustle bob up and down. He held her arm when they crossed the street and hurried her along when she was too busy looking in a shop window to watch traffic.

Stores had begun to close when they reached their carriage with the final armload of purchases. The driver took them from Mitch while Rachel contemplated the display in a nearby window that she'd considered earlier in the day.

"The more I look at those candlesticks…" she mused. "Maybe we should have a closer—oh, there's Claudia. She told me she and Graham would be together today."

Mitch spotted Rachel's friend among the thinning crowd on the sidewalk. A man was with her, the "perfect" Graham Bixby, Mitch reckoned. He knew the Bixby family by reputation, thanks to Stuart Parker. Solid leaders in the community, good businessmen.

But Graham didn't look anything close to perfect at the moment. He looked irritated.

Claudia spotted Rachel and spoke to Bixby. He seemed further irritated, but walked down to meet them. The men shook hands as introductions were made.

"I see you've wasted a day, also," Graham said to Mitch, gesturing at the packages piled in the Branford carriage.

"How did your china pattern selection go?" Rachel asked.

"A waste of time," Graham grumbled, throwing Claudia a disdainful look. "It took her hours to get ready, leaving us no time to accomplish anything."

"I said I was sorry, Graham," Claudia said in a small voice.

Graham seemed not to hear and continued speaking to Mitch. "Now we're here and the stores are closing. I told her I only had today. Now I'm going to have to rearrange my schedule to come back and get this handled."

Graham's complaint brought an uncomfortable silence to the group.

"Claudia, come look at these candlesticks with me," Rachel said, gesturing down the block.

Claudia looked relieved. "Of course—"

"No." Graham gave her a sharp look. "I don't have time. Haven't you heard a word I've said?"

Claudia's cheeks flushed.

"We'd better go, too," Rachel said quickly.

Mitch picked up on her intentions, bade the other couple a goodbye and headed back down the block with Rachel.

"Don't you want to look at the candlesticks?" he asked as they passed the shop window.

Rachel shook her head. "No. Not anymore."

Graham Bixby had managed to take the joy out of the moment for everyone. But Mitch wasn't ready to let it go so easily.

"Let's go have a look." He gave her a knowing smile. "I think they will reflect the correctness of the hostess's personality quite well."

She gazed at him, seemingly surprised that he remembered some of what she'd told him earlier. "Is that so?"

"Without overburdening the table, of course," he added.

She smiled, and Mitch's heart swelled with a sense of accomplishment no business deal had ever brought.

Chapter Twelve

"You ate at the Peacock Tea Room."

Noah's voice caused Mitch to pop up from behind the open door of the icebox, juggling an armload of food. In the darkened, cavernous kitchen he saw the boy standing near the worktable, a single overhead fixture lighting the area.

Mitch retrieved a bowl of eggs from the icebox, then closed the door with his knee.

"Why else would you be eating in the middle of the night?" Noah asked, gesturing to the food Mitch placed on the worktable.

Mitch couldn't deny that he was hungry, or that the Peacock Tea Room had not been an enjoyable experience, beyond the fact that it pleased Rachel to eat there. Small tables crowded with silver, crystal and china. Tiny portions of odd foods. Women in big hats with big hips. Mitch had been one of only two men in the place and he'd drawn more than his share of stares when he'd walked in with Rachel.

"I think your sister is trying to starve me to death," Mitch said, going through the cupboards. The supper she'd had the cook prepare tonight only made him hungrier.

"Mrs. Callihan will make whatever you want," Noah said, waving his one arm toward the adjoining servants quarters.

"I won't be here that long. No sense in causing the cook any trouble. She's got enough to do as it is." Mitch surveyed the food he'd assembled on the worktable. "Hungry?"

Noah's gaze dropped to the ham steaks. He glanced away and shook his head.

Mitch understood. The steaks required two hands. Noah wasn't about to ask for help cutting his meat. Even if Mitch performed that chore without comment, it would still embarrass Noah, as it had the first night Mitch had supper in the Branford home and his meal alone had been served already cut into bite-size chunks.

"I'm making omelets," Mitch said, though that hadn't been his initial choice.

"Uh, yeah, okay," Noah said.

He pulled a stool up to the worktable and watched while Mitch diced the ham, onion, olives and peppers, shredded cheese and cracked eggs into a bowl.

"Where'd you learn to cook?" Noah asked.

"Picked it up here and there," Mitch said, pouring beaten eggs into the sizzling skillet. "Get us something to drink, will you?"

A few minutes later the two of them sat at the worktable, plates of fat omelet, warmed-over biscuits and frosty glasses of milk in front of them.

They ate in silence, Mitch surprised at how quickly Noah cleaned his plate. Maybe the boy was as hungry for something other than vegetables, fruit and peculiar cuts of meat as he was. Maybe he should talk to the cook, after all.

When they finished, Mitch took away their plates and opened the pie safe.

"Look what I found." He held up a cake covered with thick icing.

"I'll get more milk." Noah slid off the stool and poured each of them another tall glass.

They finished off a slice each, then Mitch cut them another.

"I know why you're here," Noah said after a few minutes. "You're not an old family friend, like Rachel and Uncle Stuart said. I've never heard of you before."

"It was their idea. They didn't want anyone knowing your father wasn't capable of running the family business."

"You think Georgie did something with the family money, don't you. You think that's why he disappeared."

"I'm not here to pass judgment on anybody. I'm just here to find out what's wrong and figure a way to fix it," Mitch said, taking another bite of cake. "What about you? What do you think about your brother?"

Noah looked up at him, a little startled, as if no one had asked his opinion in a very long time.

"Makes sense," the boy finally said around another bite of cake. "Why else would he run off? I guess we won't know for sure until we find him. Rachel's determined to locate him. Bring him back. Make things the way they were."

"I guess that'll make her happy," Mitch said.

"Will you finish your work here soon?"

"Won't be much longer," Mitch said, scraping the last few cake crumbs off his plate.

"Are we going to buy Rachel's factory?"

Mitch paused. "What factory?"

"The one Mr. Prescott owns," Noah said, licking the icing off his fork. "She'd been asking Georgie to buy it for a couple of months."

"Rachel?" Mitch frowned. "What does she want it for?"

"Beats me." Noah shrugged. "Why don't you ask her?"

Mitch rose from the stool. He intended to do just that.

Pulling the coverlet under her chin, Rachel stared at the ceiling of her darkened bedchamber. She hadn't been sleeping, just lying there thinking. Thoughts floated through her mind at random, it seemed, yet always led back to the same place.

Mitch.

Their shopping trip. His unexpected attentiveness. His easy way with their driver and the shop clerks. The five dollars he'd given a dirty-faced newsboy.

The stares they'd received at the Peacock Tea Room.

Rachel knew most all of the women in the Tea Room; the place was a favorite among her set. They'd all watched as the two of them had wound through the restaurant to a little table in the back.

They'd thought him handsome, Rachel knew. How could they not? Her heart fluttered a bit at the thought.

And the two of them made a striking couple. She'd caught glimpses of them together in the glass display windows as they'd strolled the streets.

But the ladies of her social circle wouldn't stop there. Rachel knew that, all too well.

Who was that man? she was sure they'd wondered. They'd undoubtedly whispered among themselves, cast furtive glances and exchanged eyebrow bobs trying to figure out who, exactly, Mitch was. Where was he from? Why was he here?

Did he belong?

Rachel's stomach churned into a little knot as the old feelings—learned from her mother—came back to her. Being watched, judged, evaluated on the tilt of a hat, the script on a calling card, the silverware placement at a luncheon table.

Several of the women in the Peacock had spoken to her, and Rachel had introduced Mitch as a very dear friend of the family. He'd been gracious, favoring the women with a smile that bordered on charming, a smile that Rachel seldom saw.

Nothing untoward had happened during the luncheon. In fact, she'd enjoyed sitting across from Mitch. Something about his presence was comforting. How big and strong he looked among the ruffles and lace at the tiny table. How rugged he'd seemed next to the delicate china and crystal.

But as they left Rachel once again felt the heat of curious, judgmental stares on her.

Who, exactly, had she brought into their midst? Had she overstepped the bounds of propriety by her presence with him? Did they think her—

An urgent knock sounded on Rachel's bedchamber door. Her heart rose in her throat as she threw back the covers and scrambled out of bed. It was late, very late. Had something happened?

Rachel slipped her arms into her robe and dashed across the room, her footsteps silent on the carpet. Opening the door she saw Mitch standing only inches away. He wore the trousers she'd seen him in earlier today, but no jacket or necktie. The collar of his white shirt stood open and his sleeves were rolled back.

"What's wrong?" she demanded, the words coming out in a rush. "Is it Father? Has he—"

"No, he's fine," Mitch said impatiently. "I need—"

"Noah?" Her eyes darted down the hallway.

"I have to talk to you."

Rachel gasped and her knees weakened. "They've found Georgie."

"No," Mitch told her. "And nothing's wrong. We need to talk. You and I. Now."

"Now?" Rachel leaned back a little. She drew her robe together and clutched it closed with her fist.

"It can't wait," he insisted.

She glanced up and down the hallway. "It's the middle of the night. It's simply not appropriate for me to—"

"Come on."

Mitch caught her hand and urged her out of her bedchamber, then led her down the hallway, her robe billowing behind her.

When he paused outside the door to his own bed-chamber, Rachel dug in her heels.

"I'm not going into your room," she whispered urgently. "It simply isn't done."

Mitch looked down at her. "Didn't you come into my room looking for me? The night you needed help with Noah?"

She straightened her shoulders. "Well, yes. But that was different."

Mitch rolled his eyes, took her hand again and proceeded down the hallway to the attic entrance. He led the way upstairs, snapping on the electric light as they went.

The silence of the big room closed in around them as they stood facing each other. Rachel fastened the buttons on her robe, smoothing down the front. Another moment passed and she looked up at him.

"Well, for goodness' sake, what is it?" she demanded, more than a little annoyed with his attitude and his actions. "You've gotten me up in the middle of the night, paraded me through the hallway for anyone to see and brought me to this secluded spot. What's so important?"

"Your factory."

Rachel gasped softly and sealed her lips together.

"The factory you claimed your brother wanted to buy." Mitch took a step closer. "But it was you, wasn't it. You're the one who wanted it."

How humiliating. Rachel's cheeks burned. Bad enough to be caught in an outright lie. But a lie about the factory. A business. What would her mother say?

Rachel drew herself up, facing the consequences of her very unladylike actions. No point lying anymore.

"It's true," she admitted. "I wanted that factory. I asked Georgie to buy it."

"For what reason?"

"Well, it's a bit difficult to explain," Rachel told him, embarrassed further to have to provide details of the whole sordid scheme.

"I'm sure I can follow." Mitch crossed his arms over his chest, waiting.

Rachel touched her forehead, unsure of where to start. She'd never had to explain this situation to anyone before. Not even Georgie. She'd simply mentioned buying the factory to him and he'd promised to look into it, no questions asked. And she certainly hadn't told her idea to anyone else.

"Well?" Mitch prompted her, leaning forward a little as if that might hurry her along.

"It was a number of things," she finally said. "Ships. Hotels. Giants, really. And that dear Mr. Cabell in New York. And England, of course, where—"

Mitch waved both hands for silence. "What are you talking about?"

She lifted an eyebrow. "You said you could follow."

He heaved an exasperated sigh. "Start at the beginning."

Rachel paused for a moment, then proceeded. "About a year or so ago—before the…accident—Father took the whole family to England, except for Georgie, of course. We visited the shipyards through one of Father's business acquaintances. And, oh my, those huge ships under construction were breathtaking. Have you ever seen them?"

Mitch shook his head.

"You can't believe what's being planned for the future. Cruise ships capable of carrying thousands of people in magnificent splendor," Rachel told him. "England is known for its china production. It—"

"You mean dishes?" he asked.

"Yes, but the expensive sort," she said. "It was in England that the formula for fine bone china was developed, the single most important discovery in the industry. It accounted for the phenomenal development of English tableware. Did you know that?"

Again, Mitch shook his head.

"Mother wanted a new china service so we visited several potteries there and also when we returned to the East Coast of America," Rachel continued. "That's where we met Mr. Cabell. He's the foreman of a ceramic factory in New York. Very nice man. And in New York, oh my, we saw such beautiful hotels, all with magnificent restaurants capable of servicing hundreds of people."

Mitch pressed his lips together, listening hard. He tilted his head a little, the way she'd seen him do in the study when he worked on her father's finances and was trying to make sense of things. The way he was trying to make sense now of what she was telling him.

She pushed ahead. "So when we returned home I got to thinking about everything, the ships, the restaurants, the hotels and Mr. Cabell's ceramic factory. It seemed to me that with those huge ships and grand hotels there would be a need for china services on a very large scale. It seemed to me that since Mr. Prescott's City Ceramic

Works factory already produced ceramic doorknobs and fixtures and pot handles and the like, that it could just as easily turn out china for this new, expanding market."

Mitch didn't say anything, just looked at her, his lips pressed, his brows furrowed, his head still tilted a little.

Rachel squirmed under his glower. In the harsh light of reality her idea suddenly seemed silly. Especially when told to Mitch, of all people, a "hired gun" so brilliant he routinely untangled the finances of some of the world's wealthiest people.

For an instant, Rachel wished she could disappear in a puff of smoke. But she'd come this far. She may as well humiliate herself completely.

"And I wanted to—"

"Design the china." Mitch nodded. "That's what you've been painting. Not the sunrise or landscape. Colors and designs to use on the china."

"Yes," she whispered.

Mitch shifted his shoulders. "You came up with this idea? All by yourself?"

A bolt of anger threaded through her embarrassment.

"Is that so hard to believe?" she demanded. "Is it so hard to understand that I don't want to simply set a nice table for the rest of my life? That I want something more?"

The words poured out in a hot rush, and the instant they were spoken, she should have regretted them.

Goodness, what would her mother say? What would her friends, the other ladies in her circle say? A woman involved in business?

"I know it isn't done," she told Mitch, reading what

surely were his thoughts. "That has been my concern all along. That's why Georgie was buying the factory. He would have run it, too, and I could have contributed my part quietly. But…but none of that matters now, anyway. Georgie is gone and there's no money to buy the factory."

Rachel drew a breath and looked up at Mitch, squaring her shoulders. "I do think it was a good idea."

Another moment passed with Mitch just staring at her, his brows pulled together. Finally he said, "I think it's a solid, timely, very workable idea."

Her eyes widened. "You do?"

"I certainly do."

A thrilling shiver zinged through Rachel, and for a moment, she reveled in it. Yet her excitement faded beneath the weight of reality.

"But there's still no money to buy the factory, is there?"

"No, I'm afraid not."

"Well, I guess that's that," Rachel said. "I didn't mean to lie to you about me being the one who wanted the factory. It's just that—"

"I understand," Mitch said.

From the look on his face, Rachel knew that he did understand.

"I'd better go," she said softly, then hurried down the attic steps.

Mitch fought the urge to run after her. Since arriving at the Branford home his heart had ached for her. His body had wanted her. Now his brain joined in.

He'd always known she was pretty, desirable. Now he knew she was smart.

Mitch's belly tightened and his breathing slowed. This was the worst thing that could have happened.

He'd lost himself completely to Rachel Branford.

Chapter Thirteen

"So much to decide," Rachel mused.

At the other end of the settee, Claudia set aside her teacup and nodded. "Yes, but Mother and I have been busy doing…well, doing as much as we can."

Rachel detected distress in her friend's voice. Not unusual for a young woman planning her wedding, but this sounded different. Had circumstances been otherwise, Rachel herself would have been more involved in the planning of Claudia's perfect wedding, as one of her attendants.

"You and your mother aren't agreeing on things?" Rachel ventured.

"No, it's not that." Claudia glanced away. "Graham isn't happy with some of the plans we've made."

It surprised Rachel that Graham had involved himself in the wedding planning at all. Most men didn't.

"He doesn't want pink for the color scheme."

"The ceremony is next spring," Rachel said. "Pink will be perfect for the season."

"He says it's a 'little girl's' color," Claudia said. "He insists on blue."

"But you've had your heart set on pink for as long as I can remember."

"He has a point," Claudia said, drawing herself up a little. "And I am marrying into the Bixby family. There are certain…expectations."

"Well, blue is nice," Rachel allowed.

Claudia gave her a quick smile. "Of course it is. The important thing is that we're getting married."

"The wedding will be perfect, no matter what," Rachel told her.

"Yes, it will," Claudia said, her smile growing earnest. "How are the luncheon plans coming along?"

"Everything's fine," Rachel told her, and was surprised to hear herself say that.

For so long she'd dreaded the thought of hosting the luncheon. It had seemed a chore, rather than the joy it used to be when she and her mother planned it together.

But Mitch had made her feel better about it. When he'd suggested she take over the luncheon herself, put her own personal mark on it, the occasion had taken on new meaning.

Claudia rose from the settee. "I'd better get home. Graham is taking me to supper with his parents and I dare not keep him waiting."

"Or wear something pink?" Rachel teased.

Claudia smiled in return. "I'll search my closets for the truest shade of blue. That will surely please him."

Rachel walked alongside her to the foyer and waved from the porch as Claudia's carriage drove away. She couldn't help but think once more how perfect Claudia's life was. A grand wedding. A perfect bride, even in blue. A settled life.

The tiniest thread of envy wound through Rachel. She'd experienced it before, thinking of Claudia's marriage.

How nice it will be for her friend to have a husband to turn to in times of trouble. No more lonely nights staring at the darkened ceiling, listening to the wind and worrying about things. Claudia could wake him, talk to him. Wasn't that what husbands were for?

Rachel headed back toward the sitting room. Yes, she envied Claudia her husband-to-be, but why wouldn't she? Who wouldn't want a solid partner in their life? Someone to rely on, to trust.

Loneliness wafted through Rachel, dispelling her envy. There'd been no such person in her life for so long.

Her father, always the solid foundation of their family, now ill. He couldn't help that, of course. But even Dr. Matthews didn't understand Father's almost nonexistent recovery. As if he didn't want to get well.

Noah had suffered mightily. But often Rachel had wished he could pull himself out of that misery and help. Just a thoughtful opinion would do.

Georgie had left the family outright. Bad enough that he had gone off on some adventure of his own, but to leave them to worry about his welfare was unconscionable—especially when the family needed him the most.

And, of course, there'd been the situation with Benjamin Blair.

Rachel had felt so alone these past months. What would it be like if things were different?

Her pace slowed in the hallway and her gaze strayed into the study. Mitch sat at her father's desk, working.

She'd grown accustomed to seeing him there, dependably going about his duties. He'd done more for the Branford family than any of the other men in her life.

Even if she was paying him to do it.

That didn't seem to matter, though. Rachel sensed that Mitch was a man who, once committed to a project, saw it through to the end. It was one of the things she liked best about him.

That, and the way he looked in his undershirt.

His head came up as she lingered outside the doorway and his gaze assessed her. He'd done that lately, almost every time he looked at her. As if he were pondering something of great importance concerning her.

Finally, he waved her into the room.

"I'm going out," Mitch said, coming to his feet. "I have an appointment."

After the incident when he'd been gone with Uncle Stuart for several days and she'd fussed with him about not advising her of his whereabouts, Mitch made it a point to tell her when he was leaving the house.

"Someone I met at your uncle's club," Mitch said. "Albert Taft. Do you know him?"

"His wife was devoted to a number of charities in the city. She passed away about two years ago. We all miss her, still. Mr. Taft almost never attends social or charity functions anymore," Rachel said. "What's your meeting about?"

"I don't know." Mitch shrugged into his jacket. "It was his idea."

"Excuse me, sir, ma'am," Hayden's voice intoned from the doorway. "Dr. Matthews has arrived. He's with Mr. Branford," the butler said, then departed.

"Dr. Matthews…" Rachel's shoulders sagged. "I know he's going to try and force me into putting Father in that convalescent hospital again."

"Have you thought about it?" Mitch asked, rounding the desk to stand next to her.

"There's no need to think about it," Rachel declared. "I've already made up my mind."

"I've thought about it."

Rachel looked up at him as he moved closer. His jacket hung open and heat from his body radiated outward, warming her.

"I thought about your father lying upstairs, all these days and months, in the bed he shared with the woman he loved for over twenty years," Mitch said. "How lonely that must be for him. Everything around him is a reminder of the wonderful times that will never happen again. A constant suffering for him."

"But I'm here. So are Noah, and Chelsey, when she comes back from school."

Mitch eased a little closer. "I'm no expert, but I can't imagine anything could replace the love a man feels for his wife."

"I hadn't thought of it that way," Rachel admitted. "Do you suppose that's why he hasn't gotten better?"

Mitch didn't answer, just leaned down. Gently, he brushed his knuckles along her cheek, then kissed her. His mouth covered hers in a deep kiss, blending them together with an urgent hunger that went far beyond the kisses he'd given her before. The warmth of his mouth was exciting, but comforting, too. Mellow and easy, familiar.

When he ended their kiss, he didn't pull away. His mouth hovered near hers for a long moment.

"I'd better go," he said.

Rachel nodded. "I'll think about what you said… about Father."

"I'll be back in a couple of hours," he said, then left the study.

The trolley had ceased service for the night and a scant few windows along West Adams Boulevard were lighted as Mitch walked toward the Branford home. His appointment with Albert Taft had been brief and ended hours ago. Mitch had forgone a hansom and chosen to walk home instead. He had a lot to think about.

Taft owned a quarry, among other things, inland about thirty miles. It wasn't doing well. Neither was Albert Taft.

The man drank too much, Mitch had decided shortly after arriving at their meeting, so it was no small wonder the quarry was failing. Ordinarily, Mitch would have mentally scoffed at the situation. A quarry, with its treasure trove of essential building materials in close proximity to the fast-growing city, and Albert Taft couldn't manage a profit.

But Mitch has sensed something deeper wrong with Taft, something well beyond poor managerial skills. Rachel had said his wife had died; he still mourned her.

He'd offered to hire Mitch to work his magic on the quarry, figure out what was wrong, exactly, and come up with a plan to fix it. Nothing Mitch couldn't easily handle, and the fee he would collect would put him within the financial range of buying his own business. He'd worked toward that very goal for so long, and now...

Mitch drew in a breath of the cool night air, hoping it would clear his head and stop the odd feeling that had plagued him lately, a feeling that he couldn't seem to shake. Dread and expectation, fear and joy all rolled together, squeezing him from the inside out. A craving he couldn't seem to satisfy.

Mitch turned down the Branford driveway and stopped still in his tracks. He looked up at the grand house with its marble and stained glass, its manicured lawns, and Mitch knew what was wrong.

He should never have come here. He should have stuck to his resolve and refused to work in the Branford home.

Because now he wanted it all.

An ache of longing filled him. He was tired of working and saving, of having the thing he wanted always just out of reach. Standing before him now was the power he'd craved since that cold, rainy night when he was five years old. He could have it.

He'd always known that the money, the wealth he could accumulate on his own. But he'd never manage to get the final ingredient he needed for true power: social acceptance.

Yet there it stood before him now in the form of the Branford family. A solid, reputable, socially accepted family who moved with ease among the city's elite.

There was only one way for someone like Mitch to be a part of that world. His friend Leo Sinclair had teased him about it weeks ago when the two of them had arrived at the Branford home. At the time, Mitch had refused to even consider that option. He'd been offered it many times from past clients and had refused each time.

But now it was different. He'd lived in that house, seen firsthand what that life would bring.

He didn't want to do without it anymore. He was tired of waiting. This was his best opportunity to have everything he wanted. Now was his best chance.

Rachel was his best chance.

It seemed silly to worry about the safety of a man so big he barely fit through doorways, Rachel decided as she lay in bed, staring up at nothing. Yet Mitch lingered in her thoughts. His meeting with Albert Taft might have run longer than expected. He might have met up with some of the other men and they'd—

Rachel stopped her own thoughts. She didn't want to consider just what sort of activities might keep grown men occupied until the wee hours of the morning. Especially with Mitch involved. She had no claim on him, but still…

Her own thoughts forced her from the bed. She slipped on her robe and left her room, silently descending the staircase, heading for the library in the rear of the house. She intended to retrieve the book she'd left there earlier in the evening.

But as she headed down the hallway, she saw a faint light glowing in the doorway of the study. She crept closer and saw Mitch seated at the desk.

Relief swamped her. She'd not heard him come in. She'd lain upstairs and worried about him for nothing.

He looked as if he'd been there for hours. Jacket off, collar open, necktie loosened, he worked by the dim light of the desk lamp, hunched over a tablet, writing things down. She'd never seen him look this determined. As if he wanted to capture his thoughts on paper before they escaped him.

Perhaps she shouldn't bother him. The thought raced through Rachel's mind as she turned to go. But he seemed to sense her nearness and stopped his writing. He lifted his head, not seeming surprised to see her.

Mitch studied her for a long, hard moment, making Rachel aware of her state of dress. Nightgown and robe, hair down, bare feet. Yet it wasn't this that seemed to dominate his thoughts. It was something more, something deeper. It startled Rachel.

"What's wrong?" she asked, walking into the room.

Mitch glanced down at the tablet. "Nothing. I'm just finishing up here."

She supposed she should be relieved, yet something in his manner still troubled her. "You're certain?"

"Yes...no." Mitch put aside his pencil and looked at her for a moment, as if holding his breath, contemplating something that even by his own standards, was gargantuan.

"I was going to tell you in the morning," he said, "but...but I may as well do it now, since you're here."

A hot wave of foreboding crept up Rachel's spine. She crossed to the desk and stood in front of him.

"What? What's wrong?"

"Nothing's wrong." A few seconds passed before he went on. "I'm finished here. My work. It's done."

Rachel's heart lurched. What had he been so reluctant to tell her? A thousand possibilities flashed in her head. The family was, despite his assurances, penniless? They'd have to move, sell everything? Become the talk of the city?

She gripped the edge of the desk. "How bad is it?" she asked, managing only a whisper.

He looked at her for a moment, as if not understanding her question. Then his expression changed.

"Everything's fine. The family finances are back in order," Mitch said. "I told you everything would be all right."

Rachel's hand went to her throat, afraid still to believe what she'd heard. "You're sure?"

"I told you, I'm very good at this," he said, gesturing to the tablet.

"So the family still has money?" she asked, needing the reassurance. "It was just a bookkeeping error?"

Mitch shook his head. "No. I'm afraid not."

"Then where…where did our money go?" she asked.

He hesitated, as if he were as reluctant to give the answer as she was to hear it.

"Over the course of the past few months, all the family assets were mortgaged," Mitch said. "And all the cash was withdrawn from the banks."

"But whatever for?" Rachel asked. "Who would do such a thing? Aren't there charges of some sort that can be brought?"

"Not in this case," Mitch said. "It was your brother."

"Georgie?" Rachel shook her head. "No. No, he wouldn't have done something like that to us."

"There are documents, Rachel," Mitch said softly. "I've seen them. There's no mistake."

She stared at him, trying to let his words sink in. She couldn't—simply could not—believe that Georgie had deliberately deceived the family.

Yet Mitch had no reason to lie. She knew that in business there were, in fact, papers that had to be filed for such things. Evidence that could be traced. And, of course, Georgie had disappeared without a word.

"Oh, dear…" Rachel touched her fingers to her forehead as the truth of the situation washed through her.

At that moment, she was glad her father was too ill to know what her brother had done, how he'd betrayed the family's trust and left them in this awful situation. Glad, too, that her mother wouldn't know, either.

But what if everyone else found out?

The terror ripped through Rachel, causing her heart to ache anew. It was common knowledge that Georgie was her mother's son from a previous marriage. Though he'd been given the Branford name, there was no blood tie. This would be but another poor reflection on her mother.

"There's no need to worry about the family finances. The situation can be managed," Mitch said. "Your father has a large estate. It's just a matter of restructuring assets."

Relief calmed her. "Thank goodness."

"I've worked out a detailed plan to cover the next year," Mitch said. "I'll go over it with Parker, make sure he understands it and can explain it to whoever takes over."

Rachel stilled. "Takes over?"

"Yes. My work here is done," Mitch said. "I'm leaving."

"Leaving?"

"Tomorrow."

Rachel's world seemed to crumble beneath her.

"But—but you said you'd take care of everything."

"I have taken care of everything." Mitch tapped his finger on the tablet in front of him. "It's right here. The financial plan I've devised will get you through the crucial next year, and everything will be back on track."

"You said you'd stay," she told him.

"Until my job was done. This is what I do, Rachel. I figure out a recovery plan, then move on."

Her heart raced. "But you can't just abandon us."

"I've done all that I can do here."

"This puts me right back where I started. I don't know anyone capable of taking over the business," Rachel said. "I don't know who to turn to, who to trust."

"Your uncle can help you."

Rachel shook her head. "There must be some way I can get you to stay. I'll increase your fee."

Mitch pushed out of the chair. "That's not how I work."

"I'll double it again. Triple it."

"No."

She squeezed her hands into fists. "There must be some way I can get you to stay. Something I can do. Something I can say."

"Say you'll marry me."

Chapter Fourteen

Rachel's eyes widened. "You want me to—what?"

Mitch just looked at her, the shock, the panic on her face. He hardened his heart.

Rachel canted her head, as if not sure she'd heard him correctly.

"Did you say 'marry' you?"

He couldn't back down now. Besides, he didn't want to.

"Yes. Marry me."

Rachel leaned closer, as if the diminished distance between them might somehow make her hear better, understand more clearly.

"Are you suggesting that I marry you as a way to keep you here?" she asked.

He didn't know what sort of reaction he expected from her. A profession of love? A declaration that she'd fallen for him? None of that showed in her expression.

Mitch didn't care.

"I'll stay, take care of things," he said. "If you'll marry me."

Rachel's spine stiffened and her chin went up.

"You'd hold my family's future hostage?" she demanded. "To get me to marry you?"

"The marriage will benefit us both," he said, ignoring a pang of conscience.

"Ah, yes. Your plan to be wealthy and powerful," Rachel said. Her eyes narrowed. "Was this your intention all along? To make yourself an intregral part of my family, make yourself indispensable, just to force a marriage?"

Anger chased away the pain that gripped his heart.

"It wasn't me who sneaked into your bedchamber in the dead of night," he reminded her.

Rachel gasped. "I needed help with Noah!"

Mitch rounded the desk and planted himself in front of her. "You're the one who insisted I live here, under your roof. Did you encourage my involvement with your family as a way to keep me here? To make me feel important?"

"I most certainly did not!" she declared.

Mitch leaned closer. "Is it the reason you let me kiss you?"

"How dare you! You can't really believe that!"

No, he didn't. He didn't believe for a moment that Rachel was devious or conniving.

A few moments passed, cooling things between them.

"It would be a beneficial arrangement for the both of us," Mitch said, the anger gone from his voice. "I'll stay and run your family's business. You won't have to worry about any of that. Your family will be well taken care of."

"And just what sort of service do you think I'm going to provide in this bargain of ours?"

Heat surged through him unexpectedly at the thought of them sharing a marriage bed, before an odd little ache surfaced.

"Your social connections. Your help with entry to polite society," Mitch said. His gaze ran the length of her—he couldn't help himself—then settled on her face again. "As well as anything else you'd care to provide."

Her cheeks reddened but she pushed her chin a little higher. "That's it? That's the deal?"

Mitch nodded. "You can give me your answer tomorrow."

"Tomorrow?"

"I'm considering another job offer," he said. "If you don't want to go through with…this…I'll need to make other plans."

"Well, I certainly wouldn't want to hold you up," Rachel informed him. "I'll think about your proposal, and if I make my decision by tomorrow, I'll let you know."

She put her nose in the air, whipped around and stomped out of the room.

Another night of lying awake and staring at the ceiling.

Rachel sighed in the darkness. She'd always imagined that this sort of thing would come to an end, once her life was settled. She'd imagined that finding the perfect man, receiving a marriage proposal, would give her life stability.

She'd been wrong about that, too.

Rachel gulped, holding in her emotions, refusing to let threatening tears fall.

She'd been wrong about everything, even Mitch.

What a godsend he'd seemed when he first arrived. Tall, strong, handsome. Here to do battle with her family's financial troubles, to fight off poverty and public humiliation. Her knight in shining armor, to be sure.

Yet he'd turned out to be no different than any of the men in her life.

Now here she was once again contemplating the fate of her family. As it had been for months now, it was up to her to figure out how to keep the family together.

It was all within her grasp now, of course. She had but to accept Mitch's marriage proposal. Everything would be fine, if she did. Rachel knew in her heart that Mitch could easily take care of the family finances, keep them on sound financial footing, ensure their future.

So she was getting what she wanted. But at a much higher price than she'd ever expected to pay.

Yet it was for her family. Would any price be too steep?

Rachel snuggled deeper into the covers and rolled onto her side, watching through the window across the room as the moon glided through the night sky.

She needed to sleep. She needed to be prepared for tomorrow when she spoke with Mitch. There'd be no surprises.

He probably knew that already. For Rachel this was neither a difficult decision nor a hard choice. Not where her family was concerned.

She squeezed her eyes closed and a shudder ran through her. What would it be like to be married to Mitch?

And, oh, what would people say?

Last night in the study when Mitch had made his marriage proposal, Rachel had felt vulnerable, exposed, discussing the matter while wearing only her nightgown and robe. Now, fortified by her undergarments, she was ready to tackle the situation in earnest.

She closed her bedchamber door and headed down the hallway. It was early still, the house quiet. As she often did, Rachel glanced at the door to Mitch's room. Open. He was up and about already and the servants were inside, going about their chores.

Her footsteps slowed as a shiver ran though her. The gall of that man. The arrogance. Demanding her hand in marriage in exchange for her family's future.

Perhaps she was no better for agreeing to it.

And there was always the possibility that their union might turn out just fine, Rachel thought as she descended the staircase. That notion had come to her last night along with so many others.

Maybe she and Mitch could have a marriage—a real marriage. He had so many of the qualities she admired in a man. His hard work would insure the security of her family. She wouldn't have to worry anymore, at least about money.

And she was fond of him.

Rachel froze at the foot of the staircase. Fond of him? Was that it?

She wished she could talk to Claudia, see how she felt

when Graham was near. Did her heart beat faster at the sight of him? Did he wander into her thoughts at all hours? Did he make her wonder what it would be like to—

With a startled gasp, Rachel stopped her runaway thoughts. Voices drifted down the hallway, coming from the study. She looked inside to find Mitch and Uncle Stuart working at the desk. Mitch seemed to sense her nearness. He cut off his conversation and pushed to his feet.

He looked neat, as always, combed, scrubbed, polished. But there was an uncharacteristic tightness around his eyes. He seemed tired. She wondered if he'd been up half the night thinking about their situation, as well.

"Good morning, Rachel." Uncle Stuart gave her a hug.

"You're here early," she said, feeling the reserve in his embrace.

"I understand there's a big decision to be made," he said.

Her gaze flicked to Mitch. He'd told Uncle Stuart about the marriage proposal? Before she'd given him her answer?

"It's a generous offer on Mitch's part," Uncle Stuart said. "Certainly it's what the family needs right now. And, it's only for a year."

"A year?" Rachel looked at her uncle, then at Mitch. He remained beside the desk, silent.

"That will allow for plenty of time to find someone to take over permanently. We're working out the details of the agreement now," Uncle Stuart said, gesturing toward the desk.

Rachel's heart rose in her throat. "You're writing a...a contract?"

"It's prudent," Uncle Stuart said. "There's a financial consideration for Mitch, plus—"

"He's being paid to marry me?"

"We can't expect him to give a year of his life to the business with no monetary compensation," Uncle Stuart said, somehow making the notion sound reasonable. "Plus, there's a provision for safeguarding the Branford estate and—"

"So he doesn't steal from us?" Rachel asked.

"And to keep Mitch's own personal finances strictly separate." Uncle Stuart looked down at her. "If, of course, you've decided to accept the offer."

A thousand emotions whirled through Rachel, but the prevailing one was anger. At that second, she wasn't sure just who she was angry at—everyone, perhaps.

But Mitch was the person standing in front of her.

Power and wealth. That's what he wanted. He'd told her so the first time they'd walked though the garden together. He'd made no apologies or excuses. That was his plan.

Humiliation coursed through Rachel. What a fool she'd been only a moment ago to think that she had feelings for Mitch. Or that the two of them might someday have a real marriage.

What a fool to think this man was different from all the others.

She drew herself up. "I'd like to speak with Mr. Kincade privately."

"Yes, of course. You two have some…matters…to discuss." Uncle Stuart left the room.

Rachel crossed to the desk. Mitch sank into the chair and she felt a rush of superiority standing over him.

"I require information before I make my final decision," she told him. "Personal information about you."

"My background." He nodded. "After all, there's the concern over what people will say?"

He made her concern sound trite—and to him, perhaps it was—but Rachel refused to give him the satisfaction of blushing.

"Well?" she demanded.

"I asked you to marry me, not the other way around," Mitch told her.

She remembered then how he'd made a point several times of insisting that he picked his clients. He never allowed them to pick him.

Apparently he felt the same about a marriage proposal.

But Rachel had her own deep feelings. And they included suffering the shame of public embarrassment.

"I will not have my family humiliated by a scandal if something untoward should become known about you," she said.

Several moments dragged by with Mitch staring at her until Rachel thought perhaps he might not answer, that the entire marriage proposal might be abandoned.

"You needn't worry," Mitch said.

"But—"

"You needn't worry," Mitch said again, this time with such force that she knew she'd get nothing else out of him.

Though she didn't want to leave her questions unanswered, there seemed no use in pursuing them.

"The arrangement will have to be kept quiet," Mitch told her. "No one can know."

Rachel nodded. "Believe me, I'm not anxious to have this become public knowledge."

"That means we have to act as if we're married," Mitch insisted.

"There are certain standards you'll be expected to live up to," Rachel told him. "If, of course, you think you can be trained."

She was angry and hurt, and Mitch didn't blame her for the insult. Yet he wouldn't back down. Nothing, absolutely nothing, would keep him from getting what he wanted.

Rachel gestured to the papers on the desk. "If you and Uncle Stuart have worked out all the details, then I guess that's it."

"And what about…us?" Mitch's gaze strayed from her face to her bosom, then up again. "We will be man and wife."

She gave him a scathing glare. "If I decide I require those services from you, Mr. Kincade, I'll let you know."

"So you're agreeable?" he asked, his heart beating a little faster. "You'll go through with the marriage?"

"Yes," she told him. "You're hired."

Chapter Fifteen

Married.

With a heavy sigh, Rachel looked down at the thin band of gold that wrapped her finger. Her mother's wedding ring. Rachel had selected it from the velvet-lined box that held her mother's jewelry—Rachel's jewelry now that her mother was gone—only moments before she and Mitch had departed for the church this afternoon. It fit well enough. But Rachel's stomach knotted at the sight of it.

Did one sleep in a wedding ring? Rachel didn't know. She'd bathed and dressed in her bedclothes already, and now slipped the ring off her finger and dropped it into her jewelry box that sat atop her bureau.

It seemed as good a reason as any not to wear the thing.

With a sigh, she sat down on the bench in front of her vanity and plucked the pins from her hair. Since last night when Mitch had delivered his ultimatum—she refused to think of it as a marriage proposal—she'd found herself wishing that Georgie would come back, that he would speak up for himself, explain things. Surely mortgaging the family assets was part of a grand business deal he'd put together. She couldn't believe he'd actually do anything to hurt the family. If only he'd come back everything would be fine.

At the church, standing at the altar, Rachel had fantasized that Georgie would crash through the door, shouting that everything had been put right, that she didn't have to marry Mitch.

But that didn't happen.

She'd been left with no choice but to take her vows before God in His house of worship. Vows she knew she wouldn't adhere to—it wasn't in the contract.

Rachel sighed glumly. On top of everything else, she'd sinned. She'd probably go to hell, too.

With long, languid strokes, Rachel ran the brush through her hair, letting it fall through her fingers and sweep around her shoulders.

It was only a year. She'd get through it, somehow. There would be functions she and Mitch would be required to attend together. It was expected of them socially, as a couple. Plus she had to fulfill her portion of their wedding contract and provide Mitch with entry into their social circle.

Other than those occasions, she had no need to see him, interact with him. She could go about her life as always, with little regard for him.

Surely Mitch intended to do likewise.

Rachel saw her shoulders droop in the mirror. Even those thoughts didn't lighten her mood.

Her perfect marriage floated through her mind. The

one she'd dreamed about all her life. The dress, the flowers, the parties, the reception. All the things Claudia was enjoying. Rachel would have none of it.

She'd get through this difficult time, she vowed. A year would pass. They would quietly divorce and go their separate ways and she would never see him again.

Never see Mitch again? The notion caused another sort of emotion to jab her, though she couldn't name it or know where it had come from. Everything seemed so confusing.

So to make things easier on herself, she would simply avoid Mitch as much as possible. Yes, Rachel decided, that's what she'd do. At the moment, never laying eyes on the man again seemed good.

A quick knock sounded on her door and before she could rise from the stool, Mitch stepped into the room.

Stunned, Rachel gasped. "What are you doing here?"

"Surely you haven't forgotten," Mitch said. He closed the door behind him, then raised a champagne bottle and two glasses. "It's our wedding night."

Rachel surged to her feet, fumbling to close the buttons on her robe all the way up to her chin.

"I'm certain I made myself clear on this matter," she informed him, tying the sash around her waist in a double knot.

Mitch paused in the center of the room and gazed around, taking it all in.

"You did," he agreed. "But I knew you'd want me here tonight, of all nights."

"You're mistaken," Rachel declared, as she twirled her hair into a quick knot and jabbed pins through it.

He sauntered to the sitting area at the far end of the room and placed the bottle and glasses on the little table between the settee and chairs.

"You have a balcony." Mitch opened the French doors.

"Don't go out there!" Rachel dashed across the room and caught his arm. "The neighbors know this is my room. I sit outside a lot. Good gracious, what will they think, seeing you here?"

Mitch paused, allowing her to stop his progress, though she knew she was no match for his strength.

"That's my point," he told her.

"You want people to know you're here?" she demanded, suddenly horrified. Goodness, what had she gotten herself into?

"Actually, I'd think a little gratitude would be in order," Mitch told her.

"You're disgusting."

"We agreed to keep up pretenses, remember?" Mitch shrugged. "What would people think of a new wife whose husband didn't come to her on their wedding night?"

She hadn't thought of that. Why would she?

"So you're just doing this for my own good?" she asked.

"You commented yourself about how the servants talk."

"Fine," she told him. "You've made your appearance. You can leave now."

"Rachel," he said softly, "these things take a little longer than the few minutes I've been in here."

"Oh." Rachel felt her cheeks heat. "How long, then?"

"Hours."

"Hours?" She backed away, looking him up and down. Good grief, what could a husband and wife do that would possibly take that long?

Mitch leaned in a little. "If it's done right."

A wave of heat crashed through Rachel. An odd feeling she didn't understand. Yet she was pretty certain she knew the meaning of the look on Mitch's face. She'd seen it before, when he'd kissed her.

She felt vulnerable and exposed in her nightclothes, even with them buttoned up tight, covering her from ankle to wrist to throat. She went to her bureau and dug out a scarf.

"You can stay." Rachel draped the plaid, woolen fabric over her head and tossed the ends over her shoulders, then pointedly checked the time on the mantel clock. "One hour. No more."

"I don't believe I've ever been timed at this before," Mitch mused.

He shrugged out of his jacket and dropped it on the settee, causing Rachel to gasp.

"What are you doing?" she demanded.

"Getting comfortable." He lowered himself onto the settee, then pulled his tie loose and opened the top button of his shirt. "What's wrong? Don't think you can control yourself?"

"You sicken me," she declared, as she dug through another bureau drawer. She scrounged to the bottom and found the pair of Noah's socks that she sometimes slept in during the cold winter months. Balancing on one foot, then the other, she pulled them on, tugging them over her ankles.

"Champagne?" Mitch asked.

She saw him filling a glass and hurriedly yanked on a pair of gloves, then dashed over.

"I don't think that's a good idea," she said. "Consumption of spirits tends to make some men...excited."

Mitch paused with the glass at his lips. His gaze cut to her and he did a double take, seeing her in the orange plaid scarf, lavender wrapper, red gloves and black socks.

"I believe I can control myself."

"Well, all right, if you're sure," Rachel said.

He sipped his champagne, then filled the other glass.

"Have some," he said. "After all, it is our wedding night. And we each have something to celebrate."

Rachel eyed the glass sitting on the little table. "I don't usually drink...though I imagine I'll be doing more of it in the coming year."

She eased into the chair that faced the settee and picked up the glass.

"How did your meeting go with Albert Taft?" she asked, thinking it good to center the conversation on business.

"Problems with his quarry. He wants me to take a look at the books."

"So that was my competition? Mr. Taft and a rubble-filled hole in the ground?" Rachel sipped the champagne. "He wanted you to work for him, but you chose to marry me instead. I'm flattered."

Mitch twirled the glass between his fingers. "Were you pleased with the ceremony this afternoon? I know it's not what you've always dreamed of."

"Hardly," Rachel said, taking another gulp of champagne.

He'd offered to delay the ceremony until Rachel could plan a small wedding, but she'd refused. No sense putting it off, she decided. No sense trying to make something pretty out of it. And, she had a year to remain married to him. The clock was ticking.

"You looked nice today," Mitch said.

"I despise that dress. It's ugly and I hate it and tomorrow I'm going to rip it into shreds and set it on fire."

Rachel knew she was being catty and insulting, but she couldn't stop herself. She chugged the last of her champagne and glanced at the mantel clock. "You have fifty-two minutes."

Mitch refilled her glass. "Did you speak with your uncle Stuart about your father?"

Somewhere between accepting Mitch's marriage proposal in the study this morning, and dragging her hated "wedding dress" from the back of her redwood closet this afternoon, Uncle Stuart had cornered her about her father.

"He spoke with you about it first, I gather," Rachel said, taking another swig of champagne.

Mitch nodded. "He mentioned it this morning. He's very concerned about your father's well-being."

"Uncle Stuart recommended a place," Rachel said. "A facility held in the highest regard, located in the mountains near Lake Arrowhead. Lots of clean air. Top-notch care. Not far from here. Close enough for frequent visits."

"But you're still not convinced it's the right thing to do?"

Rachel stared down at her glass, then looked away. "I keep thinking about what you said. About how difficult it must be on Father to stay in the room they shared, knowing Mother is gone."

"The change might do him good."

"It might," she allowed.

"How are your friend's wedding plans going?"

Why did he have to be so nice, so considerate, when she was trying so hard to be mad at him?

"Claudia is getting a little more help than she really wants," she said, thinking of Graham's intrusive decisions. Rachel drained her glass. "The engagement party is scheduled. We'll have to attend, the two of us together. Have you been to an engagement party before?"

Mitch shook his head. "Do you think I can be 'trained' in time?"

She'd forgotten that she'd hurled that insult at him in the study, yet couldn't bring herself to back away from it.

"We'll start tomorrow," Rachel said, setting aside her glass. "I'll bring along a big stick, just in case."

"Now I'm excited," he told her.

The deep tenor of his voice sent a shock wave through Rachel. Her gaze met his and he seemed to see inside her. Seemed to know that he'd set her heart to beating faster and caused warm ripples to pulse through her.

"Time's up," she announced and rose to her feet.

Mitch stood and shrugged into his jacket. He looked at the clock. "My hour isn't up yet."

"We're out of things to talk about," Rachel said, leading the way to the door. "I don't know what else we could do."

"How about this?"

Mitch swung her around and enfolded her in his arms. Pulling her tight against him, he kissed her. Stunned, Rachel hung in his embrace as his lips moved over hers.

But this wasn't the sort of kiss he'd given her before. His mouth covered hers, hot and wet until she moaned softly and parted her lips. She couldn't help herself. Then he slid inside, acquainting himself with her intimately.

Still tight in his embrace, he leaned her back and pushed the scarf from her head. He plucked the pins out and her hair spilled free.

Rachel pressed her palms against his chest as her head spun. His kiss overwhelmed her, yet she had no desire to pull away.

His hand slipped lower and cupped her breast. Rachel gasped against his mouth. Mitch moaned and deepened their kiss as his fingers seemed to burn through the fabric of her nightgown and robe. He squeezed gently and slid his thumb over her breast as he angled himself against her. The hardness of him pressed against her thigh. Rachel gasped once more.

When he lifted his head and backed away, Rachel held on, sure she'd fall without his strong arms around her. They gazed at each other. Mitch's eyes burned hot. Somehow, Rachel knew that she looked the same.

For an instant, she thought he'd kiss her again—did she want him to do just that? But he released her and disappeared out of her room.

Rachel collapsed against the closed door wondering what more her wedding night could have offered.

Chapter Sixteen

Mitch eased back in the desk chair and gazed out the study window at the midmorning sunlight. At the side of the house he saw the crew he'd arranged for; he'd spoken to the foreman already, who was now upstairs.

Rachel had left an hour ago, headed for Claudia's house and another round of wedding talk. Mitch was sure, though, that their own marriage would dominate the conversation.

He didn't have to wonder what details Rachel would tell even her closest friend; she was as anxious as he to keep the circumstances of their nuptials quiet. He never had to wonder about Rachel's intentions on that score.

But he didn't feel married, Mitch thought, slumping lower in the desk chair. He didn't know what married should feel like, yet he was pretty sure it had nothing to do with the long night he'd endured, hard and achy, alone in his own bed.

He hadn't really expected Rachel to allow an intimate relationship between them, given the circumstances surrounding their union. He couldn't blame her for her decision.

Yet how would he ever manage a whole year of seeing her, smelling her, being close to her, imagining what color underwear she wore everyday?

She'd been insulting and cutting in her remarks to him last night in her room, and he couldn't blame her for that, either. Her words didn't bother Mitch; he was just glad she was still talking to him.

He didn't doubt that she'd keep up her part of the bargain. She would see to it that he was properly prepared—trained, as she'd put it—for acceptance by the city's upper crust. But it would go so much better if she didn't hate him in the process.

The woman drove him to distraction. Even last night when she'd thrown on nearly every article of clothing she could get her hands on had done nothing to diminish his desire for her.

Such innocence. As if that ridiculous getup could keep him from wanting her.

Mitch's body hummed with renewed desire. What a loving task it would be to acquaint her with the joys of intimacy. Slowly, gently, with all the patience he could muster—and Mitch had a great deal of patience. He'd take his time, see to her pleasure, make sure she enjoyed it. Why wouldn't he?

It would only pay incredible dividends in the future. And a year was a very long time.

Mitch pushed himself upright in the chair, his own thoughts jarring him back to reality.

What the hell had he been thinking? Making love to Rachel? Impossible.

He hadn't married her for that reason. He could find release for his lustful desires at many places in the city. At Stuart Parker's gentlemen's club several such locations had been recommended to him, though he hadn't availed himself of those places yet.

He wanted Rachel for something much more valuable.

With the determination that had gotten him this far in life, Mitch forced into his thoughts recollections of years gone by. The hardship. The hurt. That's what he needed to think of.

In his mind, Mitch projected himself into the future and envisioned all the things that would soon be his, made possible by the power he'd have. That's what was important. Not some fantasy about bedding down with Rachel. She was a means to an end, nothing more. He'd worked too hard for too long to lose sight of his goal now.

No matter what color underwear she wore.

"What is the meaning of—of—that!" Rachel demanded as she charged into the study.

Mitch looked up from the ledger in front of him, trying, she was sure, to appear innocent.

He eased back in his chair and looked her up and down, as he always did, as if trying to discern something from her appearance, though Rachel still couldn't imagine what it was. But she did wish he'd stop doing it. It made her tingle when she didn't want to.

"What's what?" Mitch asked.

"That!" Rachel gestured wildly through the house toward the second floor. She'd just returned from Claudia's, gone to her bedchamber and made the startling discovery.

At Claudia's, Rachel had immediately told her friend about her marriage to Mitch. Claudia had been shocked and a little hurt that Rachel hadn't told her ahead of time or asked her to stand up with her.

But Rachel quickly explained that she wanted a simple ceremony out of respect for her family situation. It's the story Rachel planned to tell everyone. Claudia understood completely. Then she'd launched into her own upcoming wedding.

The two of them sat together for hours looking at dress patterns, color swatches—all in shades of blue, the color Graham insisted on. It seemed the groom had an opinion on almost every aspect of the wedding and Claudia explained all of them to Rachel; she was trying hard to make the ceremony exactly what her husband-to-be wanted. Claudia's mother joined them later for lunch and happily provided the details of the upcoming engagement party.

It had been a perfect afternoon for Rachel. Then she'd come home to this.

Mitch nodded. "Upstairs? You're upset about it? I thought you'd be pleased."

"Pleased?" Rachel's eyes narrowed. "I insist you do something about this at once!"

Mitch rose from the desk with a grace that always surprised Rachel, even now when she was appalled by his behavior. He moved with confidence, almost arrogance, so sure was he of his own strength. Long arms and legs, muscles everywhere. Wide shoulders and what surely was a hard chest.

Rachel could have found out just how strong his chest was last night if she hadn't had on those gloves. Her palms were right there, pressed against him, and she could have discovered just—

"Coming?" he asked, stopping ahead of her.

Rachel ducked around him, hoping that he mistook the flush on her cheeks for anger. Because she was angry with him, she reminded herself.

She led the way up the staircase and down the hallway, clipping off her steps with determination while he sauntered beside her, leisurely keeping pace. She charged into her bedchamber and pointed at the door that had been cut into the wall during her absence.

"What is the meaning of this?" she demanded.

"It connects your room to mine," he said.

"Your room is down the hall," she declared, pointing again.

"My room is here." Mitch opened the door and gestured to the adjoining room.

Though the chamber was located in the family wing of the house, it was rarely used. There simply wasn't a need for it except on rare occasions when the Branfords entertained more overnight guests than the opposing wing could accommodate. Rachel and her mother had often discussed taking out the bedroom furnishings and turning it into a music room, or small library, but had never gotten around to it.

And now Mitch had not only moved in and taken over, he'd installed a connecting doorway to Rachel's room. As if he could simply come and go when it suited him, just as he'd barged into her room last night.

"What is the meaning of this?" she demanded, then didn't give him a chance to respond. "I want this door sealed, closed—permanently. I insist upon it."

"I thought this would make you happy."

Rachel looked at him as if he'd lost his mind. "Why on earth did you think that?"

"Because you can come and go from my room in complete secrecy, at your leisure."

"I'll do no such thing!" Rachel declared, another hot rush accompanying her words. She gestured to the door once more. "I want this door boarded up immediately."

Mitch tilted his head. "I don't think that's a good idea."

She threw him a scathing look. "This is for my own good? Is that what you're suggesting?"

"Servants talk," he reminded her. "Unless you don't mind being whispered about, with everyone wondering why your husband never comes to your room at night."

Rachel cringed, as surely he knew she'd do, at the thought of the most personal aspect of her life becoming fodder for the servants and, eventually, the city's rumor mill.

"You know I can't allow that," she told him.

Mitch leaned down a little, until she felt the heat of his body against hers. "This way, no one will know what goes on in here between the two of us."

"Nothing will be going on," she insisted. "I want this door locked—permanently."

The tiniest grin pulled at his lips. "Don't think you can trust yourself to stay on your side?"

The nerve of this man! Rachel fumed and she thrust out her palm. "Give me the keys. Both of them. At once."

Mitch slid his hands into his trouser pockets, first one and then the other, then patted his jacket side pockets and finally his shirt. Rachel's gaze followed his every movement.

There was that chest of his again. Darn, if she hadn't worn those idiotic gloves last night she could have pressed her palm full against him, let her fingertips roam and discovered what lay beneath his shirt.

It wouldn't have been so outlandish, would it? Given what he'd been doing to her at the time?

Mitch pulled two keys from his vest pocket and placed them in her hand. His fingers brushed her palm, sending a jolt up her arm.

Rachel ignored the sensation and closed her fist around the keys, the metal warm against her palm.

"Thank you," she said crisply. "I intend to keep these at all times so that you can never come through that door."

"Really?"

The subtle challenge in his voice sent a hint of alarm or expectation—something—through Rachel. She saw the sharp intake of his breath and his chest expanded. She braced herself.

Mitch stepped back, drew his leg up and smashed his foot into the connecting door. The casing shattered. Wood splintered. The door flew open and banged against the wall.

Rachel's mouth fell open as Mitch whipped around. He leaned down until they were face-to-face.

"If I decided to claim my husbandly right, nothing would keep me from you."

He gave her one last hot look, then stormed out of the room.

Rachel watched him go, too stunned to move.

Chapter Seventeen

He couldn't face an entire year of the sort of meals Rachel had instructed the cook to prepare.

Mitch left the supper table hungry, as usual. Bad enough that now he faced the most daunting challenge he could imagine, that he slept next door to a woman he couldn't touch, and that his love life had been reduced to wishful thinking.

But he couldn't—simply could not—continue to function on the pitiful little meals served in the Branford house. He'd have to do something about it.

Mitch knew that the problems experienced by the family made life for their staff difficult, also. The servants knew everything that went on with the Branfords and they, too, were troubled by them. For that reason, Mitch hadn't wanted to make things harder on the cook and her staff by requesting changes to the menus and meal preparations.

All that had changed. He would be here for a while, a year, anyway. He couldn't take it anymore.

Mitch glanced back into the empty dining room and the meal he'd abandoned. He wasn't even sure what it was. But there wasn't a potato or drop of gravy on the table and he had to change that.

No wonder Noah wasn't growing, he thought as he headed toward the study. The boy still kept to himself much of the time. He never came downstairs for a meal. Mitch rarely saw him. But he heard him in the upstairs hallway and on the staircase at night sometimes, when Mitch went to the attic to work out with his punching bag.

Maybe that was something else that needed to be changed around the house, Mitch thought.

Silence hung heavy as Mitch went from room to room. Lights burned low, casting long shadows. He supposed Rachel was in her room; that's where she'd spent most of her time lately.

He found Noah in the library slouched on the settee, dressed in trousers and a white shirt, the sleeve knotted below his shoulder, as always. A bottle of whiskey was in his hand.

The boy watched him cautiously as Mitch pulled a chair over and sat down in front of him.

"Your sister is starving me to death," Mitch said. "But it's you and me now. Two against one. I'm going to talk to the cook. Are you with me?"

Noah looked completely lost, as if no one had asked his opinion on anything in so long that he didn't know how to respond. He drew back a little and clasped the whiskey bottle closer to his chest.

"Yeah…I guess," he said.

"Meat—real meat. Potatoes. Gravy," Mitch said. "Cakes and pies for dessert. Every night."

"All right…"

Mitch gave him a brisk nod. "I'm going to need your help around here, too."

Noah glanced down at his knotted sleeve and shrugged helplessly. "I can't…"

"You can add figures, can't you?"

"Well, sure, but—"

"Then you can help with the family business," Mitch told him. "You'll get a tutor, also, and meet with him every day."

Noah frowned. "I don't want a—"

"And no more of this." Mitch plucked the whiskey bottle from his hand.

"Hey!" Noah lurched forward, but didn't grab for it. He glared up at Mitch. "Just because Rachel married you doesn't mean you can take over."

"Yes, it does."

Noah fumed silently.

"You've poisoned yourself long enough with this stuff, Noah. No more."

The boy's anger simmered and Mitch could see his mind working, wanting to take the whiskey bottle back, considering fighting for it.

Mitch stood up. That's all he needed to do. Long ago he'd learned that his height alone was often enough to bully most any man into doing as he said.

Oddly enough, though, his height didn't affect Rachel that way. When he stood up in front of her, she simply stretched herself up taller and faced him squarely.

As if he'd issued some sort of challenge that she was anxious to confront.

But right now Noah backed down, as Mitch knew he would.

"Your family needs you," Mitch told him. "Come to the study tomorrow morning."

Noah glared up at him.

"If I have to come get you tomorrow morning, you won't like it," Mitch said. He left with the bottle and went hunting for Hayden. He found him in the dining room with Rachel.

"Lock this up," Mitch said, handing the whiskey bottle to the butler. "Lock up all the liquor in the house."

"Yes, sir," Hayden said, taking the bottle.

"What's going on?" Rachel asked.

"Search everywhere, especially Noah's room," Mitch said. "There're probably bottles hidden all over the house."

"And the key to the liquor closet?" Hayden asked, his gaze subtly shifting from Mitch to Rachel.

"You keep it, Hayden," Mitch said. "Serve the liquor when appropriate, but none to Noah. Not a drop. If he gives you any trouble, come get me."

"Yes, sir." Hayden disappeared from the room.

Rachel waited until the butler's footsteps faded before turning to Mitch once more.

"I asked you what was going on."

Mitch glanced around. There were two entrances to the family dining room, plus the door that led to the kitchen. Rachel knew at once what he was thinking, and she appreciated his discretion.

He jerked his chin toward the door. Rachel nodded

and led the way through the house to the study. Mitch closed the door behind them. The lamp on the desk glowed yellow, throwing the room in a warm light.

He didn't take his usual seat behind the desk. Instead he paced back and forth in front of the window. Though it was dark outside, gaslights could be seen burning along West Adams Boulevard illuminating the trolley and the carriages that clipped along. Across the street, the neighbor's houses were lit top to bottom with glowing windows.

Mitch stared out for a few moments, then turned to Rachel. "I can't stand by any longer and watch your brother throw away his life," he said.

"He's been through a great deal," Rachel reminded him. "Dr. Matthews said that—"

"I don't give a damn what Matthews says."

Rachel paused, surprised to hear the hint of anger in Mitch's voice.

"Dr. Matthews has dealt with Noah's problem for a long time," Rachel said. "He knows what's to be expected of him."

"And where has it gotten Noah?" Mitch demanded. "He pushed away all his friends, he never goes out of the house, he creeps around this place like a ghost and he drinks himself into oblivion."

Rachel sighed. Mitch was right. She knew it. But she didn't know what to do about it.

"I don't disagree with you," she said. "But what should I do?"

"Change everything," Mitch said. "What's going on now obviously isn't working. Do the opposite."

Rachel smiled gently. "Is that what you advise your business clients?"

He gave her a quick nod. "If it's warranted, yes."

She admired his confidence. She always had. Right from the moment she laid eyes on him, Rachel knew Mitch Kincade didn't lack conviction.

For so long she'd worried about Noah. Despite Dr. Matthews's assurances she'd known that her brother wasn't getting any better, wasn't adjusting to the loss of his arm, wasn't learning to cope and move on with his life.

"That tutor he had before," Mitch said. "Get him back here. Tomorrow. Have him come every morning."

Rachel recalled the shouting matches between Noah and Mr. Hudson that had escalated to her brother throwing every piece of glassware he could get his hand on at the man until he left and never came back.

"I don't think Noah will like that," Rachel pointed out.

"Good. It's time he did something he didn't like," Mitch said. "He'll help me with the family business, too."

Rachel shook her head. "Noah's been through so much. I don't think we should push him into too many things."

"He's been babied too long."

"He's lost his arm, for goodness' sake."

Mitch stepped closer, a look on his face more intense than Rachel had seen before.

"A lot of people have problems, Rachel. A lot of people suffer hardship. A lot of people would be happy that all that was wrong was that they'd lost an arm."

And what hardship had Mitch suffered? The thought raced through Rachel's mind. What had happened to

him? What had he been through that would make him
even think such a thing, let alone say it aloud?

A pang of regret echoed through Rachel. What other
mysteries did Mitch hold? And would she ever learn them?

She shook away the notion and focused on her
brother again. Everything the doctor had recommended
had failed.

Noah wasn't getting any better. Maybe she should do
the opposite, as Mitch suggested.

"All right, then," she said, drawing a fresh breath.
"We'll try it your way."

Mitch watched her for a moment, as if he'd expected
more of an argument.

"I think it would be good if we shared meals together
at the table." Mitch looked unsure of himself for the first
time in their conversation. "That's what families do,
isn't it?"

Rachel glanced away, feeling a little guilty. Her family had always eaten together, supper especially. Her
mother had insisted upon it. Their family meals weren't
etiquette drills from their mother, or quizzes on current
events from their father, but quiet, relaxing times that
the family shared privately.

Lately, though, Rachel had stayed away from the
supper table to avoid her new husband. She hadn't
thought about Noah at all. But Mitch had, and it surprised her.

"Yes, we can do that," she said. "The family always
ate together…before."

Mitch looked at her for a long moment, his expression unreadable. What was he thinking? She had no idea.

But she did know that she owed him a debt of gratitude for helping with Noah. And Chelsey, too, for that matter. Rachel had gotten letters from her sister already and she sounded happy, truly happy. Rachel would never have let her return to school if it hadn't been for Mitch. And it had been the right thing to do.

"These family problems," Rachel said softly. "I'm sure they were the last thing you expected when you came here."

Mitch turned away and went to the window. He slid his hands into his trouser pockets and gazed out at the darkness.

Rachel stepped closer. His shoulders were wide and straight enough that surely they could carry a lot of weight, even as many family problems as Rachel had. But it wasn't right to burden Mitch.

"Thank you for all you've done. It's not expected, but greatly appreciated," Rachel said. "And I apologize for involving you in the family problems."

"Don't apologize for having problems," Mitch said, still gazing outside. "Problems mean that you have people in your life. People living real lives, with joy and excitement and heartache, depending on each other, helping each other. Not silence, walking in straight lines with your head down, waiting for it all to be over with…"

Mitch stopped and looked back at her. Even in the dim light she saw the pain in his expression. He'd said too much. Revealed something of himself that he didn't want her—or anyone, apparently—to know.

Rachel's heart ached for him. She wanted to go to him, press her palm against his cheek, throw her arms around him and hold him close. By comparison, she was slim and small, yet she could shoulder this just-revealed burden of his easily. She knew she could.

But he wouldn't let her. Without another word, Mitch moved past her and out of the study.

She almost went after him. She wanted to. But something told Rachel that it would do no good. Mitch had always been secretive about his past and she'd been content to let him have his way.

Now she wished she'd been more insistent before she agreed to their marriage. Because now that he had what he wanted, why would he ever reveal his past to her?

Chapter Eighteen

It was the most difficult decision she'd ever made.

Rachel stood in the doorway as the family carriage pulled away. Inside were Dr. Matthews, the nurses, Uncle Stuart and her father.

Her father. Tall, strong, fearless Edward Branford, now thin and shriveled, a mere shadow of his vibrant self, heading for a convalescent hospital.

Making the decision to allow him to go had been heartwrenching for Rachel. She'd put it off as long as she could, then finally, after one of her long afternoons at her father's bedside, she'd known what she had to do.

The opposite. That had been Mitch's advice for Noah. If the current course of action wasn't working—and clearly it wasn't with her father—then do the opposite.

Only time would tell if her decision was the correct one.

Sadness gripped Rachel's heart as the carriage turned onto West Adams Boulevard. The sole certainty, at the moment, was that yet another member of her family was gone.

She sensed Mitch move closer behind her and, with effort, choked back her tears. He'd waited outside her father's bedchamber this morning while Rachel had said her goodbye, and stayed at her side as her father was loaded into the carriage. Mitch hadn't said much, just stood close keeping an eye on everything, then watched with her as they pulled away.

At least she'd gotten to see her father leave. Not like the others.

Images of all the important men in her life flashed in Rachel's mind bringing with them the hurt they'd created and instilled in her heart. Tears filled her eyes. She pressed her fingertips to her lips and held her breath, as if that might hold back her emotions. Then she felt Mitch's hand on her shoulder and she broke down.

He turned her into the circle of his arms. Rachel sobbed against his jacket. He pulled her closer.

And what a natural place that seemed to be. Sheltered in his strong arms, tight against the hard wall of his chest. Safe, to cry out all the anguish in her heart. Rachel knew she could stay in his embrace forever.

But Mitch wouldn't be here forever.

Rachel pulled away and looked up at him, fighting to push away the comforting halo his embrace had wound around her.

"You're just like all the others," Rachel said, gulping back tears. "Georgie, Benjamin and now Father—Noah, too, in his own way—"

"Who's Benjamin?"

The name sliced through Rachel, tearing at the slim hold she had on her emotions. It had been well over a year since he'd courted her, called on her, claimed to care for her, only to walk out. She'd thought the incident was behind her. Yet his name came easily amid the list of the men in her life who had abandoned her.

And now she was looking at Mitch, yet another man who would do the same. He'd told her so. Even given her the date. She had it in writing.

"Benjamin Blair—the last man who walked out on me," Rachel declared, the sadness turning into anger. "At least you had the good grace not to claim you love me."

Mitch shook his head, concern causing him to frown. "What happened?"

"He courted me for months. We were a couple. Everyone expected to hear an engagement announcement," Rachel told him, anger and hurt bringing on tears again. "Then the train accident. Mother dead, Father ill, Noah crippled. My entire family was in turmoil. And what did Benjamin do? He left. He wrote me a letter explaining that the tragedy was simply too much for him to bear, and he left for Europe."

Mitch's frown deepened. "He walked out?"

"Don't you understand? Every man in my life leaves me!" Rachel sobbed harder. "And you intend to do the same. I even know in advance when you're leaving. You wrote it into your contract—no surprises there."

Mitch didn't respond. He just looked at her.

She wiped away her tears and choked back another sob.

"But don't expect anything from me in this coming year," she told him. "Oh, I'll keep to our agreement. I'll give you what you want. But don't for a moment think I'll go out of my way for you, simply because I'm your wife."

A moment passed while Mitch simply looked at her, as if absorbing her anger along with her words.

"That's understandable, Rachel." Mitch spoke softly, with no anger or malice in his tone. "But you should know that, in the year we have together, if you want to cry again, you can use my shoulder. If you want to share an unkind rumor, you can tell me and know it won't go further. If you wish for anything, you can come to me and I'll do everything in my power to get it for you. Simply because I'm your husband."

Another onslaught of emotion overtook Rachel. She'd just said the most horrible things to Mitch, and he was being nice to her.

It was too much to bear.

She burst into tears again and ran to her room.

Pink dress. No, not pink, exactly. Rose colored? Not the same shade he'd seen in the other dresses she'd worn. This one was different. Deeper, richer. With red trim along the hem and cuffs, and down the front.

Rose dress. Rose underwear?

The thoughts ripped through Mitch's mind in the few seconds it took Rachel to walk from the entrance of the dining room to her chair at the breakfast table.

Mitch got to his feet, circled to the other side and pulled out her chair.

Rose dress, rose underwear. It made sense. What else could it be? The only other color on the dress was—

Red.

Desire bloomed in Mitch with the certainty of the rising sun peeking through the dining-room window, made worse by the lovely view of her bottom descending into the chair. And her trim waist, of course, along with the gentle curve of her back, her long graceful neck, the few loose strands of her dark hair that he wanted to curl around his fingers.

And red underwear beneath everything? Mitch's mouth went dry.

"Thank you."

Rachel's words broke through his thoughts, her tone suggesting she'd said them more than once. Mitch glanced around and saw Noah, in the chair next to his sister, staring at him, and the servant at the buffet giving him an odd look. He gave up his grip on the chair—and his view—and returned to his own place.

"Good morning," Rachel said to Noah.

The boy grunted and continued to pick at his food. Mitch hadn't gotten much more conversation out of him when he'd walked into the dining room and found Noah already seated at the table.

But the boy was there, as Mitch had instructed. He intended to have Noah help audit the family books—busy work, really—under Mitch's direction after the morning tutoring session ended.

But Mitch was more glad to see Rachel at the breakfast table—relieved, actually. After yesterday when her father had left for the convalescent hospital, he wasn't sure if the hurt she'd felt wouldn't cause her to abandon their agreement.

Without Rachel's help, there was no reason for him

to be in the Branford household. The contract Stuart Parker had drawn up detailed their financial arrangement, but nothing could compel Rachel to do as Mitch asked if she chose not to.

The old familiar ache rose in Mitch. Helpless. Powerless. At the mercy of someone else. But this time something more twisted his insides.

The red underwear? No, he decided. But what?

Rachel looked refreshed this morning, Mitch saw, as one of the servants filled her coffee cup. No sign of the tears she'd shed yesterday, or the heartache caused by that bastard Benjamin Blair and the other men in her life who had abandoned her.

She did notice the change in the breakfast menu Mitch had asked the cook to make. Both his and Noah's plates were filled with eggs, bacon, potatoes and hot biscuits. Rachel raised an eyebrow at their meals but didn't say anything.

"Excuse me," Noah mumbled. He rose from the chair, tossed his napkin on the table and left the room.

"He seems to be trying," Rachel offered, serving herself fruit and a muffin from the platter on the table. "How did you manage?"

"I can be a compelling presence," Mitch told her with a tiny hint of a grin. He nodded toward the tablet she'd brought into the dining room with her and placed beside her plate. "Another project? Something for the luncheon?"

"Actually, my next project is you."

"Am I that big a chore?" Mitch asked, trying to read the list Rachel had written in the tablet.

"You'll need more clothing," Rachel said, sipping her coffee and glancing down at her tablet. "Business suits, of course. Casual suits, too. Formal wear for Claudia's engagement party. Shoes, hats, coats."

"Will I have a say in the colors?"

"No."

"How about the fabric?"

"No."

Mitch glanced down at his necktie. "Is there something wrong with the way I look now?"

Rachel sat back in her chair and looked across the table at him, her gaze roaming critically over him. Mitch felt a little uncomfortable under her scrutiny; Rachel seemed to enjoy it.

"Did you pick out that suit and necktie yourself?" she asked.

He hesitated a moment. "Well, yes."

"Actually, you look very nice," she said. "Better than most men who select their own clothing."

For some reason, Mitch felt inordinately pleased by the compliment.

"I'll have the tailor come over for your measurements. He'll bring fabric swatches with him." She gave him a little grin. "I suppose you can have a look, if you want."

"I don't want to overstep my bounds," Mitch said, finishing his coffee.

Rachel glanced at her tablet again and her demeanor changed, as if she were moving on to something else.

"It's appropriate that we send out an announcement, of some sort, about your…marriage," she said. "I'd like to discuss it with you, if you have time."

For Rachel and her—red, was it?—underwear, he'd make time.

They finished breakfast and he followed her into the library and over to the wall of books that rose from floor to ceiling. She leaned her head back, searching the titles, then stretched up to select the one she spotted.

Mitch moved in, reached over her head and plucked the book from the shelf. He angled close, getting a good whiff of her hair as her skirt brushed his leg. Little things, but he'd take them.

To his surprise, she didn't move away, just stood there near him as he handed her the book. Their gazes held for a long moment while Mitch's mind ran wild with speculation.

She was thinking something. He could always tell. And when she looked like this, Mitch found he couldn't wait to hear what she had to say.

"I said some unkind things to you yesterday," Rachel said.

"Is this an apology?"

"No. I'm not sorry I said them, but I shouldn't have been so mean about it. You didn't deserve that."

Her honesty disarmed him at times.

"You didn't deserve to be abandoned, certainly not by that Blair character," Mitch said. "And by the way, if you should see him again, I'd be more than happy to punch him in the face for you."

Color flushed her cheeks and the most alluring smile spread over her mouth. She dipped her lashes. "I don't believe anyone has ever offered to punch someone for me."

"Believe me, it would be my pleasure," Mitch told

her, managing to hold back his true opinion of the man who'd walked out on her. "I know how hurtful it is for you to be talked about. That story must have made the rounds through the city in record time."

"Coming on the heels of the devastating news about my family's loss, there was mercifully little gossip about Benjamin's sudden departure," Rachel explained. "It was a poor reflection on him, rather than me."

"Still, a painful memory," Mitch said.

She shrugged. "I rarely think of him and when I do it's with indifference. I suppose that means I never loved him in the first place. Anyway, whatever feelings I had for Benjamin are long gone. When I look back, I wonder why I ever agreed to be courted by him in the first place."

"Pursuit of the perfect wedding?" Mitch asked. "Like your friend Claudia?"

"Perhaps."

Another moment passed in silence. Mitch wondered if her thoughts had, in fact, drifted back to Benjamin Blair. Annoyance and anger rose in him with a startling intensity. Rachel and another man?

She gave herself a little shake as if shooing away whatever her thoughts had been and smiled up at Mitch.

"Ready to get started?" she asked, holding up the book.

Mitch saw from the title that it was a book on etiquette.

"Just one thing first," he said.

Then he leaned down and kissed her.

Chapter Nineteen

Dinner fork. Salad fork. Both on the left side of the dinner plate. Spoons on the...right?

Mitch opened his eyes and consulted the diagram in the book lying open on the kitchen worktable. Rachel had used the book this morning to review the procedures—and there were many—required for sending their wedding announcement. She'd explained it all to him.

Right after he'd kissed her.

Mitch squinted at the book as the words swarmed together. He'd come here to the kitchen this late at night, when he was certain the cook and her staff had retired for the evening, so he could practice in private. Using the diagram in the book, he assembled all the pieces of china, silverware and crystal he'd need.

But he couldn't keep his mind on his task any more now than he had this morning in the library with Rachel. All he could do was think of her and their kiss, while speculating on her undergarments.

"Damn…"

Mitch bit off a worse curse and focused on the etiquette book again. Enough of those sort of thoughts. Rachel was keeping to their agreement—the agreement he himself had insisted upon—so he damn well ought to do the same.

He dragged up a stool and eased onto it, staring down at the diagrams and the explanations.

He did well enough with table manners. He'd been taught a little; the rest he'd gathered by watching other diners around him. He had no way of knowing whether or not their manners were correct, though.

He couldn't bring himself to ask Rachel for help. Not with this. Even though she'd agreed to help him with entrance to the privileged world of the wealthy and powerful, his pride caused him to keep this to himself.

What would she say…if she knew the truth?

Mitch forced his thoughts back to the book and its detailed description of a proper table setting.

A space of sixteen to twenty inches should be allowed for each guest at the dining table, this area being called the "cover." Mitch shook his head. It needed a name?

The cover was marked with a service plate, a napkin folded and laid on the left and a place card centered just above the plate.

Mitch glanced at the plate he'd taken from the cupboard. All right, that seemed easy enough. His gaze skimmed the next paragraph.

Forks, tines turned up. Knives with the cutting blade

facing the plate. All silverware positioned an inch from the table edge. No more than three forks and two knives at any one cover—thank goodness for small favors—and dessert spoons and forks brought to the table when needed.

Mitch drew in a breath and turned the page. Glassware. The water glass should be placed directly above the tip of the knife, other glasses lined up to the right and slightly below the water glass. No glass—regardless of beverage—should be filled more than three-fourths full and they should never—

Mitch pushed off the stool. Good Lord, how could the simple act of eating a meal generate so many rules? How did diners not come away with indigestion?

Thank goodness he didn't have to set the table, only eat from it.

An old, uncomfortable feeling crept over him. At least setting the table could be done in relative privacy. Eating in the presence of society's upper crust was another matter entirely.

Mitch gazed around the kitchen. All this thinking about dining properly had made him hungry.

He rummaged through the ice box and cupboards, then went to work making himself a stack of pancakes. When he turned the last one out onto the plate, Rachel stepped out of the shadows, startling him. She had on the same lavender robe and nightgown he'd seen her in on their wedding night.

No underwear.

"I thought I smelled something cooking. I was in the library looking for a book. Are those pancakes?" She glanced around the room. "Where's Mrs. Callihan? Did you make those yourself?"

"I was hungry," Mitch said as he set the plate on the worktable.

"I don't believe I've ever seen any of the men in my family cook," Rachel said, moving to his side. She looked up at him and raised an eyebrow. "You don't seem like the cooking type."

"And what type do I seem?" he asked, adding chunks of butter between the pancakes and dousing them with syrup.

"Even the financial work you do doesn't seem right, though you're very good at it, as you've mentioned several times," she said. "I'd think something more physical. Like the boxing you do. In fact, if I were as strong as you—just for a day—"

She stopped and, as usual, Mitch had to know what was on her mind.

"What would you do?" he asked.

Rachel glanced around the kitchen, then rose on her toes and stretched up. He leaned down and she whispered in his ear, "I'd beat the tar out of everybody who'd ever hurt me or my family."

Mitch grinned at the fanciful look on her face.

"Including me?" he asked.

"You'd be first."

"You're welcome to try now." Mitch spread his arms. "I'll even give you an advantage. I promise not to fight back. You can do whatever you want."

Rachel paused, considering it for a moment. Then she uttered a short laugh. "I think you might enjoy that."

Mitch couldn't hold back a wider grin.

"But it must be nice," Rachel mused, "being so strong. Never having to be afraid."

"There are all kinds of strengths," Mitch said. "And more than one sort of fear."

"What are you afraid of?" she asked, as if she couldn't imagine he'd have an answer at all.

"Glassware. Forks. Which one? Used when?"

The words popped out when he hadn't meant them to. Something about being around Rachel caused him to lose control. He had to stop letting that happen.

She gestured to the place setting he'd assembled on the other end of the worktable. "Surely your mother taught you table manners."

How naive of her to think that everyone had a mother who would do just that.

If only it were true.

"I can help you, if you'd like," Rachel said, nothing judgmental in the tone of her voice.

Why had he thought she would be critical or think less of him? Rachel wasn't like that with anyone. Yet his pride hadn't let him take the chance.

He considered his options. She'd offered help. He needed the help. And if he agreed, she'd stay here in the kitchen a while longer.

"If you have time," Mitch said.

In a flash, Rachel assembled a proper place setting— she hadn't needed to look at the diagram, he noted—and drew two stools together.

"We'll practice with your pancakes," she said, centering the plate between the silverware. "First, I'll demonstrate the correct way. Then you can do it yourself."

She took the stool in front of the place setting and Mitch sat down on her left, their knees tucked beneath the table.

It didn't escape his attention that Rachel seemed more relaxed around him tonight, especially given that she was in her nightclothes. When he'd walked into her room on their wedding night she'd thrown on nearly every article of clothing she could get her hands on.

Perhaps she perceived the kitchen as a safer place than her own bedchamber. That this location somehow made him immune to her allure. If so, she was hopelessly wrong.

Visions of the two of them atop the worktable, plates and silver crashing to the floor filled Mitch's head. Was that covered in her etiquette book? He very much doubted—

"Are you listening?"

Mitch shifted on the stool. "Yeah, sure. I'm listening."

"First of all, the napkin should be draped across your lap." Rachel placed the napkin accordingly.

"Got it."

She laid her left hand in her lap. "The hand you're not eating with goes here."

He mimicked her action, but she caught his wrist.

"Your own lap."

"Oh."

She went on to explain something else about place setting, but Mitch's thoughts wandered to her profile and the curve of her chin. To her thick hair, gathered in a ribbon and curling down her back. To her small, delicate hands holding the fork.

Fascinating. Every facet of her being, every curve, every movement. It seemed that each time he looked at her, something new and intriguing caught his eye.

"Your turn," Rachel said.

He hadn't been listening but he followed along as she rose from the stool. They traded places, Mitch now seated in front of the plate of pancakes. He positioned the napkin, selected a fork—the appropriate one, thank goodness, since Rachel didn't correct him—and cut off a bite of pancake.

"Want some?" he asked, holding up the fork. "I'm very good at this."

She smiled. "Let's see about that."

He expected her to fetch a fork for herself, but instead she leaned closer and parted her lips. Mitch's simmering desire ratcheted up several notches as he slid the bite of pancake, dripping with butter and syrup, into her mouth.

Her lips closed. They slid together as she chewed. Then the very tip of her tongue swept her bottom lip and Mitch thought he'd hoist her onto the worktable right then and there.

She nodded thoughtfully. "You really are good at this."

"You have no idea."

"Aren't you going to have some?" she asked, gesturing to the plate again.

He cut off another bite, gripping the fork with all his strength, and shoved it into his mouth. If the food tasted good, he didn't notice. All he could think of was Rachel beside him, close enough to touch. And he wanted to touch her so badly.

"You've got a little syrup on your lip," Rachel said. But instead of reaching for a napkin, she dabbed at the corner of his mouth with her finger.

Mitch captured her between his lips. She gasped but didn't pull away. He caught her hand and drew her fingertip into his mouth, then kissed his way to her palm.

He burned for her. Wanted her as he'd never wanted any other woman in his life.

His gaze met hers. She sat stunned, but didn't pull away. Mitch got to his feet and drew her up against him. She came willingly, locking her arms around his neck as he covered her mouth with a hot kiss.

He plucked open the top few buttons on her robe and nightgown, then slid his hand inside. She gasped again as his fingers closed over her breast, and to his delight, she arched against him.

Mitch deepened their kiss as his hand explored her softness, her curves. He groaned as her fingers splayed over his chest, burning hot through his shirt. He shifted, pressing himself against her, wanting her with—

"Enough of that, you two."

Rachel jerked upright and gasped. Mitch, lost in the haze of desire, took another second to realize that Noah had come into the kitchen.

He kept his arms around Rachel and turned her away, sheltering her while she closed up her nightgown and robe.

"You two are married," Noah pointed out as he sauntered across the room. He got a glass from the cupboard and filled it from the milk pitcher in the ice box. At the worktable he balanced the glass on the plate of pancakes and picked it up with one hand.

"So go upstairs," he said and left.

Mitch's heart thundered in his chest as he looked down at Rachel.

"Shall we?" he asked.

Chapter Twenty

She hadn't gone upstairs with him last night, as Mitch had asked, nor had she been the least bit flattered by his invitation. In fact, for a moment, Mitch had thought she might actually slap him.

Which he might have enjoyed.

Mitch closed the ledger and rose from the desk chair making an effort to put last night out of his mind. Once again, he failed miserably.

After Rachel had dashed from the kitchen, he'd spent hours in the attic attempting to work off his frustration at the punching bag. Then he'd spent several more hours tossing and turning—alone—in his bed before finally dozing off around dawn only to awaken and hear Rachel next door going about her morning routine. The rush of bath water, the creak of her closet door, low chatter with her maid.

Images played in Mitch's mind now as he stared out the study window, same as they had earlier this morning.

Rachel in the tub. Warm soapy water. Thick towels, pink cheeks, damp tendrils curling around her face. The day's clothing choice, dress and, of course, undergarments.

Mitch's blood pumped hotter at the thought. He hadn't seen Rachel this morning. She hadn't come down for breakfast. What clothing had she selected for today?

Wondering over the color of his wife's underwear was beginning to take over his life.

Footsteps behind him interrupted his thoughts, thankfully, and Mitch turned to see Noah enter the study. So far the boy had showed up to help with the family business every day since Mitch had told him to do so. He met with the tutor, also, with no significant problems.

Mitch hadn't expected any. More than anyone else in the house, he understood Noah's actions. He knew what drove him, what he ran from. And for that reason, he was confident Noah wouldn't give him any trouble.

Mitch had moved a small writing desk into the study for Noah to use and made a point of putting it near the window, facing the front lawn, the driveway and the street beyond. He'd been surprised at how quickly Noah caught on to the work he assigned him. Busywork, at first, adding figures and verifying totals. But Noah had started asking questions reminding Mitch that his father had proved himself a smart businessman in amassing the Branford family's extensive holdings. Perhaps Noah had inherited his father's business sense.

Georgie and his underhanded business dealings that had emptied the family bank account stayed in the back of Mitch's mind, though, and he kept a close eye on everything Noah did. Noah and George were, after all, half brothers.

"I'm leaving in a while," Mitch said. "Your sister and I are going to some sort of charity function this afternoon."

Noah pulled a ledger from the stack and flipped it open on the desktop. Mitch continued to marvel at how sure-handed he was, how well he compensated for the arm he'd lost.

"It's at the Monterey house. They have it every year," Noah reported, then shook his head. "And every year she's…with child…again and everybody pretends to ignore it."

"Does Madeline tell you the neighborhood gossip in her letters?" Mitch asked.

Noah glanced up at him, wary for a moment, then sat down at the desk. "Sometimes."

"Will she be at the Monterey home?"

Mitch waited, certain he could see Noah's thoughts in the expressions that played across his face. Waiting—hoping, perhaps?—that Mitch would ask Noah to accompany them to the charity event. Or perhaps considering, at long last, sending Madeline a letter for Mitch to deliver personally.

But Mitch didn't offer. He wouldn't push Noah. It was too soon.

Noah looked away. "She'll be there. Her family goes to everything."

He picked up a pencil and went to work adding columns of figures. Hayden appeared a few minutes later, advising Mitch that Rachel was ready to go.

He shrugged into his jacket and the butler passed him his bowler as he left the study and found Rachel waiting in the foyer.

She stood in front of the mirror, leaning forward ever so slightly, adjusting the angle of her hat. Her dress was the color of rich cream, accented with bands of deep blue at the hem, collar and cuffs.

She looked beautiful. Mitch's heart ached a little at the sight of her.

He followed her outside to their waiting carriage and climbed in after her. If she was annoyed that he took the seat next to her, she didn't say so.

But her expression told him that she was unhappy about something and he figured it stemmed from their "etiquette" lesson last night. He didn't have to wait to find out for sure. Rachel seldom held back her feelings.

She kept her chin up and her lips pressed tightly together for another moment, then spoke as the carriage pulled away from the house.

"We can't have a repeat of last night in the kitchen," she said.

"Last night?"

"Don't play innocent," she said, cutting her gaze to him.

"Oh, yes." Mitch nodded. "When we kissed."

Her cheeks flushed ever so slightly. "We did more than simply kiss, if you'll recall."

"I recall that you did this." He captured her hand and pressed it to his chest, then lifted his other hand. "Then I did this—"

She caught his fingers, stilling him, then pulled her own hand away from his chest.

"It was inappropriate," Rachel said. "And we agreed we wouldn't do that sort of thing."

"We didn't agree," Mitch pointed out. "You made the choice and I respected your decision."

"Is that how you'd characterize your behavior last night?" she challenged.

"That wasn't part of your table etiquette demonstration?"

She turned away but Mitch saw her press her lips together even more tightly, struggling to suppress a smile. He couldn't recall when anything had pleased him more.

"I assure you, Rachel, I have the upmost respect for you," Mitch told her. "You and your underwear."

Her head whipped around. "My what?"

He cringed mentally, wishing he could bat his words out of the air.

Rachel tugged at her skirt as if he could see straight through the fabric and scooted a little farther away from him.

"You needn't act so prim and proper," he said, annoyed with himself. "It's not like I've never seen your underwear."

She gasped. "You've been sneaking into my room? Going through my bureau? I knew I should have barred that door somehow."

"I'm not that desperate—not yet, anyway."

Rachel looked him up and down, color high in her cheeks, a mixture of fear and intrigue on her face. Was she wondering what it would be like? The two of them together, rolling around under the covers? Discovering the delight a husband and wife could share?

Or was she considering slapping him after all?

"It matches, doesn't it," he said, deciding that if he was about to get slapped he might as well make it worthwhile. "Your dresses, I mean. Your underwear is the same color as your clothing."

Her cheeks flushed anew and he wasn't sure now if she was insulted or intrigued. He wasn't sure, either, if he would get an answer.

"You've actually thought about this?" she asked.

"We are married, after all," Mitch said. "If you told me what color underwear you wore, it wouldn't be a sin, or anything."

She gazed at him as if she couldn't understand why he would have the slightest interest in her undergarments. Mitch decided to drop the subject. He was starting to sound as desperate as he felt.

"So where are we going?" he asked. "Noah said it was the Monterey home?"

"Yes. Stephen and Caroline Monterey. He's a very successful businessman. I doubt you met him at Uncle Stuart's gentlemen's club, though. Stephen is a homebody."

Which was probably why his wife was pregnant so often, Mitch thought, the notion bringing on a familiar stirring.

He wondered if Rachel had the same thought because she folded her hands primly in her lap and sat a little straighter on the seat.

"It's their annual charity event for the children at the Sacred Heart," she said. "Every year there are—"

"The what?"

"The Sacred Heart Orphanage," Rachel said. "Every year more orphans attend, and this year—"

"Children?"

Rachel jumped, startled at Mitch's demand. "Yes, children. They are—"

"From an orphanage?" He sprang to the edge of his seat, his gaze impaling her.

"What's wrong, Mitch?" She reached for him but he pulled away.

"Stop!" He pounded his fist against the roof of the carriage. "Stop now!"

"Mitch, please—"

Stunned, Rachel watched as he opened the door and swung to the ground before the carriage pulled to a stop.

Treasures, castoffs and memories crowded the attic as Rachel waited. She'd been there for hours, knowing this was where Mitch would come when he returned home.

A heaviness still gathered around her heart as it had since he left their carriage abruptly this afternoon. It was after midnight now. He'd be here soon. Surely…

Another half hour dragged by while Rachel roamed the attic, opening dusty trunks, peering into crates and boxes, recalling occasions when the family wore the formal attire now stored in the spacious redwood closet.

Such recollections usually evoked sorrow and sadness of the worst kind, memories of what her family had once been. But tonight her heart went out to Mitch, and to the family that had never been.

Footsteps sounded on the attic stairs, heavy, quick and sure. Mitch was home.

Rachel's heart lurched as she turned to face the staircase only to hear the footsteps slow. He'd seen the light on up here, she realized. Seconds passed and finally Mitch appeared at the top of the steps. He froze there, his gaze stilling her across the wide room.

He wore denim trousers, work boots and a white undershirt. He'd come to pound out his emotions with his fists, as she'd expected.

But he didn't move from the spot at the head of the stairs. She saw his hands curl into fists and his chest expand with heavy breathing. He hadn't expected to find her here. Her presence was a challenge to him. He wanted to turn, to leave, she guessed, but wouldn't back down.

Mitch squared his jaw and walked over to the punching bag, ignoring Rachel standing a few feet away. He curled his fists up and delivered a right jab to the bag.

"I saw Albert Taft," he said, following with a left cross. "I told him I'd accept his job offer and take a look at the quarry's company books."

Rachel didn't give a response and Mitch didn't seem to expect one as he shuffled his feet and struck the bag a few more times.

He glanced at Rachel. "I have the time. It won't interfere with what I'm doing for your family."

Two quick jabs, followed by two more.

"I tried to find Leo," Mitch said. "Leo Sinclair. My friend. I couldn't find him."

A few more minutes passed with only Mitch's heavy breathing and the thud of his fists against the punching bag filling the silent attic. He danced back and forth. Sweat beaded on his forehead.

Finally Rachel spoke.

"If I'd known, I would have told you ahead of time," she said. "I wouldn't have let you walk into that event and be surprised in front of everyone."

He stopped then and looked at her, his jaw set. Yet beneath his fierce gaze, she saw something more, something she was certain Mitch wanted no one to see.

"It wasn't hard to figure out," she told him softly and took a step closer. "It's why you never talked about your past, why you evaded all my questions—everyone's questions, I suspect."

Mitch turned back to the punching bag but only stared at it.

It was all she could do to keep her distance from him. His stance told her he wanted no closeness, yet she yearned to hold him right now.

"How old were you?" Rachel asked.

"Five," he said quietly. Then he drew himself up as if steeling himself against the memory, and turned to face her. "Five. I was five years old when my mother died and they sent me to that place."

"What happened to her?"

"She fell on the stairs. That's all I know. She fell and she died."

His words came out in a heated rush, but Rachel didn't back away.

"What about the rest of your family? Your father?" she asked.

"I never had a father."

"Why were you sent to an orphanage? Surely, someone else in the family—"

"No one wanted me. Or could afford to raise me."

"Couldn't afford—"

"She was a maid. A maid for a wealthy family. She worked in their home, a grand mansion, cleaning and scrubbing and polishing, day in and day out."

The outburst seemed to cost him his strength. Mitch's shoulders sagged a little and he turned his head away.

"And she was a wonderful mother," he said, barely above a whisper. "She read to me and sang to me and took care of me, even when she was so exhausted she could barely stand."

Another moment passed before Mitch spoke again.

"We lived on the third floor with the other servants. Sometimes I'd sneak downstairs for a look at the grand world that was just below us. My mother was always afraid the mistress of the house would find me there. She didn't like children."

Servants with children usually lived elsewhere. The same was true of the staff in Rachel's own home. It was unusual that Mitch's mother had been allowed to keep her son with her.

"I was told that she'd died," Mitch said. "That night a man and woman came for me. I don't know who they were. We were on the train for days. They said I was sick. They gave me medicine. I slept most of the time. They left me at the orphanage in San Francisco."

"And you never knew…?"

Mitch shook his head. "I don't know where I lived before. I don't know the name of the family my mother worked for. I do have my own name. That much I remember."

"No one ever came for you? Aunts, uncles? Grandparents?"

"No one."

"Your friend Leo Sinclair. Was he in the orphanage with you?" she asked.

Mitch nodded.

"And you were never adopted?"

He uttered a bitter laugh. "Every Sunday we were lined up and put on display for the public. People came in and looked us over, deciding if they wanted any of us. We all hoped we'd be picked."

Rachel's stomach twisted into a knot. "Picked?"

"Picked for adoption. Picked to go live with a real family, in a real home. I was always big for my age. Not cute or sweet, like some of the others."

"Never picked by one of the families?"

"Not until I got older. Then everyone wanted me because of my size. Tall, strong. I'd make a good worker for them, they figured. But by then I was long past wanting to get picked. So I made sure I wasn't."

"What did you do?"

"When a family showed up and expressed interest in me, I took the father aside and explained to him, quite graphically, that I'd—well, it involved his daughters and wife, and it was enough to send them packing."

Rachel could only imagine the sort of thing Mitch had told them.

"So you were never adopted?" she asked.

"The headmaster, who made us call him 'uncle,' let us work, as long as he got a cut of the money. I sold newspapers. I got to know some of the shop owners in the neighborhood. One of them was an older lady who ran a dry goods store. Her husband had died and she needed help. When she asked about me working there, I said something particularly disgusting to her. She just laughed and said it sounded like fun."

Rachel gasped, but Mitch smiled at the memory.

"She was like a dear, old grandmother to me—or what I'd always imagined a grandmother would be like. I left the orphanage and worked for her. She taught me about running a business, pointed me in a direction, urged me to complete my education and helped out financially as much as she could." Mitch's smile faded. "She died a few years ago."

"I'm sorry," Rachel said.

His expression hardened. "Don't pity me."

"I admire you," she said. "I admire you for all you've accomplished, with little help from anyone. And I'm sorry that I forced you to live here with us. If I'd known about your…background…I wouldn't have insisted upon it. It was selfish of me. I was only thinking of myself. And for that I owe you an apology."

Mitch didn't respond. If he wouldn't tolerate her pity, he certainly didn't want her apology. Not now, anyway.

"Did you ever try to find your family?" Rachel asked. "I mean, there must be relatives somewhere, don't you think?"

"Why would I?" Mitch shook his head. "If they cared anything about me, they'd have come for me at the orphanage and not left me in that place."

Rachel was emotionally wrung out and Mitch appeared the same. But she couldn't leave the subject behind just yet.

"From now on, I'll explain to you exactly where we're going, who'll be there, what the event is about," she said.

Her offer seemed to embarrass him, somehow. He looked away without responding.

Rachel moved closer and, as she'd done so many times before, she laid her hand on his arm and rose on her toes. He accommodated her by leaning down a little so she could whisper in his ear.

But this time, Rachel placed a soft kiss on his cheek. His gaze joined hers, and she saw the years of hurt, pain and sorrow in his eyes. She wondered if he'd ever let anyone glimpse those things in him. She doubted it.

With all her heart she wished she could gather him in her arms, hold him, stroke her fingers through his hair and make everything better for him. He deserved it, and doing so would make her feel better, too.

She left the attic not feeling very proud of the way she'd acted since Mitch had come into her life. It never occurred to her that he needed anything. Mitch was so strong, so self-assured, so independent.

She gave so much to her own family, every ounce of her emotion, strength and love, but none to him. All she did was take from Mitch. She'd given nothing back, except a promise to allow him into the world of high society.

She knew now that he needed more than that. Could she figure a way to give it to him?

And would he take it?

Chapter Twenty-One

"If you want out, now's the time."

Noah's words intruded on Mitch's thoughts. He looked up from the desk to find the boy standing at the study window, gazing outside. He'd come in just a few minutes ago after finishing his morning tutoring session.

"They'll arrive soon," Noah said, nodding toward the driveway. "The women. For the luncheon."

Mitch nodded, finally understanding. The house had been in turmoil for days as preparations for what Rachel had called the La-La luncheon were underway. Servants had been cleaning and polishing everything from the floors to the silver. The kitchen staff and gardeners had been likewise busy, all under her direction.

Mitch made a note to give the staff a raise.

"Believe me," Noah said, sounding wise and confident, "you don't want to be here when all those women show up."

Mitch had no idea why, but he decided to take Noah's

word for it. He decided, too, that the audit he'd begun on Albert Taft's company books could wait.

"Okay, then," Mitch said, rising from his chair. "Let's go. You and me. Let's make a break for it."

Noah's face paled. "No…I…"

All along Mitch had known the real reason Noah never left the house. It had nothing to do with not wanting to see his friends anymore, or shame that he'd lost his arm and was a cripple now.

It was fear. Plain and simple. Fear that he'd be a target or easy prey for a bully or thief. He couldn't fight back with any hope of winning. He couldn't protect himself or defend anyone with him.

Mitch planted himself in front of Noah. In the past he'd used his size to intimidate the boy into doing what he wanted. Maybe Noah would see that his intentions were different this time.

"You don't want to be here with all those women, do you?" Mitch asked.

Noah shook his head. "I haven't—"

A squeal of delight—Rachel's squeal—echoed through the house, interrupting him. Noah glanced out the window.

"Chelsey's home," he said, looking relieved by the distraction.

Mitch watched her climb down from the hansom cab. A bright smile bloomed on her face as she rushed toward the house. He guessed Rachel was waiting at the door.

Noah headed toward the foyer. Mitch followed. He found Rachel and Chelsey hugging and laughing.

Chelsey broke away and gave Noah a hug, then saw Mitch.

"My new brother-in-law!" She threw her arms around Mitch and gave him a big hug, smiling broadly.

Mitch smiled back. How could he not? Her happiness was infectious. And he couldn't remember when he'd ever received such a warm welcome.

"Miss me?" Chelsey asked playfully, stepping back.

"It's been quiet around here with you gone," Mitch admitted. "You're here for the luncheon?"

"Of course." Chelsey's smile turned devilish. "If not, why, what would people say?"

This brought a laugh from all of them—even Rachel. She linked her arm through her sister's.

"Everything is going smoothly so far," Rachel reported. "But I still need your help."

Behind them the front door swung open and the hansom driver set Chelsey's satchel inside. Mitch paid the fare along with a generous tip, and sent the man on his way.

"I want to get a peek at the luncheon tables first, see what you've done different this year." Chelsey headed toward the wing of the house that held the ballroom, the only location big enough to accommodate the event.

"Wait until you see the new linens," Rachel declared, following.

"Noah and I are going out," Mitch called.

Rachel whipped around. "You're…you're what?"

"I need a haircut," Mitch said. "We both do."

Worry and concern darkened Rachel's features. "Noah, I can cut your hair—"

"Men go to the barbershop, Rachel," Mitch told her.

She looked panicked now. "But the barbershop is blocks away and—"

"I know, I know. I don't know my way around the city very well yet." Mitch dropped his hand onto Noah's shoulder. "Noah won't let me get lost. I'll stay right beside him every step of the way. We'll be inseparable."

They both turned to Noah, waiting, but he didn't answer. Mitch saw the fear in his eyes and the struggle to cover it.

"I won't wander off," Mitch said. "You won't have to come looking for me all over town."

Noah gulped and looked up at Mitch, a glimmer of trust and faith playing about his features, understanding that Mitch was really saying that Noah would never be left alone.

"Well, okay…" he said.

Mitch found Hayden and had him retrieve Noah's things from his room. As he stood in front of the mirror in the foyer fixing his necktie—surprisingly well, with one hand—Rachel drew Mitch aside.

"He'll be fine," Mitch said, anticipating her words.

"But he hasn't been out in months." She cast a worried look at her brother. "And he only has one arm, Mitch, what if something—"

"Do you feel safe when you're out with me?" he asked.

She looked startled. "Of course."

"He will, too." Mitch touched her arm. "I'll take good care of him."

"And what about next time?" Rachel proposed. "You can't escort him around town forever."

"Stop fussing over him," Mitch told her. "This is hard enough for him without you questioning his decision."

Rachel pressed her lips together as Noah walked

over. She drew a breath and stepped back while Hayden helped both Noah and Mitch into their jackets and they put on their bowlers.

"You look very handsome," she declared, straightening Noah's necktie. She did the same to Mitch. "And so do you."

Hayden opened the door.

"When will you be back?" Rachel asked, worry still in her voice.

"Not until late," Mitch said, easing Noah out ahead of him. "There's a girlie show down at the wharfs that goes all night so we'll—"

"Mitch! Don't you dare take him there!"

"Enjoy your luncheon," he called, as he pulled the door closed behind them.

The luncheon for the Ladies Association of Los Angeles had been an unqualified success. Rachel beamed with pride, enjoying the quiet moment, as the servants moved around the ballroom, clearing everything away.

"Beautiful," Chelsey declared, standing next to her. "Everything was perfect."

For the occasion Rachel had chosen a Spode fine china pattern of cornflower blue and ivory with gold trim that her mother purchased on a whim in England but never warmed to. Rachel had finished each table dressing with an ivory cloth that carried a hint of blue, all of it sparkling with candlelight and brightened with fresh flowers.

"Did you see the look on Aurora Chalmer's face when she walked in?" Chelsey asked, smiling.

"Her and just about everyone else," Rachel added.

The critical looks on the faces of some of her guests had not gone unnoticed when they'd arrived. Would the luncheon measure up to those her mother had done? their expressions seemed to ask. Had Rachel's mother done a proper job of training her daughter so that she could carry on the tradition?

From the oohs and aahs Rachel heard, those questions had been answered brilliantly. Even Mrs. Chalmers had offered her congratulations before leaving.

Having Chelsey here was a pleasure, too, Rachel thought. She'd been a pillar of support throughout the afternoon, easily assuming her hostessing duties, as they'd both been taught. Chelsey had bubbled over with excitement and news from school, too. Rachel knew she was happy there and that she'd done the right thing by letting her return to her classes.

Thanks to Mitch.

With the final tablecloth carried away, the servants disappeared leaving Rachel and Chelsey alone in the room. The large windows let in what remained of the afternoon sunlight, allowing a gloom to settle over the room.

Chelsey drew in a breath. "This luncheon's done. What about next year's?"

A whole year from now. Rachel hadn't considered it. She thought ahead to the occasion. What would her life be like then?

An odd feeling crept over Rachel, anxiety, excitement—and a little fear? She wasn't sure, except of one thing: the coming year would take its time in getting here.

Claudia came into her thoughts. Her best friend

poised for her engagement party and her wedding next spring. For her the year would be filled with wonderful events, excitement, parties, then culminate in a perfect marriage. And after that? Wedded bliss, a home of her own and a family.

Envy tainted Rachel's thoughts again. Since they were girls, the two of them had fantasized about their future weddings, their husbands, their homes and children. They'd decided on colors and flowers, neighborhoods to live in, even names for their babies.

But she and Claudia couldn't be on more separate paths now. Rachel's life had taken a turn she'd never anticipated.

"Will you repeat this theme at next year's luncheon?" Chelsey asked. "Or do something different? And, will you be able to top yourself?"

"I guess we'll have to see what next year brings."

Chelsey nodded, her thoughts turning back to the present when she asked, "What was wrong with Claudia today? She seemed upset."

"Wedding jitters, I guess," Rachel said, though she knew exactly what had upset her friend. When Claudia arrived, Rachel had noticed her distress immediately. Reluctantly, Claudia confided that Graham was upset with her over more of the details of the engagement party.

"Trudy asked me to come over this afternoon," Chelsey said. "I'd like to stay for supper if her mother asks."

"Have fun," Rachel said, as her sister hurried out of the room.

Rachel moved to the window and gazed outside. In the distance she saw her neighbor's lawn and house.

Noah and Mitch came into her mind again—they'd fluttered in and out all afternoon—and she wondered when they would return home. Logically, she knew there was no need to worry about her brother, not with Mitch at his side. Still, she couldn't keep the concern from her thoughts.

She wished they'd come back soon. Aside from easing her anxiety about her brother, she wanted to tell Mitch all about her triumphant luncheon. He'd given her the courage to make changes—even gone shopping with her to pick out the linens.

Suddenly the thought of next year's luncheon soured in her mind again.

Next year, Mitch would be gone.

Yet the luncheon would go on. Next year, the year after, the year after that. She'd be hosting the ladies association—forever.

Did she want that?

The notion took Rachel by surprise. Her mother had treasured this occasion, this opportunity, and Rachel had, too. Until now.

Perhaps she needed a different future for herself. Rachel smiled, as her mind cast about for just such a possibility.

At the furthest reach of her imagination, Rachel pictured herself taking a completely different path. Never marrying again?

She indulged herself in the idea. Perhaps she'd buy the ceramic factory, after all. Despite what everyone would say, she'd run it herself. She'd learn the business. She would make sure she knew how to do it all, so that no one could ever sabotage its operation and leave her penniless and at the mercy of someone else.

Rachel gasped aloud at her own thought and the mental image of Mitch that followed. Isn't that what he wanted, too? To do something distinctive with his life? Build his own wealth—and power—so that no one could take it from him?

A warmth grew around Rachel's heart. Perhaps she and Mitch weren't so different after all.

Hayden interrupted her revelation.

"Excuse me, madam. You have a visitor in the study."

She couldn't imagine who would come by. Nearly everyone she knew had just left.

Claudia, she realized. She'd probably lingered in her carriage until the other ladies left so she could return and talk privately with Rachel about Graham's latest complaint.

But an unwelcome thought occurred to Rachel as she made her way down the hallway. Perhaps her day hadn't been an unqualified success after all. Had Mrs. Chalmers or one of the other ladies come back to offer some helpful suggestions?

A darker prospect came to her. Was it news of her father? The doctor had kept her informed of his progress and she'd telephoned the convalescent home herself on many occasions. By all accounts he was doing well. But what if…?

Rachel steeled herself as she walked into the study, then stopped still in the doorway.

Georgie.

Chapter Twenty-Two

"Georgie?"

Rachel didn't know whether to shout at her brother or burst into tears. Whether to hug him, or hit him. All those emotions swept through her as the two of them stood face-to-face in the study.

"Christ, Rachel! What the hell were you thinking?" he demanded.

She'd settled on a hug, but now she drew back a little.

"What were *you* thinking?" She threw the words back at him. "I've been sick with worry over you—so has the rest of the family. Where have you been? Do you have any idea what we've been through worrying over you? How could you just disappear? Now, of all times?"

His anger faded. "If not now, then when?" he asked.

Rachel shook her head, not understanding. Her brother looked as he always did, impeccably dressed, tall, dark haired, vaguely resembling their mother. Yet something was very different about him. It frightened her.

He drew in a breath, as if he, too, was frightened by what he'd come here to say.

"You know how things have been with the family for over a year now. Everything going from bad to worse," George said. "There was never going to be a good time to leave."

Rachel could hardly believe her ears. At times she'd worried that he'd met with foul play. She'd suspected, too, that he'd left of his own accord. But hearing the words stunned her just the same.

"You disappeared…intentionally?" she asked.

"I didn't disappear," he told her. "I moved on with my life."

Rachel touched her fingers to her forehead. "What are you talking about? Your life is here. In your home. With your family."

He uttered a bitter laugh. "This has never been my home, my family. It sure as hell was never a life I wanted—or even a life I could call my own."

"How can you say that?" Rachel asked, not understanding. "Father gave you everything."

"He did," Georgie agreed. "But why would you think I wanted those things?"

"How could you not want them? We had a wonderful life. All of us," Rachel insisted.

Georgie shook his head. "It wasn't so wonderful, Rachel. Not even before the train accident. And if you'd take a close look at everything, you'd realize that's true."

"I'm just glad Mother isn't around to hear you say those things."

"If she were, maybe she'd finally give up trying to

have something that would never be hers," George said. "Maybe she'd find the sort of life that would make her happy."

"What do you mean?"

"You knew what it was like for her," Georgie said. "Everyone who 'mattered' looked down on her. She never quite measured up. She wasn't good enough. No matter how hard she tried, she never overcame that. She was never going to. And neither was I."

"No one looked down on you—"

"Of course they did. I wasn't a real Branford. I'd been born with a different name, from a different father. Born to a woman with a tainted pedigree. Open your eyes and look around," he told her. "You'll see the truth."

Maybe she had seen it over the years. But she simply didn't want to face it. Until now.

Yet it made perfect sense. She'd known firsthand the slights her mother faced. It wasn't much of a stretch to believe that they extended to her son.

Sadness gripped Rachel. "Oh, Georgie, I never knew. I always thought Father's support of you was enough. He gave you his confidence, put you in charge of the business. I never thought—"

"It doesn't matter. Not anymore." George waved away her concern, and from his expression, she realized he truly meant it. "I've found someone."

"You have?" she asked, unable to hide her surprise. She'd no idea. "Who is she?"

"You don't know her, Rachel. She's not from your circle. I love her and I'm going to ask her to marry me.

If she agrees, I want us to leave the city, start over someplace new."

Her anger came back at the thought of losing her brother once more.

"You're walking out? Again?"

"You're smart, Rachel. Smart like Father. I knew when I left that, with Stuart Parker's help, you'd figure out how to handle everything." Georgie shook his head, looking genuinely troubled for the first time this evening. "But Christ, Rachel, I never thought you'd get married."

She didn't know how he'd found out, but the news was hardly a secret.

"You took our money," she reminded him.

"I took my share, what I was entitled to. And believe me, I earned every cent of it." He gazed at her, sorrow in his eyes. "I never meant to hurt you. I never expected you to sell yourself in marriage to save the family."

"Why come back now? To unburden your conscience?"

"I wouldn't have come back at all, if not for that husband of yours. He fired the Edgars Detective Agency—"

"Mitch wouldn't have done that. Not without talking to me first."

"The Edgars Agency found me weeks ago but kept quiet about it, for a price. I should have known something was up when the agent stopped coming around for his money," Georgie said. "When a detective from the new firm your husband hired located me, I tried the same tactic but he refused. Seems your husband had offered a bonus if I was found quickly."

"Mitch knows they found you?" she asked, truly stunned now.

"No. I asked the detective to hold off telling him until I could see you first. That's why I'm here. You have your husband to thank for this meeting."

"So this is it? And you're leaving again?"

"That depends on you, Rachel."

The months of not venturing out of the Branford house showed by late afternoon. Noah's steps slowed and his energy waned but Mitch didn't consider returning home until the boy reluctantly suggested it himself.

At first, Noah had squinted at the bright sunlight, then gazed wide-eyed at the neighborhood seen only through the windows for so long now. Throughout the afternoon, he'd stuck close to Mitch, never ventured more than a few feet away.

Now, as they walked into the foyer, Mitch knew that Noah was exhausted but he still wouldn't stop talking. As they'd strolled the streets of the West Adams District, gotten lunch and visited the barbershop, Noah had chatted about everyone and everything in the neighborhood. Who had recently married, who had a mistress, whose business was in trouble, who was expecting a new addition to the family. Mitch supposed Noah got most of his news from Madeline, but suspected he'd overheard other things from his own family or their servants.

Hayden received their bowlers in the foyer, then disappeared. Mitch expected Noah to go upstairs and fall into bed, but he stopped on the lowest step.

Noah fidgeted for a minute. "Huh, thanks for…well, thanks."

"I eat at that little restaurant several times a week. You can come with me next time, if you'd like."

Noah glanced away. "I've been kind of...sort of—"

"Afraid to go out?"

Pride and a little embarrassment caused Noah's shoulders to stiffen. "I'm missing an arm, in case you didn't notice. Why wouldn't I be afraid—hey!"

Mitch tagged him with quick light punches on his chest, shoulders, chin and jaw, until Noah leaned backward so far that he plopped down on the staircase.

"Stop it!" He batted Mitch's hand away and glared up at him. "I've only got one arm!"

Mitch held up his fist. "That's all I used," he pointed out.

Noah glared at him, breathing hard until he realized what Mitch was saying. "You've got that punching bag in the attic. I hear you upstairs sometimes, at night."

"I could show you how to box," Mitch offered.

"With only one arm?"

"Wouldn't that be a hell of a surprise for anyone who tried to take advantage?" Mitch asked.

Noah didn't answer, but Mitch was sure he could see his mind working.

"You could go where you wanted, by yourself. You wouldn't have to be afraid anymore," Mitch pointed out. When he still didn't get a response, he added, "You could walk with Madeline and know you could take care of her."

Noah's gaze came up quickly and Mitch knew he'd hit a nerve. What man—even as young as Noah— wouldn't want that?

"You could teach me?" he asked softly.

"I could teach you to be good at it," Mitch said. "We could start tomorrow."

"How about tonight?"

Mitch smiled. "Sure. Just let me find Rachel and tell her we're home. She's worried about you."

Noah rolled his eyes, then headed up the staircase.

Mitch went to find Rachel, knowing she'd be anxious to hear how Noah's excursion out of the house had gone. He wanted to hear about her luncheon, too. Throughout the afternoon he'd found his thoughts venturing back here to the house, to Rachel and the luncheon she'd put so much time and effort into. Mitch couldn't imagine how it might be anything less than a complete success.

For anyone but Rachel, that is. She wanted nothing less than perfection.

He expected to find her in her favorite sitting room but as he passed the study, her distinctive fragrance floated out. Mitch found her seated behind the desk.

How commanding she looked in the chair, though it and the desk were a little big for her. It stirred a new feeling in Mitch that he hadn't experienced before.

Something about Rachel always stirred him, in one way or the other.

She didn't get up when he entered the study. Instead she sat back and folded her hands, and watched his every step as he crossed the room to stand in front of the desk.

"You fired my detective agency."

Her voice was low and even, calm and collected. Yet it put Mitch on edge.

"The exorbitant fee you were paying them offered no incentive for them to work quickly, so I hired a firm recommended by someone at your uncle's club," Mitch explained. "I didn't think the Edgars Agency was producing the results they should."

"Well, your suspicions were true," Rachel said. "Georgie came home."

A cold chill passed through Mitch. "Your brother is here?"

"He came by earlier, after the luncheon," Rachel said. "He explained himself."

"He had a reason for leaving his family nearly penniless?" Mitch asked, an unreasonable anger building in his chest.

"He took what he thought was due him. And we weren't penniless. You said so yourself," Rachel reminded him. "It was just a matter of moving assets around."

"And you're satisfied with that?"

"Yes, I am."

His anger shifted, taking on the feel of dread and foreboding, an old feeling he could never shake.

"Georgie told me that he would take over the family business again and run it until he found a competent successor," Rachel said.

"And then?"

"And then I could get a divorce." She looked up at him. "He said the decision was mine."

Chapter Twenty-Three

"Like hell the decision is yours," Mitch told her, his anger rising. "You and I made a deal. We have an agreement."

"Yes, I know," she said, resentment creeping into her voice. "We even have it in writing."

"Not to mention vows sworn before God," Mitch told her.

"For which we'll both probably go to Hell," Rachel said. "That's not the issue right now."

"This is what you've wanted all along, isn't it?" Mitch heard the accusation in his voice, but couldn't stop himself. "A chance to go back. To make things the way they were, to some degree, anyway. You can have your brother here running things, just like he used to."

Rachel didn't reply so he figured he'd gotten his answer. His anger grew.

"I'm on the verge of having everything I want," Mitch said. "My fee from the Taft job will give me enough money to buy my own business. All I need are your social connections."

She still didn't say anything and that made him angrier.

"You gave your word! You went along with the marriage! You can't throw me back just because something better came along!"

"I didn't say I—"

"You can't pretend I never existed!"

Rachel got to her feet. He saw her expression shift and knew that he'd said too much. Her thoughts had moved away from her brother...to him, to the meaning behind his words. And Mitch couldn't bear that.

He dug deep, finding more anger, glad that it came so easily to him now.

"You are in my life for one reason, and one reason only," he told her. "I am not going to lose this opportunity. You are going to keep your word and abide by our agreement. And I don't give a damn about anything else!"

He stalked out of the study.

Mitch was still hurt by his past. He never spoke of it, had done more than most to overcome it. He'd built himself into something bigger than his beginnings.

But it still haunted him.

His anger, the ferocity of his words in the study a few hours ago left no doubt. Rachel had seen it easily. She'd seen, too, that Mitch hadn't wanted her to know.

Standing on the balcony outside her bedchamber gazing at the twilight, Rachel's heart ached anew, even worse than it had the night in the attic when Mitch had told her about his past. He'd not mentioned it since and she thought she'd done the right thing by not bringing it up. She wasn't sure what to do.

Nor did she have any idea how someone could take a child, abandon him in an orphanage and walk away. Never come back. Never check on him.

What sort of family had he come from? What kind of people would do such a thing to a helpless little boy?

Maybe if she knew the answers, Rachel thought, if she knew the truth it would help her understand her husband better. If, of course, she decided to stay in the marriage for the coming year.

Rachel drew in a breath of the cool evening air, then went back into her bedchamber.

Mitch had made it clear he didn't intend to give her any choice in the matter of continuing with their marriage. He'd worked most of his life to get to this point. He wouldn't abandon his goal. She understood that.

Rachel's heart warmed a little. She admired Mitch for his commitment, his strong will. It was one of the things she liked most about him.

The irony of the situation didn't escape her, though. So often the men in her life had abandoned her.

Now she couldn't get rid of this one.

And since she couldn't, she intended to set him straight on one matter in particular.

Rachel waited until she saw the light seep beneath the connecting door to Mitch's bedchamber. He was in his room now, finished in the attic. She'd heard the thudding of his fists against the punching bag; she thought she'd heard muffled voices, too, but couldn't imagine who would be up there with him. She went out into the hallway and knocked on his door.

Almost immediately Mitch jerked the door open. He towered over her, tall, wide, muscular, still dressed in his worn trousers and white undershirt. Sweat trickled from his forehead and dampened his shirt.

When she saw him like this, Rachel instinctively stood straighter and pushed up her chin a little. She did that now, looking him straight in the eye.

"Don't ever raise your voice at me again," she told him.

He didn't respond but she didn't expect him to. It wasn't a request. Mitch seemed to know that, too.

Rachel went back to her room and let her mind settle on her conversation with her older brother. As she readied for bed, the notion of Georgie returning to the house knotted in her stomach. He would resume his duties in the family business, handle the problems and find a competent successor to take over when things settled down. Life would be—somewhat—back to normal, back to the way it used to be. She could have that. The decision was hers.

That's what she'd wanted for weeks now.

Wasn't it?

"Rachel? Rachel, are you listening?"

Claudia's words intruded on her thoughts, embarrassing her a little because she really hadn't been listening.

"I'm sorry," Rachel said to her friend seated at the other end of the settee. "I guess I have too many things on my mind today."

"But earlier you said all was going well," Claudia said.

When her friend had arrived an hour ago and they'd settled into the sitting room with the tea Hayden brought, Claudia had asked about Rachel's family, as she always did. It had been an odd feeling to report that her father was holding his own under the care of the staff at the convalescent hospital; Chelsey had returned to school after the luncheon and had written to say she'd passed all her tests; and even Noah was looking stronger and taking more of an interest in things.

Their conversation had moved on to the preparations for Claudia's engagement party and wedding. Rachel usually loved this sort of talk, but today she couldn't seem to keep her mind on it.

How could she with so many other things floating around in her head?

"So, everything is set for the engagement party?" Rachel asked, focusing on her friend.

"Mostly." Claudia cleared her throat. "Graham told me he thought we should have better musicians…the ones his mother used at her last party."

"His mother?" Rachel cringed mentally. She'd met Graham Bixby's mother. She hadn't enjoyed the woman's company, to say the least.

"And he's right, of course," Claudia said, forcing a little smile. "His mother has excellent taste and she knows how things should be done."

"But it's your decision," Rachel pointed out. "And I'm sure the musicians you selected were excellent."

Claudia shook her head quickly. "It doesn't matter which musicians we have. Not really. And it was wrong of me to question Graham. I shouldn't have done that."

"But Claudia—"

"No, no, really. Everything is fine…now." She smiled. "You must be relieved that everyone in town has been so accepting of your marriage."

The notion stunned Rachel. "Actually, I haven't given it much thought."

Claudia giggled. "Rachel, you can tell me the truth."

She'd just done so and apparently it surprised Claudia as much as it did Rachel. The idea that her marriage to Mitch would be speculated over and gossiped about had rarely crossed her mind lately.

"Everyone understands that you've been under duress for a long time now, so a quiet wedding isn't unexpected," Claudia said. She leaned a little closer. "And Mitch is so well thought of. All the businessmen who've met him are singing his praises. And as if that weren't enough, I overheard some whispered chatter at your luncheon. It seems some of the ladies were disappointed they didn't get to meet him that day. They'd heard how handsome—"

A commotion in the hallway took their attention. Rachel and Claudia turned to find Graham striding into the room. Both of them came to their feet.

After a brief nod acknowledging Rachel, he turned on Claudia.

"What are you doing here?" he demanded.

Claudia's face paled. "I—I'm just—"

"I told you we were going out for supper tonight with an important business associate."

She glanced at the mantel clock. "Well, yes. But that's hours from now so I thought—"

"The supper was moved up. I went to your house to tell you and you weren't there. I had to come all the way over here looking for you."

Claudia threaded her fingers together. "I'm sorry, Graham, I didn't think—"

"You didn't think." He shook his head in disgust. "How many times have I heard that from you?"

"I didn't—I mean, I—"

"I can't waste any more time here," Graham told her. "From now on, I want you to tell me where you intend to go so that I don't—"

Mitch strode into the room, cutting off Graham's tirade. Rachel almost cheered at the sight of him.

He pinned Graham with his gaze. "What's the problem in here?"

Graham smiled easily and shrugged. "No problem. I just came for my wayward fiancée. No brains. Good thing she's pretty, huh?"

"Claudia's plenty smart," Mitch told him. "Which makes me wonder why she's marrying you."

A stunned silence jolted the room. Claudia recovered first and mumbled a goodbye to Rachel before Graham clasped her elbow and hurried her out of the room.

Mitch stared after them, then mumbled. "Bastard...I'd like to beat the—" He stopped and turned to Rachel, as if remembering she was in the room with him.

"Beat the feathers out of him?" She smiled gently. "You've looked as if you'd like to beat the feathers out of someone for a few days now."

Mitch grunted and jerked his chin. The gesture reminded Rachel that the two of them had avoided each other for most of the past several days.

"Or is there something else you want to do with all that pent-up energy of yours?" she asked.

On the few occasions when she'd seen Mitch, he'd seethed with a force of some sort. She didn't know what it was.

But he turned to her now and his smoldering expression seemed to see straight through her, warm her, as if he were holding her in his arms, kissing her, touching—

"What the hell does your friend see in him?" Mitch asked.

His question brought her back to reality. "He's from one of the best families in the city, he's a highly successful businessman, he's a—"

"—jackass," Mitch said.

Rachel couldn't disagree. "I've gotten to know Graham better since their engagement. I'm not particularly fond of him, I admit. But their wedding isn't for a year."

"A year, huh? A lot can change in a year."

Rachel nodded. "I've been thinking about the future."

"About your brother's offer?" he asked quickly.

This was the first time either of them had mentioned Georgie's offer to return to the family if, in fact, Rachel wanted him to. She supposed Mitch hadn't brought it up since that night because in his mind the issue was already settled: Rachel would keep her word; he was staying; Georgie was leaving and that was that.

But it wasn't an easy decision to make, though logically, it should be. For some reason, Rachel couldn't see the situation clearly just now.

"The future I was thinking of concerned Mr. Prescott's ceramic factory," Rachel said. "I wonder if it's still for sale?"

"I hadn't seen you painting in a while," Mitch said. "I thought you'd given up on the idea."

"For a while, I did," Rachel admitted. "But no matter what happens with Georgie, in a year he'll be gone and so will you. You've made it clear what you want from me. You've made your own plans. Why shouldn't I?"

"So in a year's time, when the family can afford it, you're going to buy the ceramic factory and design and sell your china?"

"Yes. And I'm going to run it myself," Rachel said, warming to the idea that had come to her days ago. "I learned that from you. I'll manage the entire operation. That way, I won't look up one day and realize I'm nearly penniless."

"And how are you going to manage that?" he asked, tilting his head a little.

Rachel had seen this expression on his face, this angle of his head many times. It meant that he was listening intently, thinking about what was being said, processing the information. Despite her differences with him, Mitch was still very business savvy, so it pleased her to no end that he was taking her seriously.

"I'm going to hire that nice Mr. Cabell who was in charge of the ceramic factory I visited in New York," Rachel explained. "He ran a highly successful operation."

"New York, huh?" Mitch stroked his chin. "California is a long way from New York. Do you think he'll move here?"

"Everyone has a price. You and I are certainly proof of that," Rachel said. "So for the right price, why wouldn't Mr. Cabell come here?"

Mitch considered what she'd said for a moment, then nodded. "Sounds reasonable. But running your own business? Aren't you concerned about what people will say?"

"There are worse reasons to be gossiped about," she pointed out.

"Running a business alone makes for a hard life. A solitary life," Mitch said. "Won't you get lonely?"

"I'm going to take a lover," Rachel said, the words popping out of her mouth before she realized it. A tremor ran through her. Good gracious, what had she said?

Mitch seemed just as shocked. So much so, that his cheeks flushed a little.

"A lover?" he asked, as if he hadn't heard her correctly.

"Yes," she told him, pulling herself up a little. "In fact, I might take a series of lovers. When I tire of one, I'll send him on his way and select another."

"I see."

Mitch nodded thoughtfully, but Rachel had seen this look on his face, also. Playful, teasing, with a hint of mischief.

"In that case," he said, "you'll want to be sure you find a lover who knows what he's doing."

"Well, of course," Rachel said, though she hadn't realized the necessity of it.

"Someone who's experienced, but not so experienced he's grown tired of the whole thing. And knowledgeable. Knowing the right places to touch in just the right ways can make all the difference."

Heat rushed through Rachel. It seemed to be radiating from Mitch, as well. Why had she started this conversation?

"Never mind." Rachel waved her hand as if to erase the words that hung in the hot air between them. "This is all too complicated."

"I could help you." Mitch moved a little closer and his voice dropped to a deep tone that sent a tingle through her. "As your husband, I'm duty bound to help you. I could demonstrate what you should look for, what to expect to insure high standards."

Rachel gazed up at him. She couldn't help herself. Something about this man drew her, held her in place. Kept her from leaving when she knew she should.

An ache rose around Rachel's heart as she realized that this was one of those times when she should leave. Despite the fanciful remark she'd just made about taking a lover, she wanted a man in her life who would stay with her, who wouldn't abandon her as all the others had. Mitch had told her in no uncertain terms that when he was done with her, he'd be gone.

The world seemed to tilt sideways for Rachel as she gazed up at Mitch and she knew at that moment why she hadn't given Georgie his answer the other night, why she couldn't make the decision that seemed so obvious.

She'd fallen in love with Mitch Kincade.

Chapter Twenty Four

He'd made it.

Mitch stood before the mirror in his bedchamber. In his reflection he saw the black trousers and tailed jacket over the white shirt, bow tie and single-breasted vest he wore. Evening clothes, Rachel had called them. He also saw the steely glint in his eye and the determined set of his jaw, both gleaming with satisfaction.

He'd done it.

After all his years of hard work, planning and plotting, sweating, clawing and fighting, Mitch had achieved his goal. Tonight was his first formal occasion. The elite of society from around the city and across the state would be at Claudia Everhart and Graham Bixby's engagement party. And Mitch would attend—with Rachel at his side—as an accepted member of their exclusive circle.

Pride swelled Mitch's chest. At last, he had it all.

Joseph, the valet he still didn't know what to do with, walked out of the large closet and gave him one last look.

"Very good, sir," he said with a nod of approval, then left the room.

Joseph's words should have been directed at Rachel, at least in part, Mitch thought. She'd selected the fabric, the color and cut of his tuxedo. It had hung in his closet along with the business suits, the topcoats and hats, the jackets and trousers for every imaginable occasion and the myriad of accessories she'd selected for him.

With a final check of his appearance, Mitch left the bedchamber. In the hallway he saw that Rachel's door remained closed. She'd been in her room since early afternoon preparing for the occasion. She wasn't late, he'd gotten ready early.

He'd completed his work on Albert Taft's company books this afternoon and needed to give his recommendations one final look before he presented them. But the problems with the quarry had been the furthest thing from his mind.

This morning Rachel had explained what to expect from the evening's events. She made the dry subject of etiquette interesting. Sometimes, he'd even stopped thinking so much about her underwear long enough to pay attention.

Rachel had told him that the hostess, Mrs. Everhart, Claudia's mother, would position herself at the entrance of the drawing room to receive her guests, while Mr. Everhart, as the evening's host, would mingle with those already assembled, seeing that everyone was happy and comfortable.

When the butler announced that dinner was served, a procession would take the guests to the dining room.

The host would offer his arm to the guest of honor, the lady who would sit on his right, and they would lead the way. The other couples would follow in line, with the hostess and her dinner partner going in last.

Mitch had reminded himself that, though it seemed like an unnecessary production, this was the sort of thing expected of everyone wishing to maintain social acceptance.

And, of course, the rules of etiquette didn't stop upon entrance to the dining room. Everything was regimented, from the service of the food—always from the left, using the left hand—to refilling glasses from the right. Dishes could be removed from the right or left singly, but never stacked.

The first course—soup could be expected—to the dessert course would be served following long-standing rules. Then there was the finger bowl to contend with, the disposition of crumbs and proper placement of the napkin. Afterward, guests could leave the table—thank God—for dancing in the family ballroom.

He'd be expected to flawlessly execute the intricate rules of etiquette. Tonight he'd be judged not on his business expertise but his social skills. It irked him that the highbrows at tonight's party, few of whom had ever known any real hardship, held that kind of power, that he needed their acceptance to succeed in their world, but it was a necessary evil. And, besides, he'd accomplished this last hurdle.

He'd navigated unfamiliar social settings before and managed well enough. Rachel had coached him on what to expect. None of it worried Mitch.

He jogged down the staircase, his feet barely brushing the risers. Tonight, nothing worried Mitch.

Because he'd made it.

He headed toward the study intending to work on his recommendations to Albert Taft when quick, light steps and the rustling of fabric took his attention. He looked back and saw Rachel descending the staircase. His breath caught.

Her dark hair was arranged in an intricate design atop her head. White gloves covered her from fingertips to above her elbows.

Her gown was a lavender silk taffeta. The cap sleeves that rode just below her shoulders were trimmed with ermine, as was the hem of the skirt. A large, single iris formed of crystal beads decorated the gown.

But it was the fit of the dress that caused Mitch's mouth to go dry. The bodice dipped low displaying the inviting swell of her bosom. The skirt was drawn tight across the front, then lifted high in back in a close-fitted style.

Desire thundered through him. She was beautiful. He wanted to hold her, to touch her. He wanted to kiss her.

He wanted to know what color underwear she had on.

When Rachel reached the bottom of the stairs, she looked him up and down. Her gaze further inflamed his want for her.

"Very handsome," she told him.

Mitch opened his mouth to reply but all that came out was stuttering and stammering.

Rachel dipped her lashes and smiled, taking his fumbling words as a compliment. She straightened his tie and stood back, gazing at him with a critical eye.

"Yes," she declared once more. "Very handsome, indeed."

"And you're…" Mitch gulped. "Beautiful."

They boarded the waiting carriage and Rachel talked about the people whom they would likely encounter at the party. Mitch might have concentrated better on her words if he could stop thinking about her underwear. And if her breasts hadn't been undulating with the sway of the carriage and gleaming in the glow of the gaslights they passed.

The guests were in high spirits when they arrived at the Everhart home, or as high spirited as people of good breeding allowed themselves to be. Mitch greeted the other guests realizing that he already knew many of the men, thanks to Stuart Parker's introductions at his gentlemen's club. Rachel stayed at his side, as was expected, and the two of them moved through the room accepting quiet congratulations on their marriage. The night belonged to Claudia and Graham and their families, and the guests wouldn't usurp that honor by bringing too much attention to anyone else.

At supper, Mitch sat between two women he'd just been introduced to and managed to make conversation as he gazed across the table to Rachel's breasts gleaming, this time, in the candlelight.

When the meal was finally over, everyone made their way to the ballroom. With Rachel on his arm, pride swelled inside Mitch. She was the most beautiful woman in the room. And she was with him. She belonged here…and so did he.

They stood together at the edge of the dance floor as

Mr. Everhart presented Graham Bixby, his future son-in-law to the gathering. Applause followed, then the dancing began.

Mitch couldn't bring himself to join the swirling couples on the dance floor. He wanted Rachel to himself.

"You're the most beautiful woman here," Mitch said as the music, laughter and chatter swelled in the room.

"I saw you looking at me during supper." Rachel gave him a disapproving frown. "I suppose I should have mentioned earlier that was unacceptable behavior."

"For a man to look at his wife?"

"To look at her face is fine. But you were looking at my—"

His gaze dropped to the swell of her breasts. He drew in a heavy breath and her cheeks flushed.

"Stop looking at me there," she whispered, her gaze darting left and right to see if any of the guests had noticed.

He lifted his gaze to her eyes. "I suppose touching is out of the question?"

"It most certainly is, so please control yourself."

Mitch leaned down and whispered in her ear. "Tell me what color underwear you have on."

She gasped and her cheeks flushed, as he'd seen her do so many times. It made him want her all the more.

Then she arched her brow. "Did you consider that perhaps I'm not wearing underwear?"

Mitch's jaw sagged as he watched Rachel walk away, her bustle bobbing as she wound through the crowd, sending his desire for her pounding in his veins. He'd never wanted any woman the way he wanted Rachel. He didn't know how he'd manage to get through the rest of the evening, seeing her in that dress, speculating on her underwear.

"Kincade."

A big hand slapped his back, jarring his thoughts. A few seconds passed before his brain engaged and he recognized stocky, gray-haired Albert Taft standing next to him.

"I don't usually come to these things," Taft said, gesturing to the crowd with a drink in his hand.

Almost every time Mitch had seen the older man, he'd been drinking. He wondered now if Taft had added something extra to the punch, but smelled nothing on his breath.

"But I decided, why not?" Taft went on. "It's time to make a few changes."

Rachel had mentioned that Albert Taft had stopped attending most social functions since his wife's death. Mitch wondered why he'd changed his mind.

Albert Taft seemed to read his thoughts. "I can't live here any longer. Too many…well, I need a change of scenery. I'm going back East. I've got a daughter and some grandchildren in New York. I'll visit them for a while. Maybe I'll take them all to Europe."

Mitch didn't say anything, but the image pleased him for some reason.

"I know it's bad form to discuss business at these things," Taft said, gesturing with his drink once more. "But since you're here…"

It suited Mitch well enough to talk about the audit of the quarry books he'd completed. Maybe it would help get Rachel and her underwear—or lack of it?—off his mind.

"I finished up this afternoon," Mitch said. "I'll have my results and recommendations to you tomorrow."

"I'm not interested in either," Taft said. "I've decided to sell the quarry."

"Then you'll need the audit results to negotiate a fair price," Mitch pointed out.

"I'm not concerned about a fair price." Taft sipped his drink. "I want to be rid of the quarry."

Mitch wasn't surprised. Albert Taft hadn't shown much interest in the quarry for a while so it followed that he wouldn't want to put the effort into improving it. Selling it was a good option, under the circumstances.

"I'll send over my report and recommendations tomorrow. That's what you paid me for," Mitch said. "You can do whatever you please with it."

"Not so fast," Taft told him. "I want to sell the quarry to you."

Mitch froze. "Me?"

"Sure. Why not? You know more about it than anyone else—including me."

Taft's accounting ledgers paged through Mitch's memory. The quarry was in financial trouble. But despite serious mismanagement and neglect it could be made profitable again. Mitch already had a list of recommendations to present to Taft that outlined how it could be accomplished.

"And you know what it's worth," Taft said.

Mitch's heart beat a little faster. He knew exactly what the quarry should sell for. He knew, too, that thanks to each and every dime he'd saved since he'd first sold newspapers on the street corner, he could afford it.

Taft drained his glass. "So? What do you say?"

"Give me a few days to think it over."

The chunk of money he'd hand over to Albert Taft would be nearly every cent Mitch had, so it wasn't prudent to accept the offer on the spur of the moment. He wanted to double-check his facts and figures. Look everything over one more time.

"Come by the house when you've made up your mind," Taft said, then walked away.

Mitch's mind raced, taking his heart along with it. A business. A business of his own. One he could afford. One he could build on. A platform from which he could launch a financial empire of his own.

He had to tell Rachel.

The thought flew though his mind, pushing aside everything else. He wanted to tell her, share the joy of this moment with her. Nothing seemed more natural.

Mitch moved along the edge of the crowded dance floor. When he didn't spot her, he checked the nearby sitting room where the women gathered. Not there, either. Heading back to the ballroom, Mitch glimpsed a lavender beaded skirt through the open door of the balcony. He walked closer, saw that it was Rachel, then stopped still in his tracks.

She was with a man. Mitch recognized him. Nick Hastings. They'd met at Stuart Parker's club. It had been Hastings who'd suggested the detective agency that had found Rachel's brother. He was a successful businessman who lived nearby.

But he was more than that. He was tall and good-looking. He was a wealthy, successful man in his prime.

And he looked perfect standing in front of Rachel.

In the dim light, she gazed up at him, hanging on to his every word. She nodded. He spoke again. She answered. Then he smiled. So did she.

Mitch's heart ached. The two of them looked so right for each other. Hastings was of her kind. Wealthy since birth. Accepted. He fit in. He belonged. Just the sort of man Rachel deserved. Just the sort of man she should have.

A stronger, deeper pain rolled through Mitch. He couldn't bear the thought of Rachel being with another man—no matter how alike they were.

Jealousy clawed at him. He wanted to bash Nick Hastings in the face, pull Rachel into his arms and carry her away.

Another wave of emotion overtook him, this one cooling his rage. In that single moment Mitch knew that nothing he ever acquired in this world would be worth a cent if he lost Rachel. Without her in his life, at his side, nothing else mattered. He couldn't lose her— he simply couldn't.

But he'd told her over and over that he was there for the money. For his fee. He'd told her—shouted it at her—that he wanted her social connections and nothing more.

How would he ever convince her that he felt differently?

Chapter Twenty-Five

Rachel paused at the door to the study, taking in the sight of Mitch and Noah standing side by side, looking out the front windows. They made her think of uneven bookends.

Mitch was tall and broad, strong and sturdy. Noah was shorter and slightly built, but his long limbs and big feet suggested the potential of growing as tall and broad-shouldered as the other men in the Branford family.

He'd lost his sickly pallor and filled out a little. How could he not after Mitch had instructed Cook to change the menu? Meat and potatoes, swimming in gravy. Rich desserts twice a day. The two of them ate like horses.

Both were impeccably dressed in dark suits; Noah's empty sleeve was tucked into his jacket side pocket, making it less noticeable.

Where Rachel had wanted to protect and shelter her brother, Mitch had pushed him in his own, quiet way. Noah in the attic, boxing. She'd been appalled when she'd found out what Mitch was doing. Now, it seemed it had paid off.

Pride swelled in her, watching the two of them. For all their opposite physical attributes, Mitch and Noah had connected. It pleased Rachel that they got along so well.

She walked closer, wondering what had taken their attention out the front window. Mitch usually noticed when she entered the room, but not this time. He and Noah spoke quietly, neither of them taking their eyes off the front lawn and driveway.

"She'll have to ask her mother first," Noah said as Rachel stopped behind them.

"She might have callers," Mitch offered. "And then she'll have to change clothes."

They glanced at each other then, rolled their eyes and turned to the front window again.

"What are you two doing?" Rachel asked.

They turned, both looking ill at ease. For a few seconds Rachel thought they might not tell her.

The two of them exchanged a look, then Noah nodded.

"Noah sent a letter to Madeline," Mitch said.

Stunned, her gaze bounced between the two of them. Noah had written to Madeline? After all these months of not corresponding with a single one of his friends? He'd taken this giant step forward—and he hadn't told her?

But he'd told Mitch, obviously. And at the moment, Rachel didn't care. She didn't feel slighted or left out. She was only glad that Noah had made the effort. She was pleased, too, that he'd chosen Madeline. Rachel had always known there was something special between the two of them. And Madeline had confirmed her suspicion with the letters she wrote twice a week, every week, since the train accident.

"Hayden took the note to her house a few minutes ago," Noah explained. "I asked Madeline if I could call on her."

Apparently, he was anxious to receive her reply since he and Mitch were standing at the window speculating about when it might be expected.

"You think she'll let me, don't you?" Noah asked. He turned back to the window. "I've been awful to her all these months and she—Madeline..."

Rachel's heart rose in her throat as she gazed out the window and saw Madeline heading down their driveway.

She hadn't bothered with hat or wrap. She took long, striding steps, leaving Hayden trailing her in the distance. Her jaw was set, her lips pressed together, her eyes narrowed. In her fist was a crushed note card.

Rachel and Mitch exchanged a troubled look as Noah raced out of the room. They followed and reached the foyer as Madeline threw open the front door and froze Noah in front of her with a piercing glare.

Madeline drew back her fist and struck Noah across the chest.

"Is that all you thought you were to me? An arm?" She screamed the demand. "Did you think that I wouldn't want you, or care about you or—or—"

She burst into tears.

Noah pulled her against his shoulder and leaned

down to press his cheek to hers. Then he wrapped his arm around her.

One arm was enough.

"Thank you." Rachel gestured across the lawn to where Noah and Madeline strolled beneath the palms. "You made this possible."

Seated close to her at the little table on the terrace, Mitch shook his head. "Should have known everybody would end up crying."

Another wave of emotion swept through Rachel and she touched her finger to her eye. Still sobbing against his shoulder, Madeline had let Noah guide her from the foyer into the sitting room. Rachel had seen a tear on her brother's cheek. She'd cried then, too. Only Mitch had remained dry-eyed, but she'd heard him gulp hard a time or two.

Now Noah and Madeline were walking through the gardens and Rachel sat with Mitch on the terrace, a pitcher of lemonade between them, chaperoning the young couple.

"They're well suited for each other, don't you think?" Rachel sighed. "They belong together."

"Then why are we out here chaperoning them?" Mitch asked. "What's the harm in them holding hands or sharing a kiss?"

"A kiss? That would only complicate things," Rachel said.

"It would certainly improve my day," Mitch grumbled.

Rachel giggled. He always knew what to say to make her feel better.

She marveled at how he'd known what to do with Noah and with Chelsey. Mitch had no training, no instruction, not even a model of what a father, brother or husband should be. He had only the slightest inkling of how a family should care for each other.

But he'd been wonderful. Not just a good provider and protector. He'd also been kind and caring, and a tremendous emotional support for Rachel during some of the most difficult decisions she'd ever had to make.

How had Mitch known these things? Did they, somehow, come naturally to him? Did that mean he wanted a wife, a family? Rachel found herself wondering that so often now.

Not that it would have any consequence in her own future, since he was leaving in a year—or perhaps less.

"How did your meeting go with Albert Taft this morning?" she asked. Mitch had told her that the older man had offered to sell him the quarry.

"We're working out some details," he said.

"What sort of details? I thought Mr. Taft was anxious to get rid of it," Rachel said.

"There are always details, Rachel," Mitch said. "Disposition of the tools and equipment. Outstanding debts. Bills that are due. Assets on hand."

"I suppose I should write some of this down," she said, "for when I get my factory."

"You're still thinking about that?"

"Of course," she said.

"And the string of lovers to go along with your new lifestyle?"

"Would that bother you?" She couldn't resist asking.

"Damn right," Mitch grumbled. "Considering that I'm your husband and I never even get to see your—"

"Don't start asking about my underwear again."

"I wouldn't have to ask if you let me—"

"Hush. Here come Noah and Madeline."

Rachel sat a little straighter in her chair as the young couple approached.

"I'm going to walk Madeline home," Noah said.

The two of them simply could not be seen on a public street without a chaperone. Rachel wasn't surprised when Mitch volunteered.

They exchanged goodbyes and the three of them set off together. Rachel eased into her chair once more and sipped her lemonade.

Mitch fit in so well here with her, with her family. He made it seem effortless and she was sure it wasn't. It was yet another of the things she liked about him.

Another of the reasons she loved him.

Rachel forced away the aching in her heart. Yes, she loved Mitch. Perhaps she'd even loved him from the first moment she'd walked into her sitting room and seen him standing next to the tea service. She loved him now, and she would love him forever. Love, her mother had always said, never died.

But Mitch had made it clear he didn't feel the same about her. He didn't love her. He'd told her he was leaving, even written the date in their contract.

While he was here, though, he intended to be a good husband, a good member of her family.

But that's all she could ever expect from him. He was here to fulfill his duties. She'd have to resign herself to that and factor it into the decision she'd make when Georgie came back.

When they returned home, Noah looked more tired than on the first day he'd ventured out of the house. Mitch supposed seeing Madeline and spending the afternoon with her had taken a toll.

On the way back home, Noah had told him that he'd asked Madeline if he could call on her. She'd said yes, of course. She'd offered to have some of their other friends over, young people Noah hadn't seen in months. But he'd declined. He wasn't quite ready for that. Madeline had understood.

"I'm going upstairs for a while," Noah said, grasping the railing and pulling himself onto the first step. "I'll be down later to work on the books."

"Forget it," Mitch said. "I've had enough for today myself."

Noah looked greatly relieved and headed up the stairs but stopped and turned back.

"Thanks," he said, "for…well, for everything."

"Madeline's a special young woman. You'd better not let her down again." Mitch grinned. "Next time she might give you a real thrashing."

Noah smiled and headed up the stairs.

Mitch went to the study, even though he'd told Noah he wouldn't. He didn't intend to do any work, he just liked being in the room. Ledgers and journals arranged in even stacks. Entries printed carefully in straight columns. Figures added up correctly. No errors.

Yet the stories behind the company books appealed

to him just as much. The man who'd started the company. Decisions. Plans. Prospects. Hope for a better future. The workers. Their daily grind. Their faith in the owners. Their hope for a better future.

His own future came to mind, as it had for so many years now. Mitch settled into his desk chair. The details of the purchase of Albert Taft's quarry were almost all hammered out. The man had been surprised by some of the aspects of the transaction Mitch had brought up, which was probably one of the reasons the quarry was doing so badly to begin with. But he was agreeable with most everything. Within another week or so, they should close the deal.

Rachel crowded into Mitch's thoughts. Mental images of her had always been pleasant, until the night of the engagement party when he'd seen her alone with Nick Hastings. When she'd turned and seen Mitch, a flash of something—sorrow, regret, guilt, maybe?—had crossed her face. Hastings had stepped forward with a handshake and a word of congratulations on their marriage, then gone on his way.

Mitch's heart still ached at the memory. He'd never experienced raw, unbridled jealousy. But then, aside from his mother, he'd never loved another person before.

During his lifetime his emotions had run the usual gamut. Friendship, responsibility, anger, envy, the need to protect, to fix things, to take charge. But never love.

So it was no small wonder that he hadn't realized he loved Rachel right away. He'd lusted after her—and still did—and he'd worried about her and he'd driven himself to the edge trying to make things better for her.

He hadn't realized he loved her until that night at the party when he thought he might lose her. Now he had to do something about it.

Mitch sat forward in the chair. How would he tell Rachel he loved her? And, more importantly, how would he get her to believe it?

It helped that he was already married to her, he decided. That gave him an advantage. So what should his next move be?

He could simply tell her. The idea stunned Mitch with its simplicity. Just say the words. But as he pictured himself making his announcement, it seemed the moment called for something more.

Jewelry? He'd never given her a real wedding ring. He could get down on one knee and profess his love. Mitch drummed his fingers on the desktop. That idea didn't feel right, either.

With a quick intake of his breath, Mitch realized what he should do. He'd write it down for her. He wrote excellent reports. Concise, accurate, to the point. Yes, that would do nicely.

He pulled a fresh tablet from the desk drawer, located a new pencil and wrote "I love you" on the paper. Then he added Rachel's name at the top, so she'd know he meant the words for her, and signed his name at the bottom for clarity.

Mitch sat back. For a profession of love, it looked a bit sparse. He drew a heart in the corner. Then, so she'd understand the breadth of his love, he drew three more hearts, one for each corner.

He frowned down at the paper. It looked like the

work of a schoolboy who had a crush on his teacher. He turned to a fresh page.

After pondering a new approach for a moment, Mitch decided to simply list all the things he liked about Rachel. That would convince her of his love. He went to work, but stopped after fourteen numbered items. It looked like a shopping list.

He tried again with another page. Back to the report idea, he decided, and set to work detailing how her beauty had taken him by surprise upon his arrival at the house, how he admired her commitment to her family, how she'd made him feel at home, how the sway of her hips had tantalized him, how her kisses had taken away his breath, how the feel of her breasts in his palm had excited him, how speculation over the color of her underwear had nearly driven him mad, how all he could think of was getting her into bed and—

Mitch stopped abruptly. He reread his report and mumbled a curse. He'd forgotten to put in that he loved her.

"Damn…"

The report method wasn't working. He'd left out the most important part, plus he'd gotten himself so worked up he could hardly think straight.

Mitch shoved the tablet into the drawer. Now what? Maybe if he—

Rachel breezed into the study.

"Mitch, I'm going over the menu for next week. Do you want chocolate—"

"I love—"

"—cake again?" Rachel stilled and looked hard at him. "What did you say?"

"Nothing."

She tilted her head. "You said something."

"I, uh, I said I love—" Mitch gulped "—chocolate cake."

"Oh." Rachel drew back a little. "Well, then, I'll keep it on the menu."

Mitch forced his lips into a thin smile. "Fine. Good. Thanks."

She nodded and left the study.

Mitch leaned forward and thudded his forehead against the desktop. "Stupid…stupid…stupid…"

He sat up and drew a breath, consoling himself with the thought that even if he'd gotten the words out, Rachel probably wouldn't have believed him. Not after all the times he'd told her his only interest in her was collecting his fee and securing her social connections.

He'd have to think of something big, something grand. Something she'd believe.

And he'd better do it quick. Before Georgie showed up asking for her decision.

Chapter Twenty-Six

"What now?" Rachel asked, though Claudia hadn't spoken a word. The look on her face as she crossed the foyer was enough to make Rachel realize that something was very much amiss with her friend.

"Nothing's wrong," Claudia said, giving her a little smile. "I just came by to ask about one of the receipes you used at the La-La luncheon. The baked squash your cook prepared was delicious. Might I use that recipe?"

"Of course," Rachel said, leading the way down the hall.

They found the kitchen empty when they walked in, the time of the afternoon when the staff had finished with lunch but hadn't started supper preparations yet. The room still smelled good, though, the scent of roasted meat and oatmeal cookies lingering in the air.

Rachel fetched a cookbook from the shelf near the back door and carried it to the worktable where Claudia had pulled up a stool.

"I'm sure it's in this book," Rachel said, settling onto the stool beside her. "I just have to—"

"Something's wrong."

"I knew it." Rachel closed the book. "What is it?"

Claudia twisted her fingers together for a moment. "Graham bought us a house."

The purchase of a home for a newlywed couple was expected. It was the groom's gift to his new bride. But Rachel had a very bad feeling about Graham's purchase.

"The home is in Pasadena," Claudia said, the words seeming painful to speak.

"Pasadena? Why would Graham go to Pasadena to—"

"I haven't even seen the house."

"He bought it without you—"

"It's next door to his mother."

Rachel gasped and reeled back. "Oh, Claudia, no…"

Tears pooled in her eyes. "I don't want to live in Pasadena. It's too far away. I won't be able to visit my mother, or you, or any of my friends. And I don't know if I like the house—he didn't even let me see it. And—and his mother…"

Rachel patted her shoulder, though it was woefully inadequate to assuage Claudia's anguish.

"I don't blame you for being upset."

Claudia's sorrowful expression deepened. She looked miserable. And with good reason.

"Are you sure you still want to marry Graham?"

Claudia straightened on the stool. "Of course. He's the perfect husband for me."

"But you don't seem very happy anymore," Rachel said.

"I have to marry him. What will people say?"

"What difference does it make what people say?"

Claudia gasped. "I can't believe those words came out of your mouth."

Neither could Rachel. But she believed them with all her heart. What difference did it make what people said? The important issue was happiness.

Thinking back over the time since Mitch had come into her life, Rachel could see that the opinions of others had slowly become less and less important to her. So slowly, in fact, that she hadn't realized how much she'd changed until this moment, looking at Claudia, knowing she was making a terrible mistake but was too concerned about the opinions of others to do anything about it.

"Father has spent a fortune," Claudia said. "And Mother has planned for my wedding for years. Years."

"Your parents want you to be happy," Rachel said.

"And what about everyone else in the city? How will it look if I cry off from an engagement to Graham Bixby?" Claudia's voice rose. "My family will be talked about forever. It could affect my father's business."

"I understand that, but—"

A knock sounded at the back door.

"—none of that is worth you throwing your life away in a marriage you don't want."

"It's not that simple, Rachel," Claudia declared.

The knock came again. Rachel looked around and,

still not seeing any of the kitchen staff, answered the door expecting to see a local grocer with a delivery.

Instead she found a tall, good-looking man dressed in work clothes and sporting a day's worth of whiskers.

"Afternoon, ma'am," he said, dragging his hat from his head and favoring her with an open, easy smile. "My name's Leo Sinclair, and I'm hoping you can tell me where I can find Mitch Kincade."

It took only a few seconds to place him. She stepped back from the door. "You're Mitch's friend. He spoke of you. Please, come inside. I'm his wife."

Leo froze in the doorway. "You're his—his wife, did you say?" he asked, looking thoroughly amused.

Something about Leo's open, honest face made Rachel smile. "Yes. I'm Rachel Branford—Kincade."

Leo's grin broadened as if he were privy to some private joke, and he bowed slightly. "I'm very pleased to meet you, Mrs. Kincade, and my sincere congratulations on your recent nuptials."

"Please come into the sitting room," Rachel said, motioning him away from the door.

"No, ma'am." Leo gestured to the kitchen. "I'll wait here—if that meets with your approval."

"Mitch left earlier for a meeting but he should be back any minute." She glanced around and, still not seeing any of the kitchen staff, said, "I'll check the study, see if he's home yet. He's anxious to see you."

Leo's general air of amusement turned to surprise. "Mitch told you about me?"

"Yes, he did," Rachel said. She introduced Leo to Claudia and left the kitchen. She didn't find Mitch in his study but located Hayden and explained the situation. When she returned to the kitchen, she found Leo and Claudia seated on stools at the worktable, sipping lemonade and laughing.

Rachel paused in the doorway, stunned by the scene. Leo spoke and Claudia leaned in, laughing and giggling. Rachel couldn't remember the last time she'd seen her look so happy.

"I'd better go," Claudia said when she saw Rachel. She held up the cookbook. "I'll bring this back later."

"Pleasure to meet you, Miss Everhart," Leo said, rising from the stool.

Claudia gave him a smile and hurried away.

"Mitch isn't back yet, but as I said, he should return soon," Rachel said. "Please come into the sitting room. We can visit until he returns."

Leo hesitated a moment, then said, "Thank you for your hospitality, ma'am. I'll wait for a while, if you're sure it's all right."

"Mitch is anxious to see you," Rachel said, leading the way out of the kitchen. "He looked for you a few weeks ago."

"He did?" Leo's tone suggested that was unusual.

In the sitting room, Rachel took a seat on the settee and Leo the nearby chair.

"You looked a little surprised when I told you Mitch and I had married," Rachel said.

"Not that I blame him for marrying you, ma'am. You're a beautiful woman, if I can be so bold to say so, and I can tell you've got a good heart." Leo shook his head. "But so did all the others."

"The others?"

Leo uttered a quick laugh. "Your papa must be one whale of a negotiator—which I mean as a compliment, of course."

"What others?"

"The other marriage offers Mitch had. One for nearly every client he took on. All of them trying to push their daughters on him, desperate to get him into their family. Him being so smart, you know, they all wanted him." Leo shook his head in wonder, looking more serious now. "Mitch let himself get picked? Never thought I'd see that happen."

The words jogged Rachel's memory. "Getting picked? That happened at the orphanage on Sundays when families came, looking for a child to adopt."

Leo frowned. "Mitch told you about that? I never knew him to tell a living soul about the orphanage, let alone the story about Billy Stillman."

Rachel didn't answer but Leo seemed not to notice.

"Nobody was too anxious to get picked after what happened to Billy," Leo said, his gaze taking on a distant look, as if he were seeing into the past. "Billy cried every night after his mother left him there. She couldn't afford to take care of him. That happened a lot. When he finally got picked he was so happy. All he wanted was to be part of a family again. But then, after a couple of weeks, they brought him back."

"The family who adopted him returned him to the orphanage?" Rachel's heart broke at the thought. "He must have been devastated."

"Hanged himself," Leo said. "In the stairwell. We all

saw him there, twisted up in a bedsheet. Mitch, being the biggest, climbed up and—well, none of us boys were too keen about getting picked after that. Especially Mitch, though. He made sure nobody ever took him. That way—"

"—nobody could bring him back." Rachel's head and heart ached at the knowledge of what Mitch, and all the other boys, had gone through.

"That's why I'm saying that something else must be going on with Mitch," Leo said. "He wouldn't have let your papa pick him to marry you. He just wouldn't have done that."

"Actually, our marriage was Mitch's idea."

A big smile bloomed on Leo's face. "Well then, that could only mean one thing. Mitch finally fell in love."

"No, it's not like that," she said, as much as she'd like to believe it. "Our marriage is a business arrangement. Mitch doesn't love me."

"But you love him?"

"Yes," Rachel said, and it felt good to tell someone what was in her heart. "I do love Mitch. But he doesn't feel that way about me."

"Yes, he does. Believe me, Mitch wouldn't be here, he wouldn't have married you if he didn't love you."

"Then why won't he say so?"

"He's not likely to do that," Leo said. "Not after the way he was raised. You can see that, can't you? Have you told Mitch that you love him?"

"Well, no," Rachel admitted. "Mitch said right from the beginning that he didn't care about me. He and my uncle drew up a contract stating—"

"A contract?" Leo's smile returned. "Figures. Probably had a clause about him leaving, didn't it? A date when he'd go—a date he picked himself, right?"

"Well, yes."

"What better way for him to safeguard his feelings?" Leo said. "He must love you a lot if he went to all that trouble."

"Do you really think so?"

Leo nodded. "But if you want to find out for sure, you'll have to be the one to say the words first. Mitch will never do it. I promise you that."

"Then I guess it's up to me."

Chapter Twenty-Seven

Since Leo Sinclair's visit yesterday, Rachel had done nothing but think. About her life, her future…and about Mitch, of course.

She found those same thoughts running through her head this morning as she sat in the sitting room looking over the list of needed grocery items Mrs. Callihan had compiled. The house was quiet. Noah was in the library with his tutor and Mitch had gone to another meeting with Albert Taft. Yet Rachel couldn't concentrate on her chore.

When Mitch had finally returned yesterday, he'd been stunned to find Leo in the sitting room with her. He'd looked worried, at first, but glad to see his old friend. The two of them had holed up in the study for hours. Rachel didn't know what they discussed but she heard deep male laughter. It made her realize that she seldom heard Mitch laugh and it had pained her conscience a little. She, along with most everyone else in his life, had given him little reason to do so.

Since Georgie's visit, Rachel hadn't known what to do about the question her brother had put before her. She knew she loved Mitch, though. She'd thought she'd tell George not to come back…if only she knew whether Mitch felt the same about her.

She'd been safeguarding her feelings for Mitch, she realized. She'd done the same as he'd been doing about her.

Yet she had less reason to hold back than he did. So why was she doing it?

Those same thoughts had rambled around in her head all of yesterday afternoon, during a sleepless night and continued to plague her this morning.

She couldn't shake the notion that telling Mitch she loved him, wanted him to stay, wanted a real marriage, might be a terrible mistake. Would he say he loved her in return so she would send Georgie away and he could stay for the coming year, as their contract dictated? She didn't think Mitch a deceptive person, but wealth, power and social position were the things Mitch had worked toward all his life and he had them now. He wouldn't give them up easily, and understandably so.

Mitch had done so much to help her and her family. He'd helped her make the decision to send her father to the convalescent hospital, and by all accounts, he was improving daily. He'd convinced her to let Chelsey attend school again, a decision that had been good for all of them. He'd connected with Noah as Georgie never had. Georgie had been busy, of course. But Mitch had shouldered those same responsibilities and had still found time for Noah. And, of course, he'd saved them from public humiliation by putting the family business back on course.

Rachel set aside the grocery list and drew a breath. She knew in her heart what she must do.

She'd learned from a total stranger that her husband loved her. He hadn't told her himself, yet why would he? She'd treated him like a hired husband much of the time.

So it was up to her to help him work his way through the hard shell he'd built around his emotions. She didn't want to be alone. Leo had said Mitch loved her. Maybe, just maybe, that was true. Maybe he would stay with her and they'd have the sort of life she'd always wanted. It was worth taking the chance on.

But would Mitch believe she'd changed her mind? How would she convince him?

She didn't know. But it would certainly help if she knew for sure—other than through Leo's opinion—that Mitch really loved her.

By the time Rachel worked her way through the entire grocery list, she heard the door chimes and headed toward the foyer. As she expected, Claudia stepped into the vestibule carrying the cookbook she'd borrowed. She looked upset. Rachel cringed inwardly. Good gracious, what had Graham Bixby done now?

Claudia gave her no chance to ask because she blurted out, "I think I'm in love with Leo Sinclair."

Rachel's gaze flew to Hayden, still lingering at the door. He quirked his brows in their direction so she was sure he'd overheard. Rachel hooked her arm through Claudia's and hustled her into the nearest room, Mitch's study.

"What on earth are you talking about?"

Claudia clasped the cookbook to her breasts and smiled dreamily. "Leo Sinclair. He's positively enchanting. Funny and interesting. And he was so nice. He said the sweetest things to me—nothing out of line, of course. But he made me feel so—so—happy."

Rachel hadn't missed Leo's charm yesterday, either. Even dressed in his work clothes and needing a shave there was something alluring about him. Yet she suspected there was something more at work here.

"Maybe Leo seems so wonderful because Graham is so…well, not-so-wonderful?" Rachel suggested.

Claudia's expression soured. "Graham…"

"You've seen a different side of him since your engagement," Rachel pointed out. "Do you like it?"

"He's been pushy about the wedding arrangements, always wanting his own way," Claudia said. Then she exhaled heavily and her shoulders sagged. "And he's so boring. All he talks about is business. I don't know if I can bear to hear about who's-selling-this and who's-mismanaging-that for the rest of my life. Oh, and his mother…"

"You don't have to marry him," Rachel told her. "You don't have to marry anyone."

"Not marry? But what would I do with my life?"

"Whatever you want," Rachel declared. "Actually, I'm thinking of opening a business of my own in a few months."

Her eyes widened. "Rachel, you're not."

"I'm thinking of buying a ceramic factory and designing china," she explained. It felt good to say it aloud to someone other than Mitch.

"See, that's exactly what I mean," Claudia said, shaking her head. "Graham was talking about a ceramic factory being sold just last night. He went on and on. And it was all I could do to keep from nodding off."

"Whose factory?" Rachel asked, her pulse quickening. "Was it the City Ceramic Works?"

Claudia waved her hand. "I don't recall. It belonged to dreary old Mr. Taft. No, wait, that isn't right. Mr. Taft offered to sell something to Graham. Rocks, was it? But there was mention of ceramics. I think. I don't know. You see how dull Graham's stories are?"

Actually, Rachel found talk of local business interesting and she always enjoyed when she and Mitch discussed things. She'd ask him when he got home about the Taft quarry purchase and Mr. Prescott's ceramic factory.

"So what do you find interesting?" Rachel asked. "Surely you have some dream, something you'd like to accomplish on your own?"

Claudia's gaze drifted around the room for a moment. "Well, there are a few things," she said softly.

"Write them down." Rachel went through the desk drawers until she found a tablet. "Make a list of everything you'd ever thought about doing with your life and then—"

She stopped as she held out the tablet. The top page was already written on, the words surrounded by simple drawings of hearts. She saw her own name. Tears welled in her eyes.

Rachel paused in the study doorway, gazing inside at Mitch seated at the desk. Beyond him, the early evening shadows darkened the view of the driveway and street through the windows.

A little smile played on her lips. She'd decided earlier today after Claudia's visit that she would never come into this study again not expecting to find Mitch here. Not just in the coming year, but for always. She'd made up her mind what to do. And tonight she would do it, hoping with all her heart that it was the right thing.

"There're some rumors going around town," Rachel said, stopping in front of the desk.

Mitch looked up at her and closed the ledger he'd been studying. Rachel's heart warmed at the sight of him. It didn't escape her that Mitch always stopped what he was doing when she walked in, always listened.

"Let me guess," he said. "It's rumored that Albert Taft has his quarry up for sale. Cheap."

"You've heard?" she asked, genuinely surprised. She knew how badly he wanted the quarry. He'd met with Albert Taft many times to work out the details.

"Is this a ploy of his to stir up competition? Drive up the price so you'll have to pay more for it?" she asked.

Mitch shrugged. "I wouldn't worry about that rumor. The quarry purchase is proceeding as I'd planned."

His confidence always impressed her.

"I also heard that Mr. Prescott sold his ceramic factory," Rachel said. "Please tell me that's not true."

Mitch's gaze dipped, then returned to her and Rachel's heart fell.

"It's true, isn't it," she said, sure by the expression on his face that she already knew the answer.

"Yes, it's true, I'm afraid. I saw Mr. Prescott while I was out today. He sold the factory. Sorry. I know you're disappointed."

Breath went out of Rachel in a heavy sigh. She'd had her heart set on designing china and, while actually running the factory herself would have taken a lot of work, she would have enjoyed it.

"Maybe the new owner won't like the ceramic business," Rachel said. "Maybe he'll want to sell in a few months."

"Maybe," Mitch said. "Any more rumors?"

"Claudia is in love with your friend Leo."

Mitch uttered a short laugh. "Leo's not exactly the marrying kind. He just came by to let me know he was heading north again."

"He could have stayed here with us, you know."

"Leo prefers drifting around to wherever the wind takes him. Not exactly the sort of man Claudia is looking for."

"I think the thing she liked most about Leo is that he wasn't Graham."

"Does this mean there's trouble with the perfect couple and their perfect wedding?" Mitch asked.

"I've decided perfection isn't all that desirable."

Mitch's brows rose. "Is that so?"

"I've decided I don't want perfection. I want you."

He froze.

"It occurred to me that if you're not perfect, then I don't have to be perfect, either," Rachel said. "It's a terrible strain, trying to maintain perfection. Look how unhappy it made my mother and brother. I'm afraid it will cause Claudia to throw away her life in a marriage she doesn't really want."

"But, Rachel," he said softly. "What will people say…?"

"I'm not concerned about that, either," she said. "But I'm very interested in another rumor I learned of. It seems that you love me."

He drew back in the chair, away from her.

She stepped closer. "Seems there is a list of fourteen things you like about me."

He glanced down at the desk drawer where she'd found the tablet he'd written on. His face paled.

"It would seem, also, that you loved me from the moment you walked into the house, that you're mesmerized by the sway of my hips and grow very excited about some other things about me."

He didn't say anything, but she didn't expect him to. She was there to tell him what was in her heart.

"I've fallen in love with you, Mitch. You're a wonderful man and I'm lucky to have you as my husband. I want us to stay married forever," she said. "I want us to be a real married couple."

His breath quickened then.

"But I want you to say the words to me. Say that you love me." Rachel felt color rise in her cheeks. She'd mentally rehearsed, but still didn't know if she'd actually be able to say the words aloud. She continued, "If you can do that and, if you're still interested, you can come upstairs and see what color underwear I have on."

She turned and left the room.

Chapter Twenty-Eight

Dumbstruck, Mitch sat frozen in his desk chair for several moments before he processed what Rachel had just told him. Then he bolted from the room, took the steps two at a time and caught her at the top.

She looked unsure of herself. Her cheeks were a little pink, and he guessed it was because of the highly charged invitation she'd issued.

It was easier to interpret Rachel's emotions than his own. Mitch didn't know which shocked him more: that she said she loved him, or that she'd asked if he wanted to see her colored underwear.

She glanced up and down the hallway, then headed toward her bedchamber. He followed her inside and closed the door. They faced each other in the dim light of the fading sunset.

"Rachel, I…I don't know what to say…."

"I told you what you need to say," she reminded him. "You do love me, don't you?"

Yes, he loved her. He'd compiled a list of the things he loved about her—he'd even written a report and drawn little hearts. He'd almost said the words to her in the study when she'd come in to ask about the week's menu.

But standing before her now with those big brown eyes gazing up at him, holding the promise of a future he never thought he'd have, Mitch couldn't get the words out.

"Do you love me?" she asked again.

He gulped. "I, uh…."

Rachel stepped closer and touched his arm. She rose on her toes, as she'd done so many times before, and Mitch leaned down, expecting her to whisper something to him. Instead she turned her ear to his lips.

He knew what she wanted. She'd made it easier for him, as she'd done with so many other things.

"I…love you," he said softly.

She looked up at him with the most radiant smile he'd ever seen—ever expected to see—in his life, and his heart soared.

"I love you, too," she told him.

He slid his arms around her and kissed her tenderly on the lips.

"You'll get used to saying it, eventually," she said to him, standing in his embrace. "I'll make sure of that."

The solitude, the intimacy of her bedchamber closed in around them.

"You're sure this is what you want?" Mitch asked.

Her cheeks flushed pink and she backed up a step, out of the circle of his arms.

"Well, yes, I did say you could see my…my underwear," she said, twisting her fingers together. "And it's perfectly proper, really. We are…married and you're… well, you are my husband."

Mitch took both of her hands in his, thinking how utterly charming she looked, shy and timid about their lovemaking.

"Why don't you go put on your nightclothes," he suggested. "I'll wait here."

She blushed again. "Well, all right."

Mitch removed his jacket, vest and necktie, and popped open the top button of his shirt as he stood at the door to the balcony and watched the evening sky. In the adjoining bathroom, he heard water running and Rachel moving around. When he heard her feet brush the carpet a few minutes later, he turned and his breath caught.

How beautiful she looked. She wore a pale blue nightgown and robe, buttoned up to her neck and tied with a sash. She'd taken down her hair and tied it with a ribbon. Her feet were bare and her cheeks were pink.

"Is—is this all right?" she asked quietly, holding out her arms a little. "I wasn't sure what was appropriate."

"It's perfect," Mitch said, his timid bride appealing to him as no other woman had.

He took her hand and led her to the bed. She stretched out and he sat beside her.

"You're so beautiful," he said, stroking his hand down her cheek.

She jumped at his touch, but he leaned down intending to kiss away her anxiety. Her eyes closed, then popped open.

"Is the door locked?" she asked, pushing herself up on her elbows.

"No one will bother us."

Her eyes widened. "But what if someone bursts in? What if they see us—"

"I'll take care of it." Mitch hurried over to the door, threw the dead bolt and returned to the bed. "There, all fixed."

She nodded and lay back on the bed once more. Mitch leaned down to kiss her again.

"Should we have a light on?" she asked, her gaze darting around the room. "It will be dark soon and…"

"Sure." Mitch went to the bureau across the room, switched on the lamp, then eased onto the side of the bed once more.

Her eyes opened wider, horrified. "Oh, dear. That's so much light. What if—"

"I'll fix it." Mitch hopped off the bed again, turned off the lamp, dashed into the bathroom, turned on the light and pulled the door almost closed. He returned to the bed and looked down at Rachel. "How's that?"

"Better."

"Anything else?" he asked.

She gazed around the room, her brow furrowed. "No, I don't suppose so."

Rachel lay back on the bed. She crossed her ankles, pressed her palms to her stomach, drew in a breath and closed her eyes.

"You may begin."

Mitch looked down at his bride. He'd expected to take things slowly but this wasn't exactly what he had in mind.

"Come on. Get up." He caught her hand and pulled her upright.

"Get up?" She drew away from him but Mitch wouldn't turn loose.

"On your feet. Let's go," he said, tugging her off the bed.

"Go where?"

"Outside."

"Outside!" She dug in her heels and leaned back as he pulled her toward the balcony. "Oh, Mitch, no. Good gracious, the neighbors!"

He looped an arm around her back, halting her retreat.

"Trust me a little, will you?" he asked. Then he smiled. "I'm really very good at this."

She gave a short, nervous laugh and allowed him to guide her out onto the balcony. He stood behind her and pulled her against him, wrapping her in his arms.

"I want us to look at the sunset," he said.

"Oh."

The sky overhead was dark but the horizon was lit with rays of the disappearing sun. They colored the scattered clouds with shades of blue and gray, and hints of blazing auburn.

They watched the sunset and Mitch held her in his embrace until he felt her relax against him. Then he leaned down and brushed a soft kiss across her cheek. She turned toward him and he covered her lips with his for a long moment. When he lifted his head Rachel smiled up at him. He lifted her into his arms and carried her into the bedchamber.

Standing beside the bed, Mitch kissed her again as

he opened the buttons on her robe and pushed it from her shoulders. He pulled loose the ribbon in her hair and ran his fingers through the length of it. She sighed and pressed herself against him. His long-simmering desire flamed.

Forcing himself to go slowly, Mitch turned back the covers and guided Rachel onto the bed. He pulled off his clothing and lay down next to her.

He kissed her and she kissed him back, as the heat between them built. He opened the buttons on her night-gown and pulled it over her head. She curled against him. He groaned; she gasped as their hands sought each other. He covered her with hot, heavy kisses. She trembled at his touch.

Lying fully against him, her warm body pressed to his, he marveled at her soft, giving lines, the way they fit close, as if they were meant to be together. Rachel moaned softly, her hands shyly finding their way over his body. Her timid movements nearly drove him crazy with want. When he could bear it no longer, he moved above her, kissing her mouth, her cheek, her neck.

Rachel grasped his shoulders and clung to him as he moved inside her. He stole her breath, made the world spin. The swirling emotions moved faster, urging her onward until they broke within her. She grabbed a handful of his hair and moaned his name as he shuddered above her.

"I'm hungry."

Mitch's words accompanied a very loud grumble in his stomach. Rachel smiled as he pushed himself up on his elbow beside her. They were still in bed, wound together in a tangle of arms, legs and bed linens.

"Good gracious, it's late," Rachel said, glancing out the window and, judging from the sunlight, realizing it was midmorning. She ran her fingers through his hair, smoothing it down. "We had…quite a morning."

"And night," he pointed out, smiling broadly. "As I told you, I'm very—"

"—good at this." Rachel smiled. "Yes, you seem to be, but I don't really have anything to compare it to."

"And you never will," he told her.

"That's because…?" She turned her head, offering her ear.

"I love you," he whispered.

"I love you, too." She gave him a quick kiss.

Mitch growled and burrowed his mouth into the soft hollow of her neck, and she giggled wildly.

She gazed into his eyes, never more happy in her life. And Mitch had never seemed so happy, either. Rachel knew that her decision had been right, that at Mitch's side was where she belonged.

"I'll go get us something to eat," Mitch said. "You stay here."

Mitch didn't want to leave her but he was starving, and he wanted to keep up his strength. He rolled out of bed, slightly amused to see his shy bride avert her gaze as he found his underdrawers in the pile of clothing at the bedside and pulled them on.

"I don't want to stay here alone," Rachel said, pulling the sheet up to her chin.

Mitch sorted through the rest of the clothing and

came up with her robe. He slipped it around her shoulders and planted a kiss on her cheek.

"We'll go together," he said.

He gathered up the rest of his clothes and went to his own bedchamber. When he returned a short while later, washed and dressed in trousers and shirt, he found Rachel in a day dress, her hair gathered in a loose knot atop her head.

Mitch slid his arms around her—he couldn't help himself—and kissed her again.

"We'll slip down the back staircase to the kitchen," Rachel said. "Then we can—"

"Come back up here?"

Her cheeks turned a delightful shade of pink that made Mitch want to carry her back to bed on the spot. She lowered her lashes, then looked up at him.

"Is that done?"

Mitch's heart thundered in his chest. He never imagined he could love someone so much.

Arms linked, they left her bedroom and headed down the hallway toward the far corner of the house where the back stairs led to the kitchen. As they passed the twin staircases, a man waited in the foyer. They both stopped.

"Georgie…" Rachel said.

Mitch's blood ran cold.

He'd never met Rachel's brother before, but Mitch knew why he was here. He'd come for Rachel's decision.

She looked up at Mitch and he studied her face trying to glean something—anything—from her expression. Would she want her brother to come back to the family, take over the business again? Or would she leave things as they were?

An old, familiar feeling crept over Mitch, crowding out the glow of their lovemaking. She'd picked him when she said she loved him, when she invited him into her heart and into her bed. Yet there stood Georgie, the brother she'd depended on for most of her life. He'd offered to come back, to work for the family, keep everything going until he found someone competent to take over. All she had to do was tell him. He'd stay. She could have that part of her family, that much of her life back. Did she still want that?

Mitch's heart ached. Yes, she'd picked him. But would she keep him after something better came along?

Rachel's cheeks turned a deep shade of red as she glanced up at Mitch. She didn't know how long George had been in the house, how long he'd waited while the two of them were making love in her room, and she was embarrassed. It was only obvious what they'd been doing.

Mitch moved ahead of her down the staircase, sheltering her from her brother's view, shook Georgie's hand and introduced himself. There was an awkward moment before they all moved into the sitting room.

Mitch stood by the mantel when what he wanted to do was plant himself next to Rachel, stake his claim on her, the house—his life. But he put some space between the two of them, leaving Rachel to talk with her brother.

They chatted about family—their father, Noah, Chelsey—testing Mitch's patience. When the conversation stalled, George got to his feet and turned to Mitch.

"I've heard good things about you. I appreciate everything you've done to help the family. But Rachel's my sister and she comes first." Georgie turned to her. "What have you decided?"

Hours seemed to drag by as Rachel looked back and forth between the two of them. Then she shook her head.

"You don't have to come back, Georgie. I love Mitch and we're going to have a good life together."

He considered her words for a moment. "You're sure?"

"I'm sure."

"All right, then." Georgie looked relieved. "I'm leaving town in a few days, as soon as some things are settled."

"What about the lady in your life?" Rachel asked. "Are you getting married?"

"Lily says she'll marry me. Thank God."

"Can I at least give you a wedding?"

"She doesn't want that, Rachel. She doesn't want a perfect house or a perfect life. She wants me. And that makes me a lucky man."

"So you're really leaving?" Rachel asked, emotion rising in her voice.

"I can't imagine I'll ever regret my decision."

"You'll come back, won't you?" she asked.

"I don't know."

"You don't have to do this," Mitch said. "Your family, your home is here. You don't have to walk away from it."

Georgie shook his head. "I'll talk to Lily. I'll think about it."

He gave Rachel a quick kiss on the cheek, then shook hands with Mitch and left. She stood watching the doorway. Mitch moved to stand beside her.

"What about you?" Mitch asked, summoning the strength to ask. "Do you regret your decision?"

"I picked you, and I'm keeping you." She gave him a warm smile. "I love you."

"I love you, too." This time he said it out loud.

Chapter Twenty-Nine

The ocean roared outside the little inn that overlooked the beach, and the cool salt air drifted in through the open window. Rachel snuggled closer to Mitch who seemed to radiate heat even now, an hour after they'd made love again. Two weeks after first sharing a bed, they'd traveled up the coast and arrived at the inn yesterday; they had yet to leave the room.

"I forgot to tell you," Rachel said. "I received a letter from Chelsey before we left the house."

She waited but Mitch didn't say anything. He lay on his back, eyes closed, one arm curled around her holding her close. She thought he'd dozed off.

He roused after a moment. "How's she doing?"

"She's coming home in a few weeks when her classes end," Rachel said, strumming her fingers through the crisp hair on his chest. "She wants to have friends stay with us during the summer."

"Will they get along with Noah's friends?"

Her younger brother had ventured out more often in the past weeks, thanks to Madeline, and had even invited his old friends to the house.

"Yes, they'll get along fine," Rachel told him. "Maybe Georgie and his new wife will come for a visit, too. But that will give us quite a houseful, especially if the doctors let Father return home by the end of the summer."

Mitch smiled down at her. "I like having a house full of family."

She smiled back at him. "Your friend Leo is welcome, too, you know."

"I was surprised when he came by again last week to say he's staying in the city for a while longer," Mitch said. "But he won't live with us."

"I hate to think of him all alone."

"He knows he can come to me anytime he needs something. Just the same as with you and your friend."

"Oh, yes. Claudia. I think she did the right thing, don't you?"

"Hell, yes."

Rachel smiled. "When all the gossip about her calling off her marriage to Graham dies down, I think she'll be fine. I encouraged her to find her dream and go after it."

Mitch eased away from Rachel. "Speaking of dreams…"

He untangled himself from her and the covers and crossed the room to the suitcase Joseph had packed for him. Rachel blatantly ogled him, the hard lines and strong muscles of his body. She never tired of seeing him naked.

He drew a large brown envelope from the suitcase and returned to the bed, stretching out beside her. "Your wedding present."

She studied the envelope but didn't accept it. "Good gracious, we're starting to think alike. Just like an old married couple."

Rachel dashed from the bed to her own suitcase, dug to the bottom and pulled out a smaller envelope, feeling Mitch's hot gaze on her the whole time. It seemed she wasn't the only one who enjoyed the view.

"I brought you a wedding present, too," she said, sliding beneath the covers again.

He looked genuinely surprised.

"Me first," Rachel said.

He looked altogether pleased with himself as she unfastened the envelope and took out a stack of documents. She gasped, seeing the familiar name on the first page. Her eyes widened.

"Is this—is this what I think it is?"

"You are now the proud owner of the City Ceramic Factory," Mitch announced.

"Oh, Mitch!" She threw her arms around his neck, hugging him hard, and planted a big wet kiss on his cheek.

"It's in your name. No one else's," Mitch said. "It belongs to you."

"But you told me it had already been sold," she said.

"Sold to me. I bought it. For you."

"But how, Mitch?" She shook her head. "You bought Mr. Taft's quarry. How could you afford both?"

"I didn't buy the quarry," he said. "I bought the factory for you instead. I wanted you to know how much you mean to me so I—"

"You spent all your money on the factory for me?" she asked.

Mitch nodded. "Because that's what you're worth to me, Rachel. Every cent I have in the world. Everything I own, everything I'll ever have."

Tears pooled in her eyes and she hugged him again. He allowed her affection for a moment or so, then unfolded her arms from around his neck.

"Enough crying," he said, wagging his finger toward the smaller envelope. "What's my gift?"

She sniffed and wiped her eyes, but didn't hand over the envelope.

"This is for you," she said. "But you don't have to open it—ever, if you don't want to."

Mitch frowned. "What is it?"

"Your family."

He stilled. His gaze darted to the envelope, then back to her.

"Your real family," Rachel said. "I hired a private detective. He uncovered everything about your past."

"And you read it?" he asked slowly.

"I didn't want you to learn anything hurtful," she explained. "I read it first so I could be prepared, just in case."

Another long moment dragged by and Rachel wondered if he would want to read about his past. She understood his hesitancy. He'd probably fantasized about it most of his life. Wondered, speculated, fretted over who his relatives might be. And why they abandoned him.

"I don't want to read it." Mitch turned away, then looked back at her. "Just tell me what it says."

Rachel smiled because she couldn't hold it in any longer.

"Your family has been looking for you for years," she explained. "You have grandparents, and aunts and uncles, and cousins. The detective talked to them and—"

"Then why didn't they come for me?" he demanded. "Why did they leave me in that—that place?"

"Let me start at the beginning," Rachel said. She didn't need to consult the report. She'd read it over a dozen times, her heart breaking anew each time, until she'd committed it to memory.

"Your father died of a fever when you were a baby. Your mother worked as a maid in a wealthy home near Albany. She was quite beautiful, according to your grandmother, and the mistress of the house suspected her husband had designs on your mother. She was a jealous woman, by all accounts."

"Were they—"

"No. According to everyone, your mother was an upstanding Christian woman. If she'd wanted to trade on her looks she wouldn't have had to work as a maid," Rachel said. "When she fell down the staircase, it was the mistress of the house who arranged for you to be shipped off."

"But why? Why would she do that?"

"Because her husband did, apparently, care a great

deal for your mother. He allowed her to keep you in the house, when no other servants could. He was fond of you," Rachel said. "But that was exactly why the mistress sent you away. You were a reminder that her husband cared for someone else. And, I think, she wanted to punish her husband."

"That still doesn't explain why my family let her do that."

"They didn't know what happened to you. After they learned of your mother's death, they went to the house but you were already gone. The mistress refused to tell anyone—even her husband—what she'd done with you. What could your family do? They were workers. Certainly no one in authority would come to their aid against a wealthy family. Shortly thereafter, the husband left and never returned. The mistress died a few years later, lonely and bitter, still refusing to tell anyone what she'd done with you."

A long moment passed and finally Mitch gestured to the envelope. "Their names are in there? All of them? My…my family, too?"

"Yes. Everyone. The detective said they were all thrilled when he tracked them down."

"How did he manage?"

"He started at the orphanage. Got a look at your records," Rachel said. "It seemed that when you were first sent there, a hefty sum was paid to the people who ran the place to keep quiet about your past. Even if your family had somehow tracked you down all the way across the country, it's doubtful they would have been told the truth about you."

Mitch shook his head. He looked tired now. Weary. The weight of his past too much to bear at the moment.

"They—the family—they want to meet me?"

"Yes. But you don't have to, if you don't want to. They don't know where you are or how to reach you. You can contact them only if you want to."

"I need to think about this for a while," he said.

Rachel put the envelope aside and snuggled closer. They lay down together and listened to the surf and calls of the circling seagulls. Mitch grew still, his even breathing and the steady rise and fall of his chest comforting. She thought he'd fallen asleep.

"You're sure this is true?" he asked. "This private detective, he's reliable?"

"Yes, it's the same agency you hired to find Georgie," she said. "I asked Uncle Stuart and he said I should speak with our neighbor, Nick Hastings. I talked with him at—"

"Claudia's engagement party?" Mitch sat up. "That's why you were talking to Hastings that night? I thought the two of you were…well, that maybe something was going on with you two."

"Oh, Mitch, really…" Rachel rolled her eyes. "Nick is an old friend and he's desperately in love with his wife. There's a rumor among the ladies that she's going to have a baby."

"She's pregnant, too?" Mitch shook his head. "Is every woman in our neighborhood pregnant?"

"Well, not all of us," Rachel said, lowering her lashes.

A familiar, devilish smile touched his lips. "I can remedy that situation," he offered.

"I'm sure you can. But let me get things started." Rachel slid her leg across him and planted her palms on his chest. "Because, you know, I think I can become very good at this."

* * * * *

If you enjoyed what you just read,
then we've got an offer you can't resist!

Take 2 bestselling love stories FREE!

Plus get a FREE surprise gift!

THE OUTRAGEOUS DEBUTANTE
Anne O'Brien

Neither Theodora Wooton-Devereux nor
Lord Nicholas Faringdon is an enthusiastic
participant in the game of love. Until a chance
meeting sets their lives on a different course.
And soon the handsome gentleman, who has
captured the heart of the beautiful—though
somewhat unconventional—debutante, is
the talk of the town! But fate is not on their
side, it seems, when a shocking family scandal
rears its head and forbids that they be united.
Now Thea must end the relationship before it is
too late by playing the truly outrageous debutante!

The Faringdon Scandals
On sale December 2005.